LORENA

$\mathcal{L}$ORENA

FRED BEAN

A Tom Doherty Associates Book
New York

This is a work of fiction. All the characters and events portrayed in this novel are either fictitious or are used fictitiously.

LORENA

This book is printed on acid-free paper.

A Forge Book
Published by Tom Doherty Associates, Inc.
175 Fifth Avenue
New York, NY 10010

Forge® is a registered trademark of Tom Doherty Associates, Inc.

Library of Congress Cataloging-in-Publication Data

Bean, Fred
    Lorena / Fred Bean. — 1st ed.
        p.   cm.
    "A Tom Doherty Associates book."
    ISBN 0-312-86061-7 (acid-free paper)
        1. United States—History—Civil War, 1861–1865—
Fiction.
    I. Title
    PS3552.E152L67 1996
    813′.54—dc20   96-24522
                                                        CIP

First Edition: December 1996

Printed in the United States of America

0 9 8 7 6 5 4 3 2 1

To my mother,
Carol MacArthur Bean

LORENA

Prologue

Outside a pale-walled command tent, the Tennessee woods were strangely quiet along Confederate lines. Within, illuminated by light from a coal-oil lantern, Colonel Philip Work of the First Texas Cavalry Regiment witnessed a sight so courageous, he knew of no other from the war that was its equal. Seated across the tent on a field cot, a bearded four-star general watched his aide dress him for battle, tying a cork leg to a stump ending only a few inches below his hip. Everyone knew he'd lost the leg after the fury of Chickamauga. A useless, shriveled arm dangled at the general's side, an old wound from Gettysburg. Lesser men would surely have retired after so many debilitating injuries, wounds that still caused him great pain. Some might conclude he was half a man, denied the use of two limbs. Those who knew John Bell Hood would attest otherwise, for it was his unyielding heart that made him who he was.

Hood inspected the laces. He spoke to Colonel Benning, an

officer he trusted to command units of flanking cavalry striking outermost wings of lengthening Union trench lines. "You may send them my answer this morning, Colonel. Their latest proposal for our unconditional surrender is unsatisfactory. Please inform the Union commander: We will fight to the death. Better to die a thousand deaths than to submit to you and your Negro allies."

Benning wrote furiously, pausing to dip his pen in a jar of ink. "Shall I send this now? Before first light?"

Hood lowered his trouser leg over the wooden limb before he allowed his aide to help him to his feet. He teetered precariously until he had his balance. "Send it," he said. "Today we shall smite them so resoundingly that offers of surrender will be ours to tender. I have seen our victory in a dream. We suffer from a serious demoralization in our ranks. Discipline has been forgotten for the sake of comfort. Stout-hearted Southerners have been given over to cowardice and desertion." His eyes swept the group of field officers assembled in his tent. "Pass the order: Any man in my command seen running from the field of battle is to be shot by his superior officer. Neither retreat nor desertion will be tolerated. Our enemy lies to the east. Any man wearing gray moving in any other direction shall be promptly executed. This fight cannot be won without the exercise of an orderly prosecution of proven military principles. My instructors at West Point gave us sound strategies, not whimsy. No battle can be successfully joined without men who are disciplined to follow orders no matter what the cost. A well-disciplined army cannot be driven from the field if it fights with courage and sound strategy, gentlemen."

Colonel Wilson Simmons seemed disturbed. His battered men from the Army of Tennessee had seen some of the deadliest action at Franklin. "They do have us seriously outnumbered, General."

Hood pushed up his tunic sleeve for an injection of morphine, being prepared by Major Hiram Roberts from the Medical Corps, and gave Colonel Simmons a look of contempt. "For the sake of higher mathematics, let us say you are correct without further discussion. As a Tennessean, I suppose it is understandable that you know nothing about the history of our Texas brigades. My loyal Texans have never entered into a conflict in which they were not seriously outnumbered. We do not keep a tally book in which we first calculate the odds against us before we engage an enemy. Battles are won by disciplined soldiers, Colonel, a lesson I will demonstrate today." He hesitated a moment while the needle went into his arm. "President Davis removed Joe Johnston from command of this army because he lacked the will to win. He had Sherman soundly whipped at Kennesaw Mountain and let opportunity slip through his fingers. This will not be the case here at Franklin. In my dream I saw our Stars and Bars flying over those trenches. We will charge their lines no fewer than eleven times, once for each proud state committed to our cause, as a symbol of our spirit to continue this war until our right to sovereignty is recognized by Abe Lincoln and his Negro-loving politicians. We shall strike a blow for all decent, God-fearing men. Let our righteous swords speak for us here. The will of God sends us into battle today."

Colonel Benning folded his dispatch. His eyes betrayed his concern. "Eleven frontal assaults, General?"

Hood spoke to his aide. "Saddle my horse, Lieutenant." He turned to Benning as Second Lieutenant Carter rushed through the tent flap. In recent weeks his regard for Benning's cavalrymen had fallen considerably. Complaints had reached him that Confederate losses in Benning's Brigade were too heavy. Now, as the rush of morphine entered his brain, Hood permitted his displeasure to surface. "I fully intend to show the Union Army our resolve in this conflict, Colonel. Some of my field commanders have failed to instill a commitment to winning engagements among their men, and as a result we have chaos, indecision under fire. I shall take it upon myself to provide that missing leadership henceforth. Today, with the sounding of our bugles, we will transform this battlefield into a field of glory for the Confederacy. The President has placed his confidence in me, and I will not disappoint him. Prepare your men for battle, gentlemen!" His steady gaze lingered on Colonel Benning a moment longer. "You have your orders. When the bugle sounds, I want every officer and soldier in this command moving toward those gun batteries. If you are repelled, let it be from the weight of lead hurled at your faces, not from the weight of cowardice." He took a deep breath. "You are dismissed, gentlemen. Await the sounding of our bugles."

Officers filed out into the predawn paling of a cloudless sky. Hood motioned for Dr. Roberts to remain. As the last field commander departed, Hood took Roberts aside.

"Prepare another injection, Doctor. Wrap it in a piece of cloth and place it in my saddle pocket. I must not let the men see me retire from this battlefield for any reason. If you can do something for my pain, I will be able to sit a saddle today."

Dr. Roberts examined Hood's eyes. "Your pupils are already significantly dilated, General. An overdose could kill you."

"Prepare the injection, Doctor. The enemy has tried to kill me with lead and failed at it. These men must be led to victory. God has willed it . . . that I will be His instrument here. I will not allow pain to keep me from leading us to our destiny. Eleven times you will hear our bugles cry before this day has ended. I will lead the attack. This war has gone on aimlessly for lack of leadership. President Davis seeks a commander, not some pampered aristocrat like Bobby Lee or a vacillating quartermaster promoted to high rank without the slightest qualifications to lead men in battle like Joseph Johnston. At long last the President has recognized my abilities as a field commander, and I shall not be guilty of disappointing him in the slightest."

"Very well, General." Roberts turned to his medical bag.

A lathered bay horse galloped through the din and gun smoke toward a group of mounted officers watching the battle through field glasses from a wooded knob. The bay's rider swayed dan-

gerously in the saddle. The thud of heavy mortars was continuous, as it had been since dawn.

"It's General Hood," Colonel Buford Jackson said, his face
blackened by burnt powder.

Philip Work lowered his glasses. "At the risk of insubordina-
tion, Colonel, no man with all his faculties would have ordered
thirteen frontal charges against those breastworks. The bodies of
our dead now serve as our most formidable obstacle."

Cannon fire thundered up and down miles of battle line north
and south. Jackson sleeved grime and sweat from his forehead
and eyes. "Our losses are indeed heavy," he said. "However, I
suggest you keep opinion as to the general's mental fitness to
yourself."

Hood galloped his horse up the hill and reined to a halt as a
canister exploded almost directly overhead. He appeared not to
notice. A configuration of leather straps held him in his saddle
seat.

It was then Colonel Work saw Hood was weeping, although
his eyes had a glassy, vacant look belying his tears. Hood looked
over his shoulder at the battlefield. Thousands of men had begun
retreating westward as Union fire seemed to intensify.

Hood spoke to the officers around him in a voice so strange
it was as if someone else addressed them. "No discipline. See how
they turn back? If I could have led them in just one more charge,
victory would be ours. They have no heart. Bravery is in short
supply on our side today."

No one answered him. Philip Work couldn't think of anything but wasted words to say to a man who failed to comprehend what was happening.

Hood lifted his horse's reins. "Tomorrow is another day," he
said. "Perhaps God will see fit to let my men drink from the cup
of courage tonight. Let none of you doubt it is God's will that
we win this battle, gentlemen. We are not here by happenstance.
For the sake of our wives and children, we must defeat them.
There is no other course the Almighty will allow."

He rode off with a curious stiffness in his spine, looking toward the heavens as one might on a warm summer day enjoying the shapes of puffy white clouds and sunshine. But there was no sun, and the cloud above John Bell Hood was a thickening gray pall of smoke burning across the Confederacy as the year 1864 came to a close.

1

When she looked in a mirror she rarely ever liked what she saw, although she knew men found her beautiful because they stared at her much too long when she encountered them on the street. She'd been slow to develop physically. Her girlfriends had grown breasts much earlier than she and found an interest in boys long before she cared for them or wanted their attention. Her mother had comforted her as best she could during this slow maturation, promising Lorena that nature would provide when it was time. She looked like her mother in many ways, the same coal-black hair and smooth complexion, dainty hands and long, slender legs. But Margaret Blaire's eyes were quite different, an emerald green, while Lorena's were a deep brown like her father's and unusually large for her face, giving her a perpetual look of surprise.

She and her mother had never been close. A void existed between them, one Lorena hadn't fully understood until she was older. Margaret had come to resent her daughter's unusual beauty and the attention it garnered from men. As Lorena grew older, they had moved further apart. Margaret worried about wrinkles and strands of gray hair, often behaving as though Lorena were to blame for the signs of aging. Her father told her privately that Margaret was going through a mental change, asking for patience and understanding until it passed. But as distance between Lorena and her mother widened, she had found other interests. After graduation from Normal School for Girls in Baltimore and three years as a seamstress in one of the city's garment houses, she made an inquiry at the Academy of Nursing run by the United States Sanitary Commission, seeking a career as a nurse. An elderly woman there directed her to a hospital run by a crusader for the mentally ill, but only after warning Lorena that student nurses were not accepted if they only sought romantic adventure, Lorena's good looks convincing the woman she couldn't possibly have genuine motives caring for the sick.

Thus it was fate that led her to Dorothea Dix. Mistress Dix ran an asylum in lower Baltimore where mental cases were sent when their presence on city streets offended citizens with strong political ties. When Dorothea first met Lorena, the older woman disliked her immediately.

"You're too pretty," she said. "And much too young. A woman under thirty has no business being a nurse. Comeliness is a distraction to poor wretches who were born unsightly by a freak of nature, or to those who are ill. You wouldn't be suitable."

"What does a person's appearance have to do with caring? Or does empathy only come in plain paper? I made no request of God to look differently, nor did any of your patients here, the ones whom you identify as poor wretches. I am not vain. I only wish to give sympathetic care to those less fortunate. In order to do this I must have proper training, a nurse's training. Give me a chance to demonstrate that I have compassion. Please don't judge me by my physical appearance . . . it's unfair."

Dorothea gave her a frightfully chilly stare. "How old are you, Miss Blaire?"

"I'm twenty-one."

"And do you have a beau?"

She swallowed. "I sometimes keep company with a gentleman by the name of Paul Johns, although I wouldn't call him my beau. He's vice president of a banking firm here. We both have concern there will be a war over slavery. Neither of us is ready to make a serious commitment until times become more settled."

"It won't be a war over slavery," Mistress Dix said. "Issues dividing this country are far more complex. I'm still doubtful a war will result from all this rhetoric. Men, especially politicians, are inclined toward flowery speech and little in the way of action."

"Paul thinks there will be a war."

"He may envision a profit for the bank."

Lorena fussed with her handbag. "If there is a war, nurses will be sorely needed. Trained nurses will be an asset to this country—" A scream on a floor above Dorothea's private office caused her to abruptly stop talking. Someone began to shout.

"Does the sound of anguish bother you?" Dorothea asked.

"Not in the slightest," Lorena replied. "I only wish there was something I could do for him."

"You hardly seem strong enough to handle a violent person. We have some patients who can be exceedingly difficult at times."

"A gentle manner might accomplish what is needed. Coaxing may work as well as strength. With the right training I would know what to do. All I'm asking is the chance to learn what you can teach me about caring for the sick and the mentally ill."

Through slitted eyelids Dorothea watched her a moment while upstairs the ranting continued. "You have a certain sensitivity I like," she finally said. "You'd have to do something about your looks . . . wear your hair in a bun so as not to emphasize some of your better physical qualities. Being pretty can be a detriment to what you're doing, and being young detracts from the confidence patients should feel toward you. There is no pay. You'll serve as one of our volunteers during your training."

"I don't need any any money. I expected to serve an apprenticeship without pay."

"Our dresses are quite plain, no frills or lace. A cap and a nurse's gown will be provided. You are responsible for doing your own laundry at your own expense. Six months will be needed to complete your training if all goes well, but if I find that you have any deficiencies of character, I'll dismiss you at once."

"I'm confident you'll find me suitable. I'll always do my best."

"You have more poise than I expected from one so young. If you find my terms acceptable, you may report for work on Monday morning at six sharp. I won't tolerate the slightest tardiness or any shirking."

"Thank you, Mistress Dix. I won't disappoint you."

With that brief meeting, Lorena's nursing career had begun. Only a week later, on the twelfth of April, war was declared when guns were fired on Fort Sumter. Five days after Sumter fell, Dorothea Dix volunteered her services to the Union. She was placed in charge of all female nurses employed by the Union Army.

Wholesale training for army nurses commenced at once by the Sanitary Commission. Among candidates for its first graduating class was Lorena Blaire.

2

Seeing her for the first time, it was as if some inner voice spoke, awakening him to her presence despite the mayhem around him, cries from the wounded, and endless bursts of cannon fire that were so close to the hospital the very ground beneath him trembled. He looked up from his work without truly knowing why he did. She came through the tent flap wearing a dark-blue nurse's gown and cap, her pretty oval face paled by the horrors she encountered when the sights and smells and sounds of a field hospital assailed her senses. He knew immediately she was new to the battlefront by the mixture of innocence and fear he saw in her expression, the terror in her deep chocolate eyes, and more simply by the absence of blood on her starched dress. Every newcomer to the battlefields wore the same frightened look in the beginning, when so much carnage confronted them all at once, the piercing screams filling the tent, the sight of blood everywhere, a terrible smell of decaying flesh mingling with chloroform and the stench of excrement and urine when death relaxed the bowels and bladders of soldiers lying in neat rows across the murky tent floor. Many of the younger nurses fainted when they were first introduced to the grim realities of war in a field hospital. No amount of preparation in a classroom nor hours of training caring for the sick was sufficient to brace them for what they found here. Bodies torn to pieces by lead and iron had no counterpart in classroom medical instruction. Experience was the only taskmaster in wartime, and to say it was a harsh introduction scarcely seemed sufficient.

His work took his attention away from her. Suturing closed a fold of skin where he had severed the tibia and fibula to amputate the lower leg of an unconscious fair-skinned boy, he noted that most of the bleeding had stopped, draining into the bucket below the operating table just a few drops at a time now. The pail was only half full, a hopeful sign that recovery might not be unnecessarily lengthy. Blood loss killed more men than vital-organ damage. A low-velocity rifle ball was far more deadly when it severed an artery, causing a soldier to bleed profusely before a surgeon was available to stop the flow.

A shadow fell across his suturing, blocking out light from a lantern on the table where his instruments lay. Irritation made him pause long enough to say, "Get the hell out of my light so I can see what I'm doing!"

A soft voice replied, "I'm sorry, Doctor. I came over to offer assistance. . . ." The shadow moved away.

He looked up from his sewing briefly to find the pretty young nurse he had seen moments earlier now standing across the table. He attempted a polite smile. "I need the light," he said much more gently, with a note of apology for the tone he had used. "If you wish to help me, then please prepare strips of bandage from that pile of bedsheets behind you." His gaze wandered slowly over her features again—her beautiful dark eyes and high cheekbones, the fullness of her lips, raven hair twisted into a bun behind her cap. "You are quite young," he observed, doubting that she would be of much use to him due to her inexperience, thus he returned to his stitching. "I presume this is your first visit along the front. It isn't very pretty to look at, but if you have the stomach for it, your services are badly needed here. Those Yankees are giving us a pounding today, and I expect it will only grow worse. Bandages and pails of hot water must be kept at the operating tables."

"I understand a nurse's duties," the woman said, neither defensive nor boastful. "I assure you I am fully trained. I can assist with closing wounds when you have completed your surgeries, Doctor. I can perform a loop-stitch closure with a proper drainage opening, using either silk suture or cotton. I know how to administer chloroform in the correct amounts."

He tied off the final stitch and clipped the green cotton thread with bloody scissors, mildly surprised by the extent of her knowledge, far more than most nurses from academies in Richmond or Atlanta. "You sound fully competent, Miss . . . ?"

"Blaire. Lorena Blaire, Doctor. I shall begin preparing the bandages at once."

He smiled at her again, this time with more feeling. "I'm glad to have you here, Miss Blaire. Good nurses are desperately needed with Hood's Texans. We had none at the beginning of this war. I'm Dr. Jonathan Cross—" He was interrupted by a distant explosion, then the patter of spent grapeshot falling on the tent roof. A ball of smoldering hot lead burned through the canvas, plopping softly onto the floor near the bucket of blood. "I hold the rank of a captain, although I have no idea why. I'm not a soldier. I was a surgeon in Fort Worth, Texas, when the war broke out. My office was in a part of town known as Hell's Half Acre. Nothing but saloons and gaming parlors, so I have some experience with gunshot wounds." He sighed thoughtfully, glancing down at the boy on his operating table. "I doubt, however, that anything can prepare a physician for something like this." He examined the stitches again. "As to the use of silk sutures, I seriously doubt there is any silk thread available to us, nor much of anything else. Morphine and chloroform are in very short supply. It is only to be used in the worst of cases. This boy was in such deep shock when they brought him in that I performed his amputation without it. It is a sorry state of affairs, Miss Blaire, but necessary. We do the best we can."

Nurse Blaire bent over the pile of soiled linen and began tearing strips into bandage wrappings. Across the tent, another soldier started to scream when a surgeon went to work on his upper arm with a bone saw. Four harried surgeons tried to keep up with the wounded being brought back from the front lines, and as the battle sounds worsened in the distance, still more were being carried to them on blood-soaked litters. Until now their number was so great that most were being placed on the ground outside the tent until a doctor could see them. Jon saw the swelling rows of wounded lying beyond the tent flap and shook his head. Hood's army was being blown to pieces by artillery. The order to pull back would surely be given soon.

He noticed that the woman began wrapping the soldier's stump with strips of cloth. Without being told, she had undertaken the next logical step on her own. "Thank you, Miss Blaire," he said, wiping his hands dry on a blood-encrusted towel lying beside his instruments. He noted that she applied each strip of bandage in a crisscross pattern before tying off the ends. "Well done," he added. "Your training shows. I'll have this boy carried to a pallet outside and look for one of the more seriously wounded." He gave her a weak grin. "I'm afraid you have arrived just in time to begin what will surely be a very long and difficult day."

Her eyes met his. Strangely, the fear he had seen in them earlier was missing. A canister of grapeshot suddenly detonated in the skies above the tent, bringing more lead rain down onto the roof. Nurse Blaire did not so much as flinch when she heard the concussion.

"I am prepared for a great many difficult days, Dr. Cross," she said evenly, meeting his level gaze with one of her own.

Something within him stirred, a vague fluttering inside his chest, a trace of almost forgotten emotions that he had been denied since the war began. Slightly uncomfortable when he knew he had stared at her too long, he left the table abruptly and

walked across the blood-splattered tent floor to begin the search
for another badly wounded soldier. He would not have to go far
to find a victim of the merciless shelling Hood's army was taking, for they lay everywhere now, covering the ground around
the tent and the only unanswered question was whether he could
find one among them whose life he could save.

"You must eat something, Doctor," she said, holding a tin plate
of steaming food that smelled faintly of garlic, standing a few feet
away at the edge of the circle of light from his small lantern. He
had been resting against the trunk of an oak tree in the darkness,
dozing, his head lolled to one side until the sound of her voice
awakened him.

"I'm really not hungry, Miss Blaire. Too tired to eat, I suppose, but thank you, anyway. Leave the plate here. I'll try to eat
it later."

"Black-eyed peas," she said, bending down to place the food
near his feet. She noticed the half-drunk bottle of corn whiskey
resting beside him. "It's all they have at the mess tent, and there
seems to be precious little to go around at that. Hungry men are
surely less inclined to fight, I should think."

He thought how her voice had a musical quality. "These
men have been near starvation for months. Our supplies never
reach us. General Hood keeps us on the move continually, to
avoid the Yankee patrols. Hood is a tactical genius by any measure, albeit at a price in human suffering. Somehow, he knows
when and where to engage the enemy to our best advantage even
though it seems we are always seriously outnumbered. Until
today. Something has changed. No orders have come to pull
back—I don't understand it at all. We are being shot to pieces
here, and still Hood remains fast in the trenches, orders yet another charge into the teeth of the Yankee gun placements. It has
become a senseless slaughter of men, which is quite uncharacteristic of General Hood."

She allowed a silence to pass.

Not far away, its canvas walls made luminous by lanterns hanging from tent poles, men groaned inside the hospital. Some called out the names of loved ones while most of the others made their agony known without words, whimpering or crying intermittently. He had grown so accustomed to the sounds that he scarcely heard them any longer.

"There is no morphine," she said in a faraway voice, "and only a small portion of a tin of chloroform. Whatever shall we do?"

Jon sighed, reaching for the whiskey, for now it seemed as precious as the medicines. "We continue to operate without any form of painkiller, Miss Blaire. We've done it before, I am sad to say. While it is a brutal thing to witness, it is a necessity of this war for Confederate surgeons and their patients. We save what lives we can and close our minds to the rest." He took a long swallow from the neck of the bottle, wishing that distilled spirits could somehow wipe away months of terrible memories.

"In the beginning, I set out to become the most skillful surgeon I could be, providing my patients with care and sympathy," he said in a tired voice, as though just the memory of it pained him. "I studied every procedure carefully and never missed a class, for I feared I might not learn some vital part of a surgeon's training that could cost my patients their lives. I made a particular effort to master learning the symptoms of every form of disease known to man, and their treatments. I studied medicines and the complex manner of compounding them, reading everything I could on the subject, asking questions of my professors and colleagues, to seek answers to so many riddles we know little or nothing about. I felt I was prepared to become a good doctor, and a competent surgeon." His eyelids fell when a rush of unwanted recollections overwhelmed him.

"Then I answered the call of duty, when Texas seceded from the Union. At the time I had no politics of my own, for I had been much too busy with my medical training to encumber myself with feelings about states' rights and slavery. My father owns slaves, and perhaps because of this I allowed a spirit of nationalism for the Confederate cause to embroil me in a controversy I truly knew little about. I only knew that an army would need doctors, and I thought it would be a way to broaden my scant experience with the healing arts, being only two years out of school." He opened his eyes, staring at the darkness. "But I confess I was totally unprepared for this, for the horrors of it. I felt I understood the realities of my profession, that death was always a possible consequence of my failures. I believed I was equipped to handle most any situation for which I had been trained, never once doubting my ability to deal with hardship. I believed I understood death on an intellectual level, that I was prepared for it. This war has shown me just how wrong I was. . . ." His voice trailed off when tears formed in the corners of his eyes; he wiped them away with a portion of his shirtsleeve darkened by blood and looked up rather suddenly. "Sorry for rambling on, Miss Blaire. I suppose I can blame it on the whiskey, and on being tired. You must be as tired as I am. Take some rest." For a moment he listened to the silence coming from the battlefield. "At dawn they will resume the fighting, unless we are ordered back. For some reason, General Hood is bent on continuing this engagement. For the life of me, I can't see what is so important about these hills around Franklin, Tennessee."

Nurse Blaire knelt down in front of him with sympathy in her eyes. She reached out to touch his arm gently; then she took a handkerchief from a pocket of her dress and dabbed his cheeks where blood from his sleeve mingled with tears. "I don't suppose it matters to generals where a battle is fought," she said. "One place is as good as another when men are asked to die. Get some sleep, Doctor. Eat the peas before they get cold. If you like, I will bring you some coffee to go with your supper."

Hearing this, he chuckled softly, partly to hide the fact that he was embarrassed to be crying in front of her. "This army hasn't had any coffee in months. And we've all eaten enough peas to turn our skins gray. I've been told by the quartermaster that peas and salt pork is all we have. Men have been sent out to forage for whatever they can find at nearby farms. Unless supply wagons reach us soon, we'll all be eating boiled acorns and horse meat for our supper."

Nurse Blaire patted his forearm, smiled, and stood up. "I will be ready at dawn, Doctor," she said. Then she lifted her skirt above the tops of her shoes and walked away into the night shadows.

Resting his head against the oak trunk, he thought about her and the day's events. Lorena Blaire had an uncommon knowledge of medicine for a nurse, and she showed no sign of being fainthearted when even the worst injuries confronted them on the operating table. He found that he truly admired her competence. And as an aside, she was one of the most beautiful women he had ever seen. Or was it simply that he had been too long away at war, too far removed from the charms of any woman for many months?

He wondered about her until his eyelids grew heavy. As he always did now, he feared drifting off to sleep, for his dreams became dreadful things, recurring nightmarish scenes from the hospital, of amputations without chloroform, the grinding of his saw through bone and marrow, trying his best to ignore the cries from his patient that became shrieks of indescribable agony when the saw struck a nerve trunk. He was quite certain he would hear those screams in his slumber until his dying day, remembering the brutality of what he had done. No man with all his faculties intact could ever forget something like that, inflicting so much suffering on another human being even if it was called for as the correct form of treatment in the name of medicine.

At times like these he considered the bitter irony of his situation. He'd spent years learning how to diagnose and treat disease: scurvy, dysentery, typhoid, diphtheria, pneumonia, galloping consumption, for which no treatment was known. While disease caused the death of two soldiers for every one dead from battle wounds, he felt he understood death when ailment was the cause. But what he could not comprehend was the hopelessness of a surgeon's plight when asked to repair bodies torn to shreds by gunpowder and shot. What he was being asked to do simply could not be done. Mangled limbs could not be repaired, and the only hope of saving a patient's life was quick amputation, before gangrene set in, before blood loss caused death. And to perform the amputations without chloroform and morphine was too inhumane to contemplate, yet he had to do it anyway in order to save lives.

He found he was weeping again. Tears rolled down his cheeks into his blond beard stubble. Gripping the neck of the whiskey bottle, he glanced at its contents, thinking how it provided the only escape he had from the madness around him. He drank deeply and closed his eyes, feeling the welcome burning in his throat. If only he could get drunk enough tonight to sleep without any more of those awful dreams. . . .

3

Lorena undressed quietly in the darkness. Clara Brooks appeared to be asleep on the pallet beside hers. Removing her gown, then her bodice, she laid them across her trunk and slipped into a flannel nightshirt and removed her highbutton shoes. She knelt upon her blankets, after making sure the tent flap was securely fastened, and finally stretched out on her aching back to rest. Breathing deeply, she heard Nurse Brooks stir beneath the bedcovers.

"How was your first day?" Clara asked, whispering, for their tent was quite close to the others. They could hear continual coughing coming from all directions—it seemed every soldier in camp was afflicted with a cough.

"Exhausting," she replied, keeping her voice low. "Sickening beyond my ability to describe it. I saw nothing less than what they told us we would see. Worse, if that is possible. Dorothea was quite right when she said these Confederates are little more than uncivilized savages. The doctors conduct surgeries without any painkillers, as though they enjoy inflicting pain. Confederates have a great sufficiency of ammunition for their guns, yet they are unwilling to invest in even a meager supply of medicines for their wounded. What I saw here today was utterly revolting. Southerners have no compassion whatsoever. It would seem most of their physicians are completely incapable of sympathy for their suffering patients."

"Dragon Dix knew what she was talking about," Clara agreed. "We all despised Dorothea for the way she conducted our training in such a rush—demanding this, demanding that, saying it was at General Grant's request that we be prepared for service quickly. I vomited three times today, when no one was looking. I did my very best to be strong, Lorena, yet I failed miserably. I never was so sick in all my life."

"It was gruesome, indeed," Lorena whispered, remembering. "However, I do have some admiration for the physician I assisted today, despite the fact that he is a Southerner. I believe he does genuinely feel something for his patients, unlike the other doctors. He wept tonight, grieving over the men he could not save. A man who weeps cannot be thoroughly corrupt, even if he is a Texan by birth. There must be some good in him."

"I saw him come outside once," Clara said, a hint of excitement creeping into her voice, "while I was throwing up behind one of the ambulances. He is tall, and quite handsome. There was something about him, a suggestion of good breeding in his face. I suppose you could call it an air, a quality. It's difficult to explain, yet I sensed somehow that he is a well-bred man."

Lorena whispered sternly, "You must not allow yourself to be distracted or forget that he is an enemy of the Union, Clara."

"I know," Clara remarked in a small voice tinged with fear. "How can I forget that we are surrounded by the enemy here? I am neither blind nor stupid. If we are discovered—"

"They will execute us, or at the very least send us to a Confederate prison. Should they begin to suspect us at all, for any reason, we are surely doomed to the most dreadful fate. Many uncouth Southerners treat their women no differently than com-

mon prostitutes, Dorothea said, and we were told what to expect if we were sent to places like Andersonville or Belle Isle. Keep
this in mind when you believe you find good breeding among
Confederate officers. They are not well-bred, or they would have
no part of this unjust war to keep their Negroes in slavery. Their
actions speak plainly enough."

"I merely observed that the doctor is handsome," Clara said
in mild protest. "When he looked at me, I felt a slight flush."

Lorena thought back to Dr. Cross a moment. "He *is* handsome in a roguish way, I suppose. But that changes nothing. Go
to sleep now. I'm very tired." She closed her eyes, exhausted yet
far from being able to sleep after a discussion of their dangerous
secret mission with Hood's brigades. Of all the Confederate generals confounding General McClellan's Army of the Potomac and
General Grant's advances toward the Confederate capital at Richmond, none was more canny or elusive than John Bell Hood, it
was said, with the possible exception of Jubal Early. General
Early had become such a nagging irritant to Grant that he neglected to keep track of Hood's movements during the previous
summer, until suddenly Hood's fearless Texans surfaced in eastern Tennessee, cutting Pope's Union army to ribbons. Thus the
spy plan had been devised by General Grant himself, to send
trained nurses behind Confederate lines to join Hood's Medical
Corps. Desperate Confederate surgeons were unlikely to question the arrival of badly needed skilled nurses with false letters of
introduction from a nursing academy in Virginia. The letters had
worked as Grant had said they would, allowing Lorena and Clara
past the Confederate sentries below Franklin, to be pressed into
immediate service with Hood's surgeons without any questions
being asked of them. The plight of thousands of Confederate
wounded made Hood's officers less cautious. Now, all that was
expected of Lorena and Clara was to send coded letters to a
Union agent at an address in northern Virginia, advising General Grant of the movements of Hood's Texas brigades. When
it was first explained to them by Dorothea Dix, called Dragon

Dix for her autocratic leadership at the helm of all nursing services for the Union Army—she was feared and revered by every nurse and volunteer in the Sanitary Commission—it sounded so simple. Dangerous if they were discovered, yet quite simple if nothing went wrong. But tonight, some of the simplicity Lorena had perceived at the onset was not quite so apparent. She found herself perspiring despite a slight night chill in the tent. If she and Clara were caught, the consequences would surely be death or the most inhumane treatment imaginable at one of the Confederate prisons. All manner of gruesome stories had come back from Andersonville to Union headquarters in Washington, of men starved to mere skeletons, men who turned to cannibalism when no food was given them, sanitary conditions too ghastly to permit the survival of swine, a morass of bodily wastes in which men slept and clung to life by the thinnest of threads. Dorothea said it was further proof of all Southerners' appalling lack of humanity, that they would treat white prisoners no differently than they did their poor Negroes.

Imagining the fate of a woman at such a place, she shuddered and tried to put it from her mind. Outside the tent, wet coughs echoed back and forth across the encampment, a reminder of how near the reality of war and imprisonment for anyone caught spying truly was. What twist of fate was it that had brought her here? A simple wish to do something for the cause of freedom for black slaves. She had always been so deeply touched by the images of Negroes trapped in slavery. Ever since she was a young girl she had known how wrong it was to imprison people to lifetimes of servitude because of the color of their skin. She had cried when her father first told her about Negro slaves—had she been six? Or was it seven?—hearing how Southerners flogged their slaves for minor disobediences, how they worked them from sunup until sundown and fed them poorly, kept them in shacks or chained up at night to prevent their escape, treatment worse than what was given to dogs. To say that such a practice should be outlawed wasn't enough. If a war was needed to end it, then war was a cause Lorena Blaire felt she understood. Until now. Until today, when she actually experienced seeing the horror of battle injuries for herself.

She remembered again how Dr. Jonathan Cross had cried when he talked about the war, this battle being fought at Franklin. It was a relatively easy thing to make mention of a war being waged over slavery and the rights of states to govern themselves, but when the aftermath of that war lay before you on blood-soaked pallets, the bodies of men torn asunder by warring armies, then an idealistic cause became grisly reality, a reality of blood and screams and pain and death that no one could fully comprehend until they saw it, smelled it, heard it, and felt it in the pit of their stomach and in their heart.

"I'm so frightened," Clara whispered softly, when she too was unable to sleep.

"So am I, Clara. We must trust in God and believe that His blessings will be upon us. This is more than a noble effort on our part to help relieve the suffering of Negroes. We have come to this battlefield with a far larger purpose—to assist with a change in the future of mankind so that men regardless of their color will be free of slavery forever. We have put our trust in the Lord. . . ."

Clara sniffled.

"Please don't cry," Lorena said, reaching across the space between them to touch the hem of Clara's blanket. "Be strong, and believe in what we are doing."

Clara seized her hand, squeezing it. "Oh, I will try so hard to be brave," she promised, choking back more tears, "and I truly do believe what we are doing is right and just."

They were silent for a time until Clara spoke, with her voice under control now. "What is the young doctor's name?" she asked.

"Jonathan Cross. He comes from Texas, a place named Fort Worth. It seems I remember reading somewhere it is a cattle town of no particular importance. He told me his practice was in a terrible sounding place called Hell's Half Acre before the war, full of gambling parlors and drinking establishments. He said he had some experience with gunshot wounds, so it must be a rowdy section of the city . . . if this Fort Worth can be called a city. I was able to judge he has low regard for personal cleanliness. He has not shaved recently, nor taken a bath. His instruments need a very thorough washing, as does his attire."

Clara smoothed the front of her nightdress beneath the thin blanket covering her from chin to toe. "I still say he is quite handsome . . . wavy blond hair and the deepest blue eyes I have ever seen, slender and yet slightly muscular, with a rugged face sure to catch any woman's eye."

While in some ways Lorena agreed with Clara's assessment of Dr. Cross, it seemed an untimely moment to give an enemy of the Union such a thoroughly positive physical appraisal. "We are at war with him and his rebellious government, Clara, lest you need a reminder of why we brave the dangers of this battlefront. It sounds inappropriate to prepare a list of attributes you find to be attractive about him."

"I was only making woman's talk," she said quietly, reproached. "I see nothing wrong with recognizing that a man is handsome."

Lorena knew it was more than that in Clara's case. Clara was terrified. Talking about Dr. Cross was merely a way to seek comfort in other things, something less frightening than being discovered as a Union spy. She came from a sheltered childhood, a family of considerable wealth, and in the beginning Lorena had believed she would change her mind when the time came to drive the buggy to Tennessee to look for Hood's brigades. Yet Clara had surprised her, remaining steadfast even when they made their dangerous drives across Virginia and parts of North Carolina to eastern Tennessee where Hood was believed to be. Then she and Clara learned that Hood had taken a stand against a huge Union force in the foothills around Franklin. Inexplicably, the general had stopped his running, giving Lorena and Clara the opportunity to find him as November of the year 1864 drew to a close.

And now they were here with Hood's Texans at the scene of

a pitched battle, where dying men were no longer simply a topic for newspaper headlines or casual conversation over tea and sugarcakes. Death was all around them. Their own lives were in real danger, and a careless mistake could prove to be their undoing.

To push aside such unpleasantness for now, Lorena turned her thoughts back to Jonathan Cross. He *was* handsome, though not to such an extent that he unnerved her when she was in his presence. His movements were interesting, for they always seemed very sure, purposeful, without wasted motion. Even when he walked among the wounded, he accomplished it with a peculiar grace. She was only slightly uncomfortable when he looked at her too long, for at times it was as if he somehow saw through her skin into her innermost self. Once or twice, when his eyes roamed up and down her body, she felt almost naked, although there was nothing in his manner to suggest lasciviousness. He had merely examined her, and yet there was some indefinable thing about the way he looked at her that hinted of something deeper. . . .

Now it was she who was allowing herself to indulge in silly flights of fancy. Dr. Cross had only glanced at her a few times— she was merely imagining that there might be more. Her heart belonged to Paul, and she silently scolded herself for thinking about another man in the way she imagined Dr. Cross looked at her today. He could scarcely be expected to work beside her without gazing at her now and then.

She forced her mind elsewhere. She thought about Paul, to soothe away any guilt for having wondered about the attentions of another man. Paul was her strength. His memory would guide her through many difficult times, comfort her, reassure her that when she returned home, someone she loved would be waiting for her.

I miss you, Paul, she thought. I wish you could be here to put your arms around me tonight.

Wishing this caused her to admonish herself again. I am made of sterner stuff, she told herself. I will not allow myself to become a mewing creature at a time like this.

Turning on her side, she listened to the chorus of coughing spells coming from the camp. And in spite of a wish not to, she felt terribly, terribly alone.

Another sound reached her. Clara was crying softly, trying to muffle the sobs behind her hands.

"Don't cry. Everything will work out as it should. What we saw today would be a terrible shock to anyone. It may help to remember the way they mistreat their slaves, Clara. They whip them unmercifully, and starve them as though they were no more than lowly beasts of the field. What we are doing here will help free thousands of poor Negroes from slavery. Try to think about them when you feel overwhelmed."

"I will," Clara promised. "You sound . . . so courageous, and I know I will never have your inner strength."

"I think of Paul when circumstances threaten to weaken my resolve. It may help if you think about Willard."

"Yes. I shall confine my thoughts to happy days spent with Willard. Our picnics. His gentle nature, his sweet caress. He is such a wonderful man. The dean of the college praises him for how well he conducts his classes. He promised that Willard will be afforded a full professorship soon. Won't it be wonderful?"

Lorena had not truly been listening, for an unwanted recollection of Jonathan Cross kept creeping back into her thoughts. What was it about him that she found so distracting? Was it his eyes? They were a piercing blue. It most certainly could not be his tangled, unshorn hair, for his golden locks were continually tousled about his head, hanging down his neck in a careless and neglected fashion. His attire was filthy, his chin unshaven, and most of the day his shirt clung wetly to his sweating skin. His tall cavalry boots needed blacking, his riding breeches were torn in a number of places. An unkempt appearance surely did nothing to distinguish anyone—had she not been told of his profession beforehand, she would not have supposed he could be a surgeon.

"Go away," she whispered when a mental image of Dr. Cross would not leave her thoughts. She was in love with Paul Johns of Baltimore, a respected banker from a good family. It was dis-

graceful to be thinking about anyone else, unladylike, unbecoming a young woman of good education and moral character.
She would not tolerate the intrusion into her private thoughts
any longer.

She forced her mind back to her momentous meeting with
General Ulysses Grant. Grant had come to the Sanitary Commission Academy of Nursing at Baltimore back in March, shortly
after being named commander of all the armies of the United
States by President Lincoln. He had conferred with Dorothea,
asking for four of her best students who would be commissioned
with a dangerous assignment: be sent south as spies behind Confederate lines with the sole objective of locating Confederate
generals John Bell Hood and Jubal Early. In pairs, the nurses
were to win the confidence of medical officers with false papers
and competent nursing skills. The only thing required of them
was to master a code and write periodic coded letters to an address in northern Virginia, in care of a woman who resided at
Gaines's Mill. Thus had come so unexpectedly Lorena's chance
to do something more than nursing for her country, and she accepted it gladly, after the hushed conversation with Ulysses Grant
in Dorothea Dix's private study wherein she and Clara, Bessie
Higgins and Ruth Ann Waldrop were given a secret commission
that Grant promised would cut the war short by months and perhaps save thousands of lives. Lorena had listened closely to General Grant's every word and, with her heart racing, tried to envision what the spying mission would be like. They would be
camped with the Confederate enemy for an unknown length of
time, always at great risk of being discovered, enduring the hardships of war with battle-weary Southerners who had little food,
it was reported, and not much else but the heart to continue
fighting. General Grant wanted an end to the war—he had given
Lincoln his word that he would end it soon if he could only surround General Lee and splinter the guerrilla armies of Hood and
Early. Finding Hood and Early, knowing their whereabouts at
all times, was a key element of Grant's strategy. It fell to four
brave young nurses from the nursing school run by Dorothea to

provide him with the intelligence he needed. There had been something about General Grant's voice that night, his manner and soft-spoken way that gave Lorena and the others confidence in him. Although he was a smallish man, thickset and bearded, not at all a gentlemanly type, he had had a sincerity and openness that Lorena liked and trusted. She had been the first to agree to the mission, a fact which doubtlessly influenced the other women to accept.

She eventually drifted into a light sleep, awakening every now and then when a groan from the hospital or a cough intruded upon her slumber. There were no more unseemly recollections of the handsome Confederate surgeon to disturb her, and for that she was most grateful.

4

Jonathan Cross walked slowly from one pallet to the next, pausing with his lantern, bending down to inspect each patient carefully as the sky brightened with faint gray light just before sunrise. Far too often, he merely lifted a soldier's tattered blanket and draped it over his face in a silent acknowledgment of death. A squad of grave-faced litter bearers followed him to remove the blanket-draped dead. A line of soldiers was forming east of the hospital, where the newly arrived nurses stood with jars of bowel remedy—a plug of opium for those with dysentery, a larger plug of blue mass for men whose bowels were obstructed. The afflicted shuffled obediently past Nurse Blaire and Nurse Brooks, muttering their medical complaints softly in mildly embarrassed voices when they were forced to explain their reasons for being in line to attractive young women.

Major James Canfield, commander of Hood's Fourth Medical Corps, stood by with his hands clasped behind his back, inspecting the work of the nurses. It had always been his belief that women had no place in a military encampment no matter what the reason, yet he had grudgingly granted permission for the two nurses to remain in camp under close supervision when the worst casualties of the war besieged his staff after only three days of fighting at Franklin. The major seemed as bewildered as the rest of the officers under Hood's command about the general's refusal to withdraw from the field when his troops were being subjected to such a merciless pounding by Union artillery. Whispers spread that Hood had taken leave of his senses—he had to be strapped to his horse every morning now due to a missing right leg, and his left arm was almost useless after being shattered by a ball at Gettysburg. It was said he often wept, or alternately ranted and pulled his hair when his troops were not able to win engagements. Jon Cross and the other surgeons had had no audience with the general as conditions gradually worsened. Major Canfield had explained that Hood did not want to hear bad news while his mind was otherwise occupied with strategy.

Jon knelt beside a boy obviously riddled with fever, for in spite of a chill November morning the soldier's face was beaded with sweat. Holding his lantern closer, Jon noted the telltale spots developing under the skin that would become pox. "How do you feel?" he inquired softly.

"Cold," the boy stammered. "Then it gits hot real sudden-like, an' I'm burnin' up, like I was on fire."

"You have typhus. I'm afraid there isn't much we can do except allow it to run its course. One of the nurses will be along later to feed you some broth." He frowned. "I'm simply curious, son. How old are you?"

"Fourteen, Cap'n. Tell me, sir, are you the doctor?"

"Yes, I'm a doctor."

Swallowing, the youth asked fearfully, "Am I gonna live?"

Given a choice between truth and words of encouragement, he replied, "If you're strong enough. You mustn't give up no matter how poorly you feel. Men with low constitutions have been known to die from typhus, while others fare much better and recover in relatively short order. It's up to you, soldier. You must face your fever as bravely as you faced those Yankee guns."

Tears began to mingle with sweat on the boy's face. "Wasn't none of us all that brave, sir. Fact is, we was all plumb scared to death. Everybody was runnin' every which way, yellin' to beat all get-out. There was dead men all over the ground, so thick we couldn't hardly walk without trippin' over bodies. Worst sight I ever saw in all my life. Tryin' to run up that hill, my boots kept slippin' in all the blood. Bobby was right in front of me when a ball struck him in the face. He turned 'round and I seen he had this hole in his forehead. He jus' fell down dead afore he could say a word. He was nearly a year younger'n me, an' he was the best friend I had in the whole world."

Jon's expression hardened unconsciously; his teeth gritted and when he spoke, his voice was hard to hear. "Someone should send a letter to his family. If you know his address, I'll see to it that you get some paper and an envelope."

"Can't write, sir. I learnt how to write my name, is all. Bobby's family lives at Prairie Hill. It's the Joneses' place at the crossroads. Calvin is his pa's name."

"I'll find someone to write the letter for you." He looked over his shoulder. Nurse Blaire and the other nurse were handing out medicines by lantern light, a task one of the orderlies could perform just as well. "Nurse Blaire!" he cried, standing so she could see him clearly among the rows of wounded lying beneath the trees. "Find some writing materials and come over here to take a letter from this soldier. Someone else can dispense the medicine for the time being."

He saw Lorena hand her jar of tablets to the other nurse and hurry through paling shadows behind the hospital tent. "A nurse will take down your letter and see that it gets to a courier," he told the shivering boy. "I'll ask her to fix you some broth with a measure of snakeroot powder. Sometimes it helps lower the fever if the typhus is not too far advanced, and it will help you get back some of your strength."

"I sure ain't lookin' to die, sir. If all it takes to git well is a strong constitution, I'll be jus' fine in a day or two. My ma always said I was mighty strong willed."

Jon recalled the soldier's story of his friend's death on the battlefield. "Where is the body . . . of Bobby Jones?"

A grim, meaningful silence followed while the boy stared up at a sprinkling of stars fading with the coming of dawn. "Out yonder, at the bottom of one of them hills. Night before last I tried to crawl out there in the dark so's I could fetch him back fer a proper burial, only they saw me, I reckon. Somebody fired a shot at me, an' I got so scared that I was gonna die fetchin' Bobby back that I commenced to crawl back quick as I could."

Nurse Blair emerged from the nurses' tent carrying a sheaf of foolscap. Jon waited while she found her way through the maze of prone forms swathed in blankets to the pale glow from his lantern. "Good morning, Miss Blaire," he said, trying his best not to sound too grave. "I want you to take down a letter—two of them, if you please. This soldier lost his friend on the battlefield, and he needs to notify the family. Then take down a letter to this boy's parents. He has contracted a case of typhus and he is only fourteen years old. I want his family to hear from him. He doesn't know how to write, although he can sign his own name."

He saw it in her eyes: disbelief when she learned the boy's tender age.

"Yes, Doctor," Lorena replied, noticably hoarse as though her throat was constricted. She smiled at the young soldier and knelt down beside him, placing the paper on her lap.

"When you have finished," Jon continued, "see to it that the letters are given to a courier." He glanced eastward, where the sun was beginning to rise above the hills. "I suggest you do it as quickly as you can, Miss Blaire, before the shelling begins. You will be sorely needed at the hospital as soon as the fighting resumes."

He was turning away to continue making rounds through rows of wounded men without his lantern when Lorena spoke to him.

"Would you grant me permission to include a short letter to my aunt at Gaines's Mill, letting her know that we made it safely to our destination?"

"Of course. I merely ask that you accomplish it as rapidly as possible. Any moment now, the cannons will commence firing at us from those hilltops. Apparently, General Hood has decided that we will hold our present position again today."

"I shall do my best to hurry," she promised, looking to the boy now. "If you will begin by giving me the name of your friend and where to reach his family . . ." she said in a gentle voice while preparing a pen with ink from a tiny lavender bottle she placed on the ground beside her.

Jon departed to pass among the rest of the wounded soldiers, peering down at one and then another, hearing the boy with typhus start to cry as he told Lorena about his dead friend. Suddenly, the first thundering roar from a distant cannon abruptly shattered the morning silence. A canister of lead whistled across skies painted pink by a brilliant sunrise; then a second explosion shook the earth as hundreds of excited shouts went up from the sleeping Confederate camp, announcing a resumption of the bitter battle on the fourth day of bloodletting at Franklin.

Casualties poured into the clearing around the hospital in waves; some were carried on litters, others were limping or crawling under their own power, and all of those who could speak were begging for medical attention and some way to lessen their pain. Jon could never have imagined so much suffering. Hundreds of retreating Confederates streamed past the hospital tents and rows of parked ambulance wagons. Men who fought courageously for the three previous days of pitched battle now merely hoped to escape total annihilation. Soldiers in deep shock who somehow were able to walk stumbled blindly past the hospital, glazed eyes fixed on some far-off tranquil hillside to the west where there were no pounding cannons or crackling muskets, no fallen bodies or dark puddles of Confederate blood. It was a scene too frightful to describe with words when Jon was able to look up from his work long enough to comprehend what was happening, seeing fear-crazed men, some from units of the Army of Tennessee along with men from Hood's brigades, soldiers driven beyond reason by terror running through the forest like herds of stampeding cattle.

Lorena gripped a wounded soldier's wrist while the bone saw ground slowly through the humerus a scant four inches below the screaming man's shoulder. Fresh blood freckled her cheeks from twin eruptions when the anterior and posterior humeral arteries were severed. Hemorrhaging continued despite a band of cloth wound tightly around the upper arm. The soldier's undamaged arm was held fast by a slow-witted youth named Goodie Carrothers who never seemed to mind his duties as an orderly, no matter how grisly. Goodie's unusual strength made him ideal for the job, and his dullmindedness was in many respects a blessing, for he seldom truly understood what was going on around him, and being almost deaf he was oblivious to all but the loudest screams.

Jon glanced quickly into Lorena's eyes, for she appeared to be losing color in her face at the sight of so much blood. "Are you all right, Miss Blaire?"

"I'm fine, Doctor. Please do not stop on my account. This poor fellow surely cannot endure much more." She raised one arm and hurriedly sleeved blood and perspiration from her brow without releasing her two-handed grip on the patient's wrist.

Three more strokes were needed to cut through the bone and the radial and medial nerve trunks. The soldier gasped, his body went slack, and he fell unconscious. Lorena let go of the severed limb and took a half step back; then she reached for her forehead in the same instant that her knees buckled. She collapsed limply on the floor of the tent before Jon could reach her. Her brown eyes rolled upward, batted once, and her eyelids closed.

Jon picked her up gently and carried her from the tent as a steady flow of soldiers retreated past him. The girl was light as a feather, loose jointed in her deep faint, her arms and legs dangling. He found a secluded spot away from the mad rush of gray-clad men beneath a giant oak tree, its autumn leaves alive with color. Lowering her to a bed of fallen leaves, he took off his shirt and rolled it into a ball to make a pillow for her head. When she was as comfortable as he could make her, he trotted back to the hospital for a rag, a pail of tepid water, and, from his medical bag, the remnants of last night's bottle of home-brewed corn whiskey.

Dr. Canfield gave him an inquisitive look, pausing before he delved a bloody hand into the chest cavity of a wounded man on a nearby operating table.

"My nurse has fainted!" Jon cried, answering the major's questioning stare with a shout in order to be heard above the screams and groans, the rattle of gunfire, the boom of distant cannons.

"Do not tarry long, Doctor," Canfield said gruffly, his brow pinched somewhere between a frown and a grimace. "As you can see we are terribly busy here. A solitary fainting nurse is not sufficient cause to leave these wounded men unattended."

"Yes, sir. I won't be but a moment." He raced from the tent so quickly that water slopped from the pail down his trouser leg and into his boot. Nearing the tree where Lorena lay, he heard a sudden burst of gunfire coming from the west, the direction from which men were retreating. The shots made no sense at first, until he saw an officer in a gray uniform aboard a charging bay horse riding back and forth in front of the retreating Confederates, firing a pistol in the air. General Hood, lashed to his saddle by leather strapping, shouted to his men, firing over their heads. "Turn back! Turn back! Fight, you yellow bastards, or you are not worthy of being called a Texan or a soldier! Follow me! I will lead you to the tops of those hills myself!"

Hood's cries had a curious effect on men who could hear him. Some halted in their tracks. Others slowed their steps, looking to one another. Gradually, the retreat faltered and then ended. Soldiers gathered to form small groups, turning back toward enemy lines, talking among themselves as some reloaded muskets and side arms. Jon saw what Hood had accomplished as he ran to Lorena's side and knelt beside her. When he noted the absence of color in the woman's face, her skin turned almost translucent, he quickly forgot about everything else and attended to her.

He wet a cloth and wiped her face, her brow, her cheeks and neck, using gentle strokes, dabbing her skin here and there where dried blood made her appear measled. For a time she lay perfectly still, unconscious, having retreated no differently than the scared soldiers, to a place where there was no suffering. Gradually, as the damp rag passed over her again and again, she awakened by degrees with eyelids aflutter as consciousness slowly returned.

"What . . . happened?" she asked weakly, trying to focus on his face.

"You fainted. Lie still a moment, until you feel better."

A look of concern crossed her face that became frustration, then embarrassment. She tried to sit up, but he caught her by the shoulder, pressing her gently yet firmly back down on the bed of leaves.

"Please do not coddle me, Dr. Cross!" she protested loudly, a flush darkening her cheeks. "I am quite capable of continuing my duties. . . ."

He grinned, and his amused expression brought an end to her outburst, her voice trailing off.

"Lie still," he said again. He took the cork from the neck of the whiskey bottle. "Drink a swallow of this. It should help to revive you."

Lorena scowled at the clear liquid, smelling it when he took out the cork. "I do not partake of distilled spirits, Doctor, not for any reason. It has a disgusting odor, and I shouldn't be at all surprised if the taste is similarly foul. Thank you, but I must decline. Now, please allow me to stand up so that I may return to our wounded." It was then she noticed that he was not wearing a shirt. Her gaze drifted down his bare chest until it seemed something startled her. "My goodness," she whispered, her flush deepening. "Why have you undressed?"

His grin only widened as he noticed her embarrassment. "My shirt is behind your head, Miss Blaire."

She reached for the shirt and handed it to him quickly. "I do wish you would put it on," she said, half closing her eyelids while she turned her head away. "Some might think it improper."

He almost laughed, but he held it in when he sensed that her embarrassment was genuine. Rocking back on his boot heels, he put on his badly bloodied shirt as Lorena got up with the aid of the tree, steadying herself against the oak trunk. Curiously, as he watched her, it occurred to him that he had been oblivious to the noise of battle while attending to her faint. He could not remember ever being so taken with a woman before. She was more than a beautiful girl . . . her remarkable beauty was only a part of the strange attraction he felt. It was something far deeper than a purely physical interest. Odd, he thought, that this should happen at a time like the present. What was it about her that fascinated him so?

Then, as though his hearing had suddenly returned, he heard shrill yells of agony and the pounding of cannons from the east. He straightened and wheeled toward the hospital, pushing Lorena from his mind when duty summoned him. He had scarcely taken more than a few hurried strides when Nurse Blaire rushed past him to enter the rear of the tent before he got there, holding her skirt above her shoe tops to keep from tripping on the hem.

5

With the dark had come a chill one might have expected from November in Tennessee, accompanied by an eerie silence across the field of battle when the relentless Union shelling finally ended. Lorena rested atop a stack of firewood, her shoulders drooping inside her wool coat, watching tiny fires flicker from a line of wooded hills on the far side of the valley. She was cold, albeit not entirely due to a change in the weather from Indian summer to fall, rather from an inner cold accompanying the knowledge that her coded letter had been sent to Gaines's Mill. The Union agent would know both she and Clara were with Hood at Franklin, thus Grant could be informed that two of his spies were in place with the Texas brigades. She had dashed off the letter hurriedly to keep from being missed at the hospital by Captain Cross or the bullish major, James Canfield. Her duty to the Union was done for the present, and all she had to do now was wait for orders to come that would tell her where Hood's army intended to move. If they meant to move at all. After a thorough routing today by Union forces, it seemed illogical that Hood would stay here to continue this losing fight. Confederate casualties were enormous—she had seen most of them for herself—yet Hood still sought a victory, sending wave after wave of infantry across the pockmarked plain where thousands of dead bloated in the sun. Even at night the stench of death drifted across the battlefield on soft currents of air, and the smell grew so nauseating that men walked about camp with damp rags over their nose and mouth. One look across the battleground littered with rotting corpses had been enough to satisfy her curiosity about what the front lines were like—a horrendous slaughter of men that she felt sure no one on either side truly understood.

A shadow came toward her from the hospital. She knew by the silhouette it was Jonathan Cross. She had been so humiliated to have fainted this afternoon, hardly the sort of stalwart behavior expected from a trained nurse.

"Good evening, Miss Blaire," the doctor said thickly, his steps slowed by fatigue and resignation. So many wounded were left untreated in the clearing around the hospital that a dozen physicians could not have seen them all. Men groaned and whimpered behind trees along the battle line. Only the most seriously hurt could be attended by the doctors, and even then many would die from less serious wounds before a surgeon could provide them with care. The task had quickly become too overwhelming by any measure, and the four weary surgeons, the medical corps aides, and the two nurses simply saw as many men as they could until exhaustion rendered them unable to stand, forcing them to rest.

"Good evening, Doctor," she replied. Remembering how he had cared for her when she collapsed, she added, "I want you to know how truly sorry I am about what happened today. I had no warning that I was going to faint. And thank you so very kindly for seeing to my comfort in a time of distress. I feel so silly, fainting like some schoolgirl."

He slumped against the stack of oak log beside her, then

drank from a fresh bottle of whiskey he took from a pocket of his gray officer's tunic. "Think nothing of it," he said. "It was no fault of your own. Today, I have seen the worst destruction of human life that any man shall ever see. More blood than ever was shed on the killing floor of the largest slaughterhouses in Chicago. Any creature made by the hand of God would be revulsed by what men have done to each other here. That valley beyond us has become a sea of mutilated corpses. Major Canfield estimates our losses at five thousand men, a fourth of Hood's army. It is the most senseless disregard for human life imaginable, growing worse with each passing day. Hood has surely gone utterly mad."

"Men are deserting," Lorena observed quietly. "I see them sneaking through the woods. But one wonders who can really blame them for leaving when the cause seems so hopeless. If they stay, they will be killed. Desertion seems a far more sensible choice when the alternative is almost certain death."

Dr. Cross drank again, staring blankly at winking campfires dotting the far hilltops. "General Hood halted a mass desertion earlier in the day himself, beseeching the men to turn back and fight. All of this for the sake of something called slavery, and the rights of a state to make its own laws."

She thought his voice betrayed a hint of sensitivity to the unjust nature of slavery, although she remembered he had mentioned that his father owned slaves. She took a risk. "There are some Southerners who say privately that men do not have the right to own another man simply because of his skin color. I suppose the issue is whether or not a Negro can be considered a man."

He nodded vaguely, which surprised her. "You have touched on the real matter for debate, Miss Blaire. Can a Negro be seen as a human being in the eyes of the law? Or are they something less, some poor creature we regard as draft animals who happen to have human characteristics—even speech. My own experience leads me to conclude that Negroes are indeed human beings, capable of the same emotions and abilities to reason, although perhaps they have slightly less intelligence. Some of my father's slaves are no different than close friends of our family, almost like siblings. In some respects many of them are simply childlike and would doubtless be incapable of caring for themselves. This may be a consequence of generations of slavery, I suppose. A slave has no need to learn how to feed himself when he is fed by his master."

"Sometimes inadequately," Lorena said, "or so I have heard. My family does not keep slaves. I have only actually seen them from a distance." She was angered by his condescension, to say that Negroes were childlike and had lower intelligence. However he did say his family treated them as friends.

"Where are you from?" the doctor asked, taking a swallow of his evil-smelling spirits.

The question made her very uncomfortable, even though she had been schooled with the answer she would give. "Gaines's Mill, northeast of Richmond on the Chickahominy River. I was born in Baltimore, until my father moved south to escape the blight in the cities. He is a shoemaker."

Her reply appeared to satisfy Dr. Cross. He merely grunted and continued to watch the display of firelight on the far side of the valley. Close to the hospital, orderlies moved slowly among the wounded feeding them soup, changing bandages by lantern light or administering spoonfuls of thick syrup derived from duckweed as a cough remedy. She thought about the boy for whom she had written the sad letters, remembering that his name was David Cobb. She had all but forgotten about him until now. "Have you seen the young boy with typhus tonight? His name is Cobb."

"Yes, I saw him again after the shelling stopped," he told her quietly, sounding grave. "His condition has been complicated by a sudden onset of pneumonia. It is unlikely he will live more than a day or two, at best. What a tragedy, although we are surrounded by so many tragedies. A fourteen-year-old child who was given a rifle and a uniform—his dead friend only thirteen. I find it unconscionable that mere boys are being asked to fight this war, yet at times like these it appears neither side has a conscience. I treated a Union drummer boy for a gunshot wound to his calf when one of our patrols found him deserted by his outfit after we routed the Yanks at Chickamauga. He was eleven years old. I asked that he be escorted to the Union line of retreat and given safe passage, after I removed the ball from his leg."

Lorena found that she was mildly discomfited, listening to Dr. Cross talk about his compassion for young soldiers and the Negro slaves belonging to his family. It was much easier when she regarded him as she had been taught to feel about all Confederates and Southern sympathizers, finding it less troublesome on her conscience when she remembered that she was part of a secret effort to defeat the unrighteous cause he believed in. "How very generous of you," she said in response to the tale about the young drummer. "I suppose you could have made him a prisoner of war."

He turned to her sharply. "Do you mean to scorn me by that sort of remark, Miss Blaire? It sounds like ridicule."

His abrupt manner startled her. "Why, not at all, Doctor. I simply said you could have done otherwise with a boy wearing an enemy uniform, regardless of his age."

"I mistook your meaning, then," he said apologetically. He stood up and came over to her, staring down into her eyes. "I am very tired, as we all are," he said, his voice hardly more than a feathery whisper. "I'm sorry for what I said. You are a highly skilled nurse, the best any surgeon could ask for, and you held up quite well under the most trying conditions. I have great admiration for your selfless sacrifice here . . . Lorena, and I offer a most sincere apology for my misunderstanding of what you said to me."

His closeness unnerved her somewhat, and the expression she saw on his face, even in the poor light from dim stars overhead, was one of genuine regret for the harshness of his accusation. But the stinging truth was that she had, in part, intended sarcasm for his story that the eleven-year-old drummer was released at his request. Yet she could not admit the truth to him. "I do accept your apology, Doctor. As you say, you surely mistook my mean-ing." She was aware that her voice had taken on a noticeable quiver while she spoke, and her fingers trembled until she closed her hands tightly in her lap. Her reaction was not the result of guilt or fear that she might be unmasked as a traitor in an enemy camp. It was a woman's kind of feeling, when a woman noticed a man—a man who was standing very close to her, awakening strange sensations within her breast that made her uneasy yet at the same time pleasantly warm inside. She became angry with herself for feeling even the slightest attraction to a Confederate. He was, after all, a part of the reason she risked life and limb to spy on a Rebel army. And there was Paul, whom she loved dearly, to think about when she allowed herself to be beguiled by a hand-some Southerner's subtle charms.

He smiled gently, further disarming her, breaking down more of her resolve to dislike him for being a Confederate.

"I'm glad that you won't hold it against me," he added. "I suppose the only excuse I can offer for my lack of sensitivity is fatigue. I can't ever recall feeling so tired, or so helpless. No mat-ter how hard I try, I simply cannot save but a handful of these men and it is a burden on my soul . . . if I have a soul left within me after today. After yesterday. Or the day before." His smile dis-appeared and he took a shallow breath, gazing past her into the dark. "I sometimes wonder if experiences like this rob men of their souls forever. . . ."

"You shouldn't feel that way," she said, coming to her feet rather suddenly before excusing herself, finding that she could not abide being in his presence any longer, the way he was mak-ing her feel. A part of her wanted to stay close to him, enjoying the warmth of his personality, his kind nature. But a darkly wicked side of her had begun to wonder what it would be like to have his arms around her, and she would not tolerate that sort of uncontrolled emotion influencing her thoughts, her actions, weakening her belief in what she and Clara were doing here. "I really must go now, Doctor. There is so much left undone." She looked for Clara and caught a glimpse of her moving about in the dark with a kettle of soup in the company of Dr. Roberts, a balding, elderly physician she had been assisting today. "Nurse Brooks could use some help from me in feeding the men, unless you have other duties you wish to have me perform."

He wagged his head and started to speak when they heard a general murmuring spread through camp, moving among the rows of tents, the soft rustling of feet and whispered voices. They both listened to the sounds for a while, puzzled by it, until Major Canfield suddenly appeared at the back of the hospital. "Captain Cross! Come to the hospital. Our orders have come to withdraw. The wounded must be loaded into ambulances immediately."

Lorena's heart began to race. Where were they going? Word needed to be sent to Gaines's Mill of their destination as soon as she could learn where Hood was taking them.

"At last," Dr. Cross sighed, turning for the tent, "although transporting some of these poor men will surely kill them. Jolts from the wagon wheels will reopen so many of their wounds. There will be no way to halt the worst of the bleeding."

She followed him toward the hospital, matching his longer strides as best she could, buttoning her coat against the cold, repeating the numerical code to herself lest she forget it. "I wonder where we will go," she said quietly as they approached the dark outline of Major Canfield.

"General Hood has given the order to fall back to Nashville as soon as companies can be formed," the major said when they came within earshot. "We are to build up our fires so the Yanks will still believe we are here until morning. The mules are being harnessed to the ambulances now." He stared at Lorena for what seemed an inordinately long interval; then his gaze went back to Dr. Cross. "Have the nurses see to the men's comfort as best they can, Captain." Pointing north, he directed their attention to a bank of dark clouds moving across the horizon. "The first winter storm is approaching, I fear. Winter in Tennessee can be a brutal business for men without sufficient clothing or blankets to keep them warm. Let us pray the storm holds until we reach Nashville. Otherwise, these poor men will suffer greatly if we are forced to march in bad weather—I expect we will see men die from pneumonia on a grand scale if it rains or snows."

Soldiers were moving throughout the campground now, although it was being accomplished quietly.

"We'll do the best we can, Major," Dr. Cross promised as he led Lorena by the arm past Major Canfield into the foul-smelling, lamplit hospital. He looked over at her when they were inside. "Pack the instruments," he said, still holding her arm, his face thoughtful yet relaxed. "See that the medical trunks are placed in the ambulances beneath the seats. I'll send Nurse Brooks and Goodie to assist you with heavy lifting." Then he gave her a grim smile. "You won't get much rest tonight, I'm afraid, but at last we're pulling back from this killing ground."

He left her, walking briskly across the tent and out into the night. Lorena hurried over to the operating table to begin packing Dr. Cross's instruments, wondering about Nashville, what it would be like, ignoring for now the groans coming from blanketed men all around her. Moments later, Clara rushed inside, and when she saw Lorena, she came over as quickly as she could.

"We're going to Nashville," Clara whispered.

"I know," Lorena replied, wrapping medical tools in pieces of clean cloth. "We must write a letter to Gaines's Mill at the first opportunity, advising Mistress Wheeler—" A movement at the back of the tent silenced her abruptly. Glancing over her shoulder, she froze when she saw Major Canfield staring at her with shuttered eyes.

He watched her for a moment, his expression made of stone. Then he turned on his heel and left through the tent flap without saying a word.

Clara's face was waxy white. "He heard us, Lorena," she stammered softly. "I'm quite sure he heard what you said about the letter to Mistress Wheeler."

6

The old woman regarded him with caution, peering through a crack in the door of her weatherbeaten shanty. She took note of the color of his uniform, saying nothing, watching him. A crudely lettered sign swung from a porch post, swinging in the wind on a rusty nail that had worked its way loose. HOME REMEDYS, it read. CURATIVES. A gust of cold wind sighed across the porch. He figured the woman knew a thousand healing secrets, learned over a lifetime. They were hidden deep within her memory, just behind those dark pinpoints at the centers of her eyes like tunnels, windows into her past. In back of those inky pupils lay a storehouse of information needed by hundreds of suffering soldiers in the slow-moving columns trudging past her house—ways to allay pain, to lessen fevers. When he told her that he was a physician, she grew wary, suspicious, eyelids hooded.

"How come yer askin' me fer medicines?" she asked quietly. Her voice, even when she spoke softly, was coarse, dry, like her throat was clotted with sand. "You did say you was a doctor."

"Quite simply because we don't have any ourselves," Jon Cross replied. "We have badly wounded, sick men and nothing to give them. I saw your sign and wondered if you might have some foxglove or duckweed, painkillers, anything we could use. . . ."

"An' what if'n I did?" One liver-spotted hand moved up to close the top button of her dress when she felt the wind.

"It would aid a lot of young men who are suffering needlessly. We have no morphine, a small amount of opiate, not much else." He heard the rattle of harness chains, the creak of wagon axles moving down the two-rut road behind him. "Our supply wagons haven't reached us for more than a month. General Hood has ordered a retreat to Nashville, and some of our wounded won't make it without something to reduce fever and help with their coughing spells. If you have anything that will do them any good . . ."

"Might, at that," she said, less guarded, "only there's some who follow yer profession who claim my potions don't work. Some say there ain't nothin' in 'em besides wishes."

"I believe in the workings of a great many home remedies," he confided, listening to the sharp crack of a whip over a team of mules struggling up the grade past the old woman's shanty. In this part of Tennessee there were no flat roads—the columns had been either climbing or descending since midnight, and the terrain was telling on men and animals as dawn came.

The woman's expression softened when she glanced beyond her porch to the lines of plodding soldiers and rattling wagons. "I brewed up a batch of laudanum this fall," she said. "Best batch of poppies you ever saw this spring, on account of it was so wet. Made plenty of gum, they did. Soon as it was powder, I mixed it with whiskey. Made a strong batch . . . best I ever brewed, but I won't sell it cheap." Her eyes narrowed again. "You gotta pay fer it with hard money, no worthless Confederate. Won't nobody take paper Confederate money in these hills."

Jon looked over his shoulder at Major Canfield, who sat his horse down by the front-yard gate, watching the house and the proceedings on the porch. "I'm afraid we don't have any money. None of us have been paid for months. I could sign an official voucher, saying that you would get your money from Richmond."

She waggled her head. "Ain't takin' no voucher, neither. I git hard money or you boys don't git none of my laudanum. I may be an old woman, but I ain't no fool. Them vouchers ain't worth spit, same as Reb money. Everybody knows this-here war is near 'bout over. Them bluebellies got you whipped. There ain't no such thing as sugar in none of the stores. No coffee, neither. Can't so much as buy needles an' thread nowhere. Yanks got us cut off, an' 'bout all we got left is what we kin grow at home."

"Those men are suffering," Jon protested, growing impatient. "They fought the Yankees to protect you, your land. . . ."

"Like hell they did! They was fightin' to keep slaves fer a few rich plantation owners! Poor folks got no stake in this-here war."

Jon heard boots come up behind him. Major Canfield and one of his aides climbed the porch steps.

"What's the problem here, Captain?" Canfield asked. "All this talk . . . ?" He directed a look down at the woman, fixing her with a cold stare. "Do you have any opium, anything we can give our wounded soldiers?"

"Not without you got hard money, I ain't," she said, as she closed the door a little more. "I got laudanum to sell, but it costs a dollar. A Yankee silver dollar. Otherwise, I ain't got no medicines fer sale."

Canfield turned to his aide, a strapping young soldier with a blunted chin. "Open this door. We have no choice but to take what we need by force, Corporal Collingsworth. Use your pistol, if it appears a gun will be necessary."

The woman shrieked as Corporal Collingsworth drew his Colt revolver and pushed the door inward, knocking her out of the way when he went inside. Jon started to object, until he saw a hard look in Major Canfield's eyes. Instead, he backed out of the way to let Canfield into the shanty and faced the road, hunching his shoulders inside his coat when he felt the stinging bite of a north wind across his cheeks and neck. Inside the house, more of the woman's shrill yells distracted him briefly from a numbing lack of sleep that had made him groggy and weak, wishing he could lie down for just an hour or two. Then a movement along one side of the shanty caught his attention, and he heard chickens squawking somewhere. Three infantrymen dressed in rags ran past the porch carrying armloads of fluttering chickens—starving men had resorted to thievery to fill their bellies. Two more soldiers followed with handfuls of eggs. Hungry men would eat—though at a possible cost of permitting a helpless old woman to starve.

He opened his mouth to order a halt to it, then gave up in resignation and turned away. What these soldiers were doing was no different from what Major Canfield meant to do by taking the woman's medicines, and he wondered what sense it made to try to stop one form of theft while ignoring another. An order to halt probably wouldn't stop the chicken thieves, anyway. When a man was driven to the brink of starvation, he would ignore any orders not to steal food when it was there just for the taking.

Walking woodenly down the steps, Jon made for his horse to be away from the woman's feeble protests and the voice of his conscience. So much of what was going on around him now seemed utterly senseless. Robbing one old woman of her livelihood and her hens was no less insane than two armies blowing each other to bits, he supposed. He consoled himself somewhat with the notion that this was wartime. The woman could raise more chickens and grow more poppies next spring. Some of the wounded they carried in their wagons were unlikely to see another springtime.

He climbed aboard his rawboned chestnut gelding and reined away from the sagging pole fence around the yard, paying only scant notice to a celebration among infantrymen crowding around the stolen chickens and eggs while they continued to march up the lane behind overloaded wagons and ambulances. Jon swung over to an ambulance and trotted his horse along beside it as he crested the hill and rode out of sight of the shanty.

Stolen or not, the Texas brigades now had a supply of laudanum for the most seriously wounded. And six chickens for tonight's soup pots, a welcome respite from black-eyed peas and bacon.

He saw Nurse Blaire bending over a wounded man at the rear of the ambulance in front of him. Heeling his horse forward, he rode to the back of the wagon and caught her eye.

"How are they?" he asked, shouting to be heard above the squeal of axles and wheel hubs badly in need of grease.

The woman shook her head, her complexion nearly as gray as the Confederates' uniforms. "Two of these men are dead, Doctor. At the next rest stop they should be removed from the ambulance to make room for others being carried on litters. A boy at the front who is riding on the seat with the driver is in terrible pain. He should be given something—he is only a boy."

"There is nothing to give him, Miss Blaire. Cover the dead men's faces and I'll have them taken out. I'll look for Goodie." He marveled at her composure. No matter how trying their circumstances became, she held herself together. Remarkable, he thought, how she seemed outwardly untouched by the grisly realities of this war. There had only been that single incident, her fainting spell . . . understandable, considering the things going on around her yesterday. Although she was quite small, delicate in appearance, she was anything but frail of constitution. And she was so very, very beautiful, so striking that he had a considerable amount of difficulty keeping his mind on other matters while she was near.

"Why are you staring at me, Doctor?" she asked, frowning when his gaze lingered.

He grinned weakly and prepared to ride off to find Goodie. "I'm sorry, Miss Blaire. I was distracted, I suppose. You are a very comely woman, and it was, indeed, bad manners on my part to stare at you. I apologize if I made you the least bit uncomfortable." He touched the brim of his cavalry hat in a lazy salute and turned his horse away from the rear of the ambulance, feeling a trace of embarrassment. Riding along the columns searching for Goodie Carrothers, he made himself a promise that he wouldn't

be caught staring at her again—she clearly wasn't the type who
was tolerant of gawking men. She probably came from a good
Southern family where correct manners were taught. He imagined that she would know all the proper etiquette required in
most any social situation: eating with her fork held correctly, dabbing daintily at the corners of her mouth with a napkin, sipping
rather than gulping from her glass. He was sure Lorena Blaire
knew all these things. They would be second nature to her. A
woman with her obvious refinement could scarcely have escaped
a proper upbringing.

A mighty gust of wind from the north brought the first big
raindrops from a bank of dark clouds scudding across the morning sky. Rain began to pelt his hat brim, his threadbare coat, the
sides and canvas roofs of the ambulances, the men marching in
uneven rows between the wagons. Jon glanced skyward. Now the
soldiers' suffering would truly begin, with the weather turned
against them. Winter was on its way, bringing even more misery
to men without coats and blankets, boots, enough food to fill
empty bellies. It had begun to seem that everything, even the elements, meant to thwart the efforts of Hood's brigades. Not only
would their courage be tested but also their endurance. He could
hear quiet murmurs of complaint being uttered as men took
blankets or whatever they had from their backpacks to cover
themselves from the rain. Icy wind blew through treetops along
the roadway, pulling dead leaves from swaying branches that
formed swirls like dancing dervishes as the leaves were scattered
over the ground. He thought how it would have made a pretty
picture—brilliant reds and yellows and every possible shade of
brown falling from skies darkening with a line of storm clouds
painted pink by sunrise. A pretty painting, were it not for the soldiers marching down this tree-lined lane; the ambulances full of
injured, dying men; the limbers and field guns drawn by half-
starved mules and horses. A battered army in full retreat turned
this forest scene ugly as a living scar moving slowly through the
Tennessee hills.

And now came the rain—a few drops at a time, smelling

damp, faintly musty, as if nature meant to wash away the scar made by the army. Clouds moved to block out the rising sun, and suddenly the forests and hills were dark. Distant thunder rumbled, a gloomy sound to accompany the gloom of men marching in the rain. The rain became a downpour as Jon rode down the columns searching for Goodie. Someone had to remove the dead from Lorena's ambulance. He wanted to keep her from experiencing the worst of this war . . . as much of it as he could. And at the same time he wondered why he would allow himself to feel so strongly about this particular young woman, why he felt the need to shelter her, protect her. He'd only known her a short time, a couple of days. What was it about her that attracted him so?

Turning up his coat collar to keep out the wind and cold, he rode into a curtain of gray rain seeking Private Carrothers among the dispirited faces following the winding road toward Nashville.

Mud gripped the wagon wheels. Weakened animals labored to free mired wheels and hooves under the snarling crack of merciless whips. Mules collapsed in full harness and had to be cut away when exhaustion and weeks of starvation rendered them unable to pull another step. Shouting, cursing drivers tried to force just one more mile from their floundering teams, or simply to reach the top of the next hill or cross the next muddy valley. And with every mile the column marked its progress with more of their dead, placed by the side of the road with their caps or hats covering their faces. It had been common practice to bury all Confederate dead at the beginning of the war, until their number swelled to unimaginable proportions across a battlefield, until the task became impossible. Men were simply wrapped in their blankets whenever conditions permitted, or left where they fell if haste or risk demanded otherwise. But as Hood's men plodded into the brunt of a growing winter storm, scarce blankets could no longer be spared for the deceased, and now dead soldiers lay along the edge of the roadway often without boots or coats or any other item of apparel needed by the living. Jon rode slowly along their trail of bodies without truly seeing them. After three long years of brutal warfare, his mind was numbed to the sight of corpses. His thoughts were on the living, on the men whose lives he might be able to save.

At the crest of a steep hill an ambulance stood off to one side under an oak tree, and behind the wagon, despite a steady downpour, a body was being removed from the rear. He urged his horse to a faster trot and rode up the hillside to the oak as the corpse was being placed at the foot of the tree. And then he saw Lorena, huddled inside a soggy blanket near one mud-caked wagon wheel with her hands pressed to her face. Jon was dismounting before his horse came to a complete stop. He rushed over to her, for he knew she was crying from the way she was trembling.

She heard his boots in the mud before he reached her, and she turned quickly, just as he put his hands on her shoulders. A sob caught in her throat . . . she looked up with tears brimming in her eyes.

"The boy," she whimpered, trying to stifle another sob. She glanced at the shoeless body lying beneath the oak, an infantryman's cap protecting the young soldier's face from the rain. Then her eyelids shut and she began to cry, shaking from head to toe.

"You're soaking wet, Miss Blaire," he said gently, resisting an urge to put his arms around her. "Let me help you back into the wagon. There's nothing more you can do here, and there are others who need your services."

She needed a moment to regain her composure before she said, "I'm sorry, Doctor," sniffling, unable to look at him, her face downcast. Her trembling became a small shiver. "I'm fine now. It was only that the boy was so young, and he suffered so before he died. He told me his name was William, that he was seventeen his last birthday. He asked for his mother just before he . . ."

She couldn't finish, and Jon understood. "There are so many of them, Miss Blaire, and we simply cannot save them. Do the best you can. That's all anyone can expect from you. From us. I experienced the same sorrows when I first came to this war. I still do, in fact, only I suppose I have become hardened to all but the worst of it. I have seen enough inhumanity, shed enough tears over it, that there are times when I feel completely wrung out by it. Anyone with a heart and a soul will be stricken by what is happening here, yet we must go on with our work. You have to find the inner strength to continue to assist the men who can be saved, and close your heart and mind to the others. Now, please, get back inside one of the ambulances before you catch cold."

She nodded, turned from his gentle grip on her shoulders, and walked stiffly through the mud toward the back of the wagon, the wet blanket clinging to her frame like a second skin. He had to hurry to catch up to her in time to help her climb in, and he found it slightly odd that she refused to look at him or acknowledge his assistance when he held her arm to steady her into the rear of the ambulance.

7

Lorena was badly shaken by the young soldier's death and she needed sleep, which only made things seem worse. She required a moment or two to collect herself. The ambulance lurched forward under the crack of the driver's whip, and in the darkness near the front of the wagon a soldier groaned when the sudden movement caused him pain. Seven wounded men lay across the floor of the wagon box, enclosed by the wooden sides and canvas roof of the ambulance. The smell of decay, of death, almost took Lorena's breath away. A young soldier named Clay Reynolds had developed a case of gangrene from a hip wound, and as his flesh rotted away he begged softly for morphine. He told her he came from a place in Texas called Pecan Grove, and he asked that Lorena notify his family in the event of his death, which he believed would come soon. In another part of the wagon lay the most heartrending of all her charges, the boy named David Cobb from Prairie Hill who was dying of typhus and pneumonia. Knowing that he was just fourteen, and that his deepest fear was that he would die alone, far from his family, she could scarcely keep herself from weeping while she attended to him. Gripping the edges of a bench where she sat at the back of the wagon, she did her best to forget about young William's death, all the other deaths, struggling to remain in control of herself, keep from crying. Her resolve to be strong was melting away. She had been so sure she could do it, manage to handle her duties somehow. This was what she had been trained to do—minister to the sick and wounded, to assist doctors with surgeries, apply splints and bandages, a hundred more procedures she'd been shown. But what Dorothea Dix and the other instructors at the academy had been unable to show them was how to deal with their own feelings when, as it was now, death was everywhere around them. What to do when her stomach started to churn, when she knew her heart would break over the death of a boy too young to have known what he died for, boys like William and David Cobb and thirteen-year-old Bobby Jones, whom she had never known. How could anyone truly prepare themselves for so many untimely deaths? This was a war being fought by children dressed up like soldiers, Confederate soldiers. Further evidence of all Southerners' inhumanity, sending schoolboys off to fight a war. But hadn't Dr. Cross taken a rifle ball from the leg wound of an eleven-year-old boy in the Union Army? Children were fighting on both sides, it seemed.

Private Reynolds groaned again. "What's the use?" she said aloud, in a choked whisper she hoped no one else could hear, screwing her eyes shut when more tears began to form and run down beside her nose. "I can't help them. No one can help them . . ."

David Cobb stirred, raising his head to look at her across the darkness inside the jolting, swaying wagon. "Anything wrong, ma'am?" he asked, his voice almost too weak to be heard above the drumming of raindrops on the roof and the dry creak of axle hubs. The rocking of the ambulance forced him to lie flat again.

Lorena left the bench quickly with a pail of water and damp rags, steadying herself when the uneven movement of the wagon bed made it difficult to walk. She knelt down beside David with a cool cloth against his forehead. The boy's dulled eyes were on hers. "Nothing is wrong," she told him gently, smiling, although her tears might have betrayed her in better light.

"Sounded like you was cryin'," he whispered, watching her as she wiped his face.

The bang of iron-rimmed wagon wheels and the squeal of axles prevented her from hearing all of what he said. "I'm doing fine, David. I do hope you're feeling better."

His brow furrowed. "Can't honestly say that I am, ma'am. I got them chills somethin' awful a while ago. That syrup did make me quit coughin' fer a spell. Feels like I got water inside my chest, only I can't cough it up."

"You have pneumonia."

The wagon rattled and bumped over rough road, wheels making a sucking sound when they went through deeper mud. David stared at her, silent, thinking about what she said. Rain fell on the canvas roof in an endless torrent.

"I'm gonna die, ain't I?" he asked a moment later. "It don't matter 'bout havin' a strong constitution like that doctor said. I got the typhus, an' now I got . . . pneumonia, to go along with it. Most everybody who gits one or the other winds up dead, an' I got both of 'em. I jus' know I'm gonna die real soon. If I could have me one wish, it would be to squeeze my ma 'round her neck real tight afore I die. Maybe shake my pa's hand, tell him that I ain't still mad 'bout that whuppin' he gave me fer goin' swimmin' with Bobby that time, when we was supposed to be pickin' cotton. Pa gave me a terrible whuppin' for bein' at the swimmin' hole. That's how come I run off from home an' joined this-here army when Bobby did. Bobby got a whuppin' too, fer goin' swimmin'. Only now he's dead, an' I'm gonna be dead same as him. Us joinin' up with the army turned out wasn't such a good idea."

Hearing the boy's story only worsened Lorena's grief and in spite of herself, she couldn't keep from crying. Tears fell down her face onto the blanket covering David Cobb, making little damp circles where they landed. "Maybe you won't die after all," she said, hoping to sound cheerful, failing at it. "I know your ma would wish the same thing, and I know that she would give you a big hug if she could be here."

David's eyes were watering now, thinking about his mother. "I wonder if you'd mind, ma'am, if I gave you that hug instead, seein' as my ma is way off in Texas at Prairie Hill."

"Not at all," Lorena replied, strangling on anguish, tears, frustration over senseless dying. "I'd like that, if you gave me a good hug," she added, her voice breaking completely as she bent down, sobbing, to put her arms around David's neck, his fevered face against her cheek. "You can close your eyes and pretend I'm your mother," she whispered in his ear. "Then I'll write to her and tell her that you sent this hug to her."

Slowly, the boy removed his slender arms from underneath the blanket and closed them around her neck. A wheel struck a stone in the roadway, jolting the wagon bed violently. Private Cobb's arms relaxed and fell to his sides. His eyes were closed when Lorena peered down at him.

A cry of utter despair passed through her tightly compressed lips, a sound masked by the steady downpour on the roof and noise made by the wagon. Suddenly she lost control of her thoughts, her actions. She stood up, whirled around, and ran to the back of the ambulance where a canvas flap hanging over the door kept out the rain. It was as if she'd forgotten where she was momentarily, that she was riding in a wagon. Shoving the flap aside, half blinded by tears, she simply stepped off the tailgate and plummeted to the ground, falling face down in a muddy wagon rut.

The last thing she remembered was how cold the mud felt on her cheeks. Then she felt nothing at all.

Clara gave her another spoonful of hot soup. Examining her surroundings, she discovered that she was lying in a tent with a lantern hanging above her. She could hear rain pounding the tent roof and sides, and somewhere in the distance was rushing water.

"You gave everyone quite a fright," Clara scolded, but when she said it, she was smiling. "You were nearly trampled to death by a team of mules. The poor driver said he almost didn't see you fall off the back of the wagon in front of him on account of the heavy rain. You must remember to watch where you are putting your feet, Lorena, dear. I suppose you must have slipped, it was raining so hard."

She had a vague recollection of running to the back of the ambulance. "Yes, I must have slipped off," she said, her voice sounding far away, as though it came from another place. "I fell in the mud . . . I remember that. I must look awful." She glanced down at herself, finding a dry blanket tucked under her chin.

"I washed you off," Clara told her, bringing more soup to her lips. "Dr. Cross examined you while you were asleep. You have much to be grateful for, that you have no broken bones."

"Dr. Cross . . . examined me?"

"Yes. He seemed most concerned about you."

"Was I fully clothed? I pray to the heavens above that you did not leave me naked, Clara."

Clara blushed a little. "You were wearing your bodice. I took off your dress and stockings. You were drenched with mud from head to toe. I removed a clean dress and bodice from your trunk, and a pair of stockings. As soon as you feel up to it, I will help you get dressed."

Lorena could feel her cheeks coloring with modesty. "Oh, I do wish Dr. Cross hadn't seen me almost naked, Clara," she said earnestly, blushing more deeply.

"He merely examined you for broken bones," Clara said. "And after all, he is a doctor. He wouldn't be the type to leer at you or do anything untoward, even if he is a Confederate. I can tell by his actions he is a gentleman. He was simply concerned for your well-being." Clara gave her a knowing look and spoke softly. "I think he is such a handsome man. His nose and his chin have a certain refinement, giving him this perpetual air of superiority, and his eyes are the very deepest blue color of any I have seen."

Lorena's face darkened. "Why must you continually carry on about him, Clara? You sound utterly moonstruck on the subject of Dr. Cross. Have you completely forgotten why we are here?"

Clara lowered her eyes. "Of course not," she whispered, a bit embarrassed. "How could I ever forget when there are so many gruesome reminders of it? I have seen so many men die during these dreadful days that I know I shall never be able to sleep soundly again. I have no appetite at all for their disgusting food, and even if I could find something I wanted to eat, I know I could never keep it down. I vomit almost continually, so please don't ever ask me if I have forgotten why we have come to this god-awful place. It is on my mind constantly. I find that I'm always on the verge of crying. . . ."

"I'm sorry, Clara. We've both been under a terrible strain. I shouldn't have said what I did." She pulled a hand from under the blanket and held Clara's forearm. "I can't stop crying over it, either. So many of the wounded are mere children, hardly old enough to need a razor, their short lives ended before they have truly begun. Just before I fell from the ambulance, a boy of fourteen died in my arms, asking that I hold him in place of his mother as he was dying. I experienced the greatest agony of my lifetime when he passed away. I can't put it into words, but I felt we became like family for that moment, the boy and I. I was his mother for an instant—I felt something change inside of me, and I know I will never be quite the same. And now I wonder if this is all a part of God's plan for us, Clara, to show us why we must help General Grant bring this terrible war to an end, to end the dying, the suffering, as quickly as possible."

Boots splashing through mud and water near the tent silenced them. The canvas flap opened and Dr. Cross came inside, his hat and coat thoroughly soaked. He saw Lorena and smiled. "How do you feel, Miss Blaire?" he asked, pausing at the entrance to pull off his hat, nodding politely to Clara.

Lorena was careful to pull the edge of the blanket over her bare shoulders before she answered, mildly irritated by the fact that Clara appeared to be close to swooning the moment

Jonathan Cross acknowledged her presence. "I feel well," she replied, at the same time discovering that she was looking at Jonathan's nose and chin after what Clara had said about them. And she became very much aware that she was wearing nothing but her bodice underneath the blanket, and in spite of herself she felt self-conscious, embarrassed that he had seen her in her undergarments.

"Nothing is broken . . . no bones," he said, "but you took quite a fall. I suppose the mud cushioned you somewhat. The ambulance driver behind the wagon you rode in told us he very nearly drove his team over you, almost failing to see you because of the rain."

"I feel fortunate, Dr. Cross. Once again I find that I'm in your debt. My foot slipped, apparently, while I was attending to Private Cobb, fetching another pail of water, although I do not recall the incident clearly. The boy died—I do remember that so vividly."

"I know," Jonathan said softly, fingering the sodden brim of his hat as he held it in front of him. "I found the boy a short while ago, making rounds through the ambulances. I asked Goodie to dig a shallow grave for him and mark it with a pile of stones while we waited for the men crossing our caissons over the river on logs. We should be moving again soon." His voice had begun to trail off as he talked about David.

Lorena felt tears welling in her eyes again, but she vowed she would not cry in front of Jonathan—she thought of the doctor by his given name now, and she found it strange that even in her thoughts she would be so familiar, since she barely knew him at all. She remembered the incident at the top of the hill when the boy named William was being taken from the ambulance. Jonathan held her shoulders while she cried. There had been something about his touch, the gentle feel of his hands. Then there was the time she found him staring at her. He had apologized, but he had also said that he found her a comely woman . . . "a very comely woman," those were his exact words. Why was she remembering the way she felt when he said that? "I'm glad you thought to bury David," she told him. "He had become very dear to me, perhaps because he was so young. Thank you, Doctor, for showing so much compassion in David's case."

Jonathan's pale eyes turned a darker shade, as if something she had said made him angry. "I am not without compassion for all these men, Miss Blaire. I am simply unable to do anything of substance to help them. Under these conditions, without medicines . . ." He put on his hat and made to leave, then hesitating as though he had more he wanted to say. He stared at her a moment, listening to the rain, his features etched deeply by glow from the lantern and the shadow of his hat brim.

Lorena felt slightly uncomfortable. "I understand, Doctor. David was a special boy. I allowed my feelings to become part of my professional duties. At the end he wanted his mother, as so many of them do. He asked that I hold him in my arms. I didn't mean to imply that you had no feelings for the others."

He appeared to be satisfied, although it was hard to judge in bad light, yet his gaze remained on her face. He stood there, watching her, until a peal of thunder exploded in the skies above the tent. He glanced at Clara, then back to her. "You are both highly trained nurses. A godsend, when so many men need help so desperately. You are to be commended for what you are doing in the name of this cause, and for your personal courage. If my temper seems short, I blame it on fatigue and frustration. Like everyone else, I'm doing the best I can." He sighed, pulling the tent flap aside to watch the rain. "We should be moving again in another hour. Goodie will come for you and take down the tent when the ambulances are ready to cross." Nodding to them both, he stepped out into the storm and walked away.

Lorena and Clara shared a look. Lorena wondered if Clara was beginning to feel the same guilt she felt, for being part of a deception that would result in defeat, imprisonment, even death for a truly sincere physician who happened to wear a Confederate uniform. She hadn't wanted to like him, or admire his dedication the way she had begun to of late. Nor had she wanted to feel any sort of physical attraction toward him, yet it was there, growing despite her wish to control it. She felt something when she was in his presence, more than a passing interest in his rugged good looks.

She willed herself to think of Paul and no one else. "Help me get dressed, Clara," she said, tossing the blanket aside. "We cannot shirk our duties lest our convictions be questioned."

But even as she said this, she continued to doubt her own convictions more and more. Slipping out of her damp bodice and into the other, she knew, however, that it was much too late for her to experience a change of heart. General Grant had been informed of Hood's direction of retreat, his destination at Nashville, in her last coded letter. The damage had already been done.

8

Chief of Staff John Rawlins watched Ulysses Grant pace back and forth between a window overlooking the street and his desk. It had been quite clear for several hours the general was deeply agitated. As was his usual habit when anything stressful occurred, Grant was drinking heavily. A nearly empty bottle of bourbon sat on a sideboard behind his desk.

Grant paused near the window, gazing thoughtfully across the lights of Washington. Despite a chill north wind, he had his window open as if he were immune to November cold. The moment a courier had come with bleak news from Tennessee, Grant opened his office window and poured himself the first of several liberal shots of sour mash Kentucky whiskey.

"He has eluded us again, John. I'm tempted to put precious little faith in the reports we've had that Hood has gone mad. A madman would lack the capacity to make an entire army disappear at the precise moment we are encircling him. We had him in our grasp, yet somehow he has slipped through our fingers.

We had him cornered in Atlanta, and he escaped Sherman by the skin of his teeth. Sherman wrote that he was delighted to learn Hood was moving toward Tennessee, offering to send him rations. I was not as pleased as Sherman over that bit of news. Wherever Hood shows up, he fights with an almost supernatural ferocity. He dealt us nothing but bloody hell at Franklin, and once again he vanishes. The same must be said of that bastard Jubal Early. He came within a whisker of defeating Phil Sheridan at Cedar Creek, then he simply disappears when enough men are put afield to crush him. While we hold the Shenandoah Valley now, it is, in my judgment, a decidedly shallow victory. Early is still on the loose, playing havoc with our railroad lines. Lee seems to be the only Confederate general we can find, and he is so deeply entrenched around Petersburg that I seriously doubt we can blast him out until spring. . . ."

Rawlins watched Grant leave the window to pour another drink as though a summation of Union Army frustrations demanded that he soothe his nerves. Although small in stature, Grant had a larger man's appetite for bourbon. "Hood reportedly lost a fourth of his army at Franklin, General. Some estimates put his casualties at close to six thousand. Observers say he ordered apparently senseless charges toward our gun batteries day after day. By any measure it was a Confederate slaughter. Interviews with recent Confederate prisoners captured from Hood's brigades contained information that Hood alternately weeps, then rants and raves. Even some of his own men insist that he has taken leave of his senses. He has but one leg and one arm, existing on opiates to relieve his pain, if the reports are true accounts of his nature. His supply lines are cut off. I'm of the opinion he will soon be rendered harmless."

Grant took a healthy swallow of whiskey, his features drawn into a dark scowl. "John Bell Hood will never be rendered harmless until his body lies below ground. It would be a serious mistake to believe otherwise. Jubal Early is a man of similar caliber. So long as he is alive with soldiers under his command, he will pose a threat to this war. Our President is occupied celebrating his reelection, and he won't want to hear bad news. I confess I lack the courage to inform Mr. Lincoln that Hood has escaped us again. We must find Hood and Early at any cost."

Rawlins lit a cigar, twisting uncomfortably in his chair as Grant continued to drink. "Perhaps the nurse spies you commissioned will send word of Hood's plans. There is truly only one direction Hood can retreat, in my estimation. He must go west. He is virtually cut off from any other course."

Grant's scowl only deepened. "We've underestimated him so many times that I've completely given up making predictions. He will do the most unlikely thing. If we believe we have him cut off from one direction, he will go that way merely to prove that he can. As to those young nurses, I frankly have little confidence in their chances of success gathering intelligence. It was a desperate measure, sending them to the enemy. Dorothea Dix is partly to blame for encouraging me in that regard. She believes quite strongly in her young women. However, I must confess that privately, I lack the same high opinion of women during wartime. They will most certainly crack under pressure." A blast of icy wind passing through the window interrupted Grant's observations for the moment. He cast a look toward his fluttering drapes and shrugged when a sheaf of papers rustled on his desktop, taking a large gulp of bourbon before he continued. "It would be foolhardy to put faith in those four nurses as a means of gathering any intelligence on Hood or Early. They will ultimately fail. My dear wife, Julia, feels otherwise, of course. What else should a man expect from another woman?"

Rawlins shivered, wishing the general would concede one more thing—that it was much too cold in his office with the window open in late November. He blew cigar smoke toward the ceiling, then tapped off a curl of ash in an ashtray. "If the nurses are discovered, they will be killed. Mistress Dix will then point an accusing finger at you, General. There could be a public hue and cry over sending young women behind enemy lines if they are found out and executed."

"It was a calculated risk," Grant conceded. "In the beginning

I had hopes it might work. However, in hindsight, it was probably a mistake. I am left with no choice but to pray they won't
be unmasked. Under the best of circumstances, no good will
come of it. Jubal Early is so clever that he most likely changes directions several times in the course of a week. John Hood, on
the other hand, is a brazen bastard who charges forward like an
enraged bull at the most unpredictable times."

"This Confederate bull may have had his horns cut off after
heavy losses at Franklin. I don't expect another charge from him
at all. I'll wager he's in full-scale retreat westward, perhaps with
Nashville as his final objective. Hood needs time to lick his
wounds."

"You'd make a lousy gambler, John. Hood is utterly fearless
under fire. He'll come straight at us somewhere . . . if only we
knew where he means to strike. He has a nose for our weakest
flank at times and places when we are otherwise engaged." Grant
took a cigar, clipped it, and struck a match to it. He smoked continually, and yet for some reason tonight he'd momentarily forgotten to keep a cigar lit. Downing the rest of his drink, he
poured another, unconcerned what Rawlins might think. He
and John had been neighbors in Galena, Illinois, before the war
and were such close friends that he didn't bother to disguise a
fondness for strong drink or tobacco. Nor did he try to hide his
lingering depression when things weren't going well, as they
presented themselves tonight after Hood's escape.

"If I may speculate, General, we have no weak flank in any
part of Tennessee now. George Thomas and his Army of the
Cumberland is advancing toward Franklin from the north. He
presently has eighty thousand men and heavy artillery. I'm sure
you recall how well George distinguished himself at Chickamauga and then at Missionary Ridge. Chattanooga fell in two
days because of Thomas and his courageous men. Should General Hood be foolish enough to strike Thomas, it'll be his undoing. Hood can't turn southeast or he'll run squarely into Sherman in Georgia. Sherman whipped him soundly at Atlanta. Hood
won't want any part of him again, I feel confident. John Logan

has him cut off from the south with forty thousand men. By our own estimates, Hood has fewer than fifteen thousand soldiers. They are underfed, poorly equipped, and may have lost the will to fight after being driven away from Franklin. Jubal Early has been chased from the Shenandoah Valley in disarray by Phil Sheridan. Sherman scattered Joe Johnston's Confederates from hell to breakfast at Atlanta, and now Sherman is marching across Georgia burning everything to the ground, leading a force of sixty thousand men. Nothing short of a miracle will stop Sherman from reaching the Georgia coast. This leaves no one but Lee himself to conquer. If we direct every available soldier from the Army of the Potomac to Petersburg, we can force Lee to leave his trenches or surrender. With enough commitment we can take the Confederate capital. Should Richmond fall, I believe it will spell the end of this war. Their backs will be broken."

Grant had been listening, puffing his cigar, drinking, no longer pacing to and fro. He scratched his bearded chin with a finger while watching Rawlins silently, thinking about what was said. "In most respects, John, your plan is sound. You have an excellent grasp of military strategy. Surrounding Lee, bombarding him relentlessly with our heaviest artillery, may force him out of his underground holes. Regiments of the First Pennsylvania Artillerymen are moving toward Petersburg now with more of their thirteen-inch mortars. They can hurl a two-hundred pound shell at Lee's breastworks. We've taken every step to cut off all supplies from reaching Petersburg and may have more success starving Lee out than blasting him from his trenches. Hungry men are more inclined to desert. But your tactics do not account for halting General Hood or General Early. These two men are the most dangerous of all Confederate leaders, and unless they can be found and destroyed, they may be able to raise larger armies and surface again. Send a courier to George Thomas, ordering him to press Hood's rear with the utmost dispatch as soon as he can be located. Send a similar order to Phil Sheridan, that he is to hound Jubal Early's trail to its end at all costs. It would be the worst possible calamity if Hood or Early joined forces with

Bedford Forrest's Tennesseans. Forrest is a horseback demon, and if he has cavalrymen mounted on fresh horses, we can look for a great many more difficult days ahead."

"Forrest is rumored to be in Alabama along the Tennessee River, recruiting more men," Rawlins said, shivering again when more cold air swept through the window. "But until Lee can be dislodged from his fortifications at Petersburg, this war may last another year, even two. I honestly don't see how it has lasted this long. We've battered them on every front and they keep fighting—even when there is no hope for Southern victory now."

Grant tasted his drink. "The answer is really quite simple, John. We are fighting very courageous, capable military men who believe theirs is a just cause. Brave men are most difficult to discourage, even in the face of tremendous adversity. Robert Lee may be the best tactician on earth. Early is nothing less than a military genius. Hood is tempestuous, but he is utterly fearless. James Longstreet fought as bravely as any man ever has. Jackson and Johnston are brilliant on the battlefield. Nathan Bedford Forrest may know more about horseback warfare than anyone. When we set out to defeat men like these, we must be as dedicated to our cause as they are to theirs. We should not expect them to simply lay down their arms and go quietly after so many years of brutal struggle, after such a terrible cost in human lives and suffering."

Rawlins stubbed out his cigar, preparing to leave the office simply because he was freezing. "I do believe it will be over soon, possibly as early as this spring," he said, standing up. "I'll send those orders to Thomas and Sheridan tonight. It would be a stroke of good luck should the nurses have contacted Bertha Wheeler at Gaines's Mill. Knowing exactly where to direct Thomas or Sheridan would be a godsend."

Grant went to his window, staring out at the city. "They are much too young, I'm afraid, for this type of endeavor, and the fact that they are women seriously dampens any hopes I have of success. You won't mention my feelings to Julia, of course. My wife, for all her virtues, believes in fantasies at times."

As Rawlins prepared to leave, they heard footsteps in the hallway, then a gentle knock on the door. Grant and Rawlins exchanged questioning looks.

"Come in," Grant said, obviously annoyed by a late-night visitor.

A tall, gaunt figure entered the office dressed in a coat and tie. He gave both men a thin smile. "Good evening to you, gentlemen. May I intrude?"

"Of course, Mr. President," Grant replied, straightening his spine to appear as tall as possible. "General Rawlins and I were discussing the latest news from the fronts. I'm sorry to be the one to inform you that John Bell Hood has escaped our flanking maneuver in Tennessee. On the eve of our attempt to close ranks around him, he seems to have vanished."

Lincoln, whose expression was perpetually melancholy in the opinion of those who knew him well, gave a sigh, closing the door behind him. He directed a passing glance to Grant's open window as he ambled toward a vacant chair opposite the desk. He sank heavily into his seat, his head slightly bowed, resting his chin on a folded hand. "What of Lee in Virginia?" he asked, his deep voice echoing off polished-mahogany walls. Rawlins thought the President looked tired.

"He continues to extend his trenches in every direction," Grant replied. "He has become a mole, deciding, it would seem, that he prefers to engage us at Petersburg for the winter. If we surround him and batter him with our heaviest artillery, he may lose some of his will to fight. His supply lines have been cut, and we are told barrels of flour are selling for four hundred dollars in Petersburg and Richmond. Firewood is almost nonexistent. We have Lee under siege. Desertion has become so commonplace that some reports put his losses at forty thousand men. We may break their spirits before we are able to destroy their breastworks and tunnels."

Lincoln appeared doubtful. "For three agonizing years we have been led to believe we could crush Confederate nationalism, and thus far there are no signs whatsoever of any weakening of their resolve to continue this war. They are somehow able to fight without rations or gunpowder, existing on sheer force of will and precious little else. General Sherman believes we can defeat them by burning down farms and cities, turning the South into a smoldering wasteland. Ambrose Burnside was convinced we could frighten Southerners into surrendering with a show of force, and George McClellan proved to be a poor successor to Burnside's indecisive nature." He looked straight at Grant now, his eyes brightened somewhat by mist that could have been tears. "I am counting on you to bring this senseless slaughter to an end as soon as you can. Take whatever steps you feel are necessary to conclude it. I've grown exceedingly weary of hearing casualty figures, and so, I fear, has the rest of the nation."

Grant placed his smoldering cigar in an ashtray. "I plan to lead the renewed assault on Lee at Petersburg personally, Mr. President. We will blast him out of his trenches while Sherman burns his way to the Georgia coast. As soon as our intelligence tells us the whereabouts of Hood and Early, we will have all we need to crush what is left of the Confederate Army."

Lincoln nodded, albeit without much enthusiasm. "Do it as quickly as possible," he said. "I find little joy being elected president of a country torn asunder by such a monstrous war. I suspect I earned a great many votes by virtue of being the only candidate Democrats wanted to see hanged. General Early is said to be in Maryland now, planning an assault on Washington. My own party questions my policies as commander in chief, and until the election I was sure I was going to be beaten. If I am to survive this office . . . if this country is to survive, we must arrive at a peace very soon. Do what you must, but end it quickly."

9

Bertha Wheeler moved her rocking chair closer to a fireplace crackling with warmth, gathering a woolen shawl across her breast when another wind-driven sheet of icy rain pelted the roof of her house. Too many of those split-wood shingles need replacing, she thought, remembering how they had begun to curl with age and some malady Brewster called "the dry rot" that afflicted wood. Yet the old Negro claimed he couldn't fix her roof without pitch and proper tools, thus she continued to suffer occasional leaks when wind blew rain from the wrong direction. Which it didn't do all that often. Since her husband's death not much got fixed around the place. James had always been handy when it came to fixing or making things, despite having only one leg. His life was ended by a Rebel rifle ball on the twenty-sixth day of June in '62, during the bloody seven days of battle around Richmond, and ever since that awful day Bertha grieved. Grieved endlessly, daily, long into the night, cursing the Confederate cause and soldiers in gray and the twenty-sixth of June and President Jefferson Davis and Robert E. Lee and a single rifle ball fired by a Rebel infantryman through the heart of James Wheeler, a Southerner himself, a Virginian, and not even a soldier. It had been a senseless act of murder, to shoot down a one-legged man simply for refusing to give up their plow mule. James had been executed, his life exchanged for the ownership of an old brown mule with a fistula.

Bertha rocked, staring into the fire, remembering. She no longer cried over it, for she had no tears left to shed after more than two years spent grieving. But she still remembered, and still felt anger over the injustice done to James, to her, to them. She knew she would feel this mixture of sorrow and anger until the day she died.

The distant rumble of thunder caused a loose windowpane to rattle somewhere in the house—James would have known how to fix that loose glass. Brewster wouldn't know how. He plowed fields and mended harness and gathered wheat in the fall, but he couldn't fix roofs or windows. James had always insisted that Negroes did not have brains large enough to teach them specialized things or how to read and write. Neither could they care for themselves on their own because their brains were simply too small to learn how to operate farms or even the simplest machinery. But while James believed Negroes like Brewster needed to be cared for, he did not believe in slavery. Unlike most other Negroes in Virginia, Brewster was not owned. He knew he was free to leave any time he took the notion, yet this was a notion Brewster never considered as far as Bertha knew. He stayed here where he was fed and clothed, at the James Wheeler farm, in a small house of his own beside the barn, never once showing any desire to go elsewhere. For almost twenty years he'd seemed perfectly content with things as they were, but lately, as more and more runaway slaves stopped by the house for food and rest, Brewster was beginning to change. He talked some about leaving "for a spell" to see what cities like Baltimore and New York looked like, maybe during the winter when there wasn't much to do around the farm. Bertha knew this was only Brewster's way of telling her he was thinking about moving off the place for good.

His mind has been poisoned by those runaways, she thought, wondering how she would manage without him. It's this damn war ruining everything for decent folks. Ending it would be an act of mercy. Ending it soon would save so many lives . . . this was one reason she had written that letter to President Lincoln, offering to do anything she could to help end the war quickly in northern Virginia so she could farm the way she and James always had instead of hiding inside her root cellar with Brewster every time another battle pockmarked her fields with cannonballs and when stray bullets cracked her windows or chipped whitewash from her house. She thought President Lincoln had never gotten her letter at all until the day over a year later, when a stranger in a dark brown suitcoat and trousers came to the farm. He'd told her his name was Willoughby and that he'd been sent to see her by none other than General Ulysses Grant himself. They'd talked most all afternoon about what she could do for the Union if she were only willing to take the risks. Which she was, indeed, because of what a Confederate soldier had done to James on the twenty-sixth of June.

A leak started to drip in the hallway, making a patter on her polished hardwood floor. The sound irritated her more than the knowledge that water would warp the floor. Gathering her shawl more tightly about her neck, she got up to put a bowl under the leaky spot, lighting a lantern before she went to her kitchen so she could see her way about the house.

She was in the pantry, looking for a proper bowl, when she was interrupted by the sounds of a horse traveling through mud coming up the lane to her house. She turned her head, and suddenly her heart began to beat rapidly. So often now Confederate deserters fleeing rat-infested trenches around Petersburg came to her place seeking food, sometimes demanding it at gunpoint. They'd stolen all her chickens this summer, and she'd hardly had any eggs since, unless she traded wheat for eggs with a neighbor. And only by threat of force had her buggy horse and the new mule remained in the barn. She kept a loaded pistol on the mantle above the fireplace, and an ancient shotgun of questionable firing capability—due to a broken nipple—she hid behind her front door. With a gun and determination, she and Brewster had managed to hang on to both animals, for without the gray mule no plowing could be done in the spring, and without her buggy horse she couldn't take any of the coded messages to Mr. Willoughby's house up on the Potomac—if any coded letters ever came. So far none had.

She hurried from her pantry and ran to the mantle to fetch James's pistol, a Navy Colt she didn't know how to reload should a need ever arise. Neither did she truly know how to fire it, not exactly, only that she was to pull the hammer back, take aim, and pull the trigger.

She crept to her front door and opened it a crack, peering out into the storm, clutching the gun beneath her shawl. A rider halted his rain-soaked horse in front of her porch, his hat brim drooping where water fell from it in torrents.

"Got letters fer you, Miz Wheeler," a familiar voice said as the horseman swung down. Lemuel Sawyer had ridden all the way from his store beside the mill to bring her letters in a winter rainstorm.

She came out on her porch still hiding the gun under a fold in her shawl. "I'm so very grateful, Lem. You shouldn't have come in such terrible weather."

Lem opened his oilskin coat and handed her two damp envelopes as a clap of thunder echoed across black skies. "You hardly ever git any letters, Miz Wheeler, so I figured they might be real important."

Bertha took them, wondering. Could these be the coded messages she was told to expect by Mr. Willoughby? "Thank you, Lem. Do you care to come inside a moment to warm yourself by the fire?"

"No ma'am, but thanks fer the offer. I'd best git back to my house afore this storm gits any worse. Ol' man Fisher claims he can tell it's gonna snow by mornin'."

"I'm much obliged, Lem," Bertha said as he got back on his horse. "I'll be by in a few days to buy some sugar."

"Won't be no need, Miz Wheeler. Them Yanks got us cut off, so there ain't no sugar nor much of nothin' else gettin' through to Richmond or Petersburg. Got us plumb surrounded, so folks say who tried to git through. Way some are startin' to talk, this war ain't gonna last much longer 'less Gen'l Lee gits some help real soon."

"I declare," she said, sounding sorrowful. "I do wish we could buy a bit of sugar now and then. Seems I haven't been able to bake a cake in a month of Sundays."

Lem waved and wheeled his horse. Bertha hurried inside with her letters and closed the door, latching it securely, returning the pistol to its proper place on the mantel before she took the envelopes over to her lantern. Her fingers were trembling as she opened the first rain-dampened letter addressed to Mistress B. Wheeler, Gaines's Mill, Virginia.

She recognized the apparently meaningless message at once as words she had to decode, memorize, and recite for Mr. Willoughby. She opened the second envelope and found the same signature at the bottom, Lorena Blaire.

"These must be important," she whispered. A drive in her buggy to the Potomac would require more than a day even in good weather, and the storm would slow her horse down considerably if roads were quite muddy. "I must take these messages to him tonight. Brewster has to harness the mare. . . ." She had another letter, given to her by Willoughby, that would get her through Union lines if she encountered any soldiers. The trip could be very dangerous for a woman traveling alone. Confederate deserters might take her horse and buggy. There were all manner of men on the prowl in northern Virginia these days— robbers and thieves, highwaymen, common pickpockets. She would have to carry James's pistol hidden beneath the buggy seat—and above all, be ready to shoot someone who meant to harm her or take the horse.

Carrying the lantern to her bedroom, she opened a trunk at

the foot of her bed, reached into the bottom, and took out both the letter granting her permission to pass through Union lines and a list of code symbols Willoughby had given her, words and letters from the alphabet that had other meanings. Kneeling on the floor, she read both messages very carefully, until half an hour had passed and her knees were stiff.

Bertha gazed out a bedroom window. "General Hood is headed for Nashville," she said aloud, albeit softly, as if the walls might have ears. "This must be terribly important news."

When she stood up her legs were weak, trembling slightly. A chain of lightning brightened the skies above her house briefly. Thunder rumbled seconds later, yet Bertha did not truly hear it or see the raindrops splattering against her bedroom window-panes. Her thoughts were on her forthcoming journey to the Po-tomac River and reciting the contents of these two letters to Mr. Willoughby. Following instructions, she burned both letters in her fireplace.

She roused Brewster from a sound sleep to have him harness the bay mare to the buggy. "Make sure the canopy is fastened as se-curely as possible," she instructed, "otherwise this wind may blow it off."

"But Miz Bertha," the old man began, peering out a window of his shack, "it be stormin' out there somethin' awful. Jus' afore dark I heared a hoot owl screech four times in a row. Everybody on dis earth know what that mean. It's gonna snow afore day-light tomorrow. You'll catch your death."

"Harness the mare," Bertha said, losing patience. "Anyone who believes owls can predict the weather has loose couplings."

Brewster nodded and sleeved into his tattered coat, mutter-ing to himself as he went out into the rain.

She felt as though her hands were frozen to the reins when a harsh voice shouted at her from the dark forest. The mare shied and snorted, coming to an abrupt halt. Spits of snow fell across the muddy two-rut road, surrounded on both sides by oaks and leafless sycamores resembling bleached skeletons with bony fingers reaching toward a night sky. Bertha was numbed by hours on the buggy seat and at first, she couldn't think clearly even when she heard the command again.

"Halt that wagon!"

Even though the mare had stopped, Bertha drew back on the reins to reach for the pistol hidden in a wicker basket near her feet. A man on a horse rode out of the trees, then three more followed to block the road in front of her. Fumbling for her gun, as frightened as she was then, she almost failed to recognize uniforms worn by these men until they were upon her.

A Union cavalry officer rode up to the buggy seat, peering beneath the canopy. "What's your business on this road, lady?" he asked, not sounding quite so gruff now. "No one is allowed to pass without proper authorization."

She left her pistol in the basket and took an envelope from an inside pocket of James's old woolen greatcoat. "I have a letter from General Ulysses Grant," she stammered, still fearful and so terribly cold that her teeth chattered. She handed the officer her envelope from the Department of the Army.

"I can't read this in the dark," the soldier said, taking out Grant's letter.

"I thought of that," Bertha said. "I have a candle, and if my matches are not too damp, I'll light it."

When the candle was lit, a scowling Union officer read each word on the paper carefully, and his demeanor quickly changed. "Sorry you were detained, ma'am, but as you probably know, we've encircled Petersburg to shut off Lee's supply lines. You should be warned this road is crawling with Reb deserters. How far do you intend to travel?"

She remembered easily. "To the Willoughby Inn at Twin Forks on the Potomac. I must get there right away, for the message I have for General Grant is of the utmost urgency."

The soldier nodded and gave back her letter. "I'll have two

of my men escort you the rest of the way, Mistress Wheeler. It's a very long way to Twin Forks. My men will see to your safety."

"Thank you, kind sir." She blew out her candle and picked up the reins while snowfall thickened around her, all the while silently repeating Lorena Blaire's message to herself, lest she forget even the slightest detail.

Remembering James and the bullet that had struck him down, she drew a comforter around her to help keep out the cold, prepared to drive all the way to Washington if necessary to make sure the news of General Hood's retreat reached Ulysses Grant.

Flanked by two Union soldiers, Bertha drove her buggy into a veil of falling snow clinging fiercely to the reins, sure in the knowledge that if James were alive, he would approve of what she was doing.

10

Rain had turned to sleet and snow. Two bridges across the Cumberland River had been destroyed by Union forces, and a third was so badly in need of repair that orders came to send infantrymen across first before wagons or cannons tested the strength of its planking. Jonathan Cross waited with the ambulances, shivering inside his coat. What was left of Hood's battered Medical Corps waited in line with the artillery, and like everyone else they were hoping the bridge would hold. Fatigue hooded Jon's eyelids. His chestnut horse held its muzzle to the ground, near the end of its endurance as was every starving animal in Hood's columns after a forced march through bitterly cold storms, across swollen creeks, traveling down bottomless mud roads to reach Nashville.

Major Canfield rode slowly through a curtain of sleet to the front of the line of ambulances, halting alongside Jon to gaze at the river in gray daylight. His sodden cavalry hat fell over his face, weighted down by ice and water.

"They're sending us across behind the infantry," Canfield said, his voice hollow. A vacant stare made his eyes appear to be glazed over. "It seems wounded men are considered to be more expendable than caissons and cannons."

Jon watched infantrymen plod across the bridge. Ice had now formed on some of the bridgework, making footing treacherous. He thought about Lorena Blaire and Clara Brooks. "I suppose, for the sake of our nurses, I should tell the women to walk across rather than remain in the ambulances." Jon's teeth were chattering. "Thinking of their safety, Major," he added, "in case the ambulances are too heavy for this bridge."

Canfield frowned. "I overheard them talking in one of the tents as we were pulling out of Franklin. I couldn't swear to all that I heard, yet it sounded like one nurse told the other they must write to a woman in Gaines's Mill, advising her of our destination at Nashville. I believe the woman's name at Gaines's Mill was Wheeling. The very moment I entered the tent they ended their discussion abruptly—a bit too abruptly it seemed to me."

More than anything else, Jon wondered about Major Canfield's suspiciousness, although he did have a vague sense that Nurse Blaire had asked him once for permission to write some sort of letter to a relative in Virginia. "Do you suspect them of betraying us to the Yankees after all they've been through? It hardly seems very logical."

Canfield glanced back to rows of parked ambulances dusted by a layer of sleet and snow. "Spying is certainly not limited to a man's talents. Whores have given away more military secrets than intercepted dispatches ever could. When a man is in the throes of passion, he is doubtless more likely to say things he might later regret. Prostitutes make excellent spies, thus I see no reason why nurses should be any less capable of learning valuable tactical information. Wounded men say all sorts of things when they're in pain. A nurse could report what she was told to any number of contacts with the enemy. I distinctly overheard one of our nurses say she needed to write a woman at Gaines's Mill, advising her of our destination. I'm almost positive that's what the young woman said."

Jon was still puzzled by Canfield's doubts about the women. "It's possible one of them merely wanted to inform a concerned family member of her whereabouts. Both seem much too young to be trained spies, although I can't say I'm qualified to judge what a spy looks like since I've never seen one. As nurses, they *have* been well trained. Nurse Blaire has been assisting me, and save for a single fainting episode, she has proven to be capable and willing to perform her duties. Perhaps when you came into the hospital it merely startled them."

Canfield grunted, stroking his unshaven chin. "I suppose it was the way they stopped talking so abruptly when I came into the tent, as though they didn't wish to be overheard by anyone. It could be, as you say, that they were only startled. When we get our hospitals established around Nashville, I'll try to re-member to ask the couriers if any of them recall anything unusual about letters from either of our nurses."

Jon had a vague recollection of something Lorena said as she was about to write a letter for a dying boy. "Nurse Blaire did ask me if she could write to her aunt, informing her of her safe ar-rival there. I saw nothing wrong with that, so I gave permission. That's about all I remember. Letters home are so frequent that I gave no thought to it."

"It may be nothing," Canfield said offhandedly, as if he had other things on his mind now, watching the bridge. "There are a number of cotton warehouses close to Nashville. We'll make use of them for our hospitals as soon as we get there. At least we should be able to keep our wounded reasonably warm, and if we experience any luck, there may be morphine and chloroform at the local hospital."

Jon squinted across the Cumberland at rooftops of the city, covered with snow and ice. "Nashville seems like a poor choice for our retreat, Major. We've been moving north, almost paral-lel to Union lines. West appeared to be a more logical choice, away from the enemy. While I'm certainly not a military man, going to Nashville doesn't make any sense to me. It does not look defensible from here."

Canfield showed a trace of impatience. "General Hood makes our military decisions, Captain. What may seem illogical to you apparently has been deemed sensible by Hood. Questioning your orders may significantly shorten your military career; however, I do share your surprise at the direction we took. The rains have washed out our tracks away from Franklin. General Hood has made the decision to travel in a direction most prudent men would avoid. Quite possibly, he means to go on the offensive somewhere to the north of Nashville, which would certainly be an unexpected move by an army almost decimated in recent weeks. In any event, we are bound for Nashville, and I strongly suggest you show support for General Hood's choice if you wish to avoid court-martial. He is at his wit's end, by all accounts. A dissenter might well be shot as an example to others."

"I'm told he has fits."

"The man has a cork leg and an arm that is utterly useless beyond filling his coat sleeve. He endures enormous amounts of pain. Dr. Roberts administers morphine by injection three or four times daily. A man denied the use of two limbs is entitled to fits. Few men in this army can lay claim to more courage or sheer determination. A lesser individual would go home and spend his final days in a porch swing."

Jon remembered a scene from Franklin. "He personally turned back a full-scale retreat by foot soldiers that last day, when the shelling was at its worst. He's not wanting for bravery, yet one cannot help but wonder if he is in full control of his senses at times. Perhaps the morphine blinds him to the truth of our dire situation here."

"I'm informed he believes we shall be sent reinforcements in a matter of days. Couriers from Richmond have promised supplies and fresh recruits. Until they arrive we make do with what there is left to us. General Hood is a resourceful man. In the years

I've served under him, he has shown an uncanny ability to pull us from adversity in the nick of time."

Jon kept private doubts to himself. Major Canfield was one of Hood's strongest supporters, making further argument a waste of time. "If the bridge holds we'll be in Nashville before nightfall. We can begin changing bandages and feeding our wounded. I'll tell the nurses now of our need for fresh bandage material as soon as we arrive."

Canfield gave Jon a stern look. "Say nothing to either one about what I overheard, Captain. If these women are involved in some sort of spying for the Union, we'll discover them soon enough, and if I'm wrong, no harm will have been done."

Jon turned his weary gelding, drumming heels into its sides to ride along the rows of waiting ambulances. Bits of windblown ice struck his face and hat, rattling softly on his coat sleeves and boots. He urged his footsore horse past columns of exhausted infantrymen shuffling toward the bridge, some without coats or boots, many with bare feet wrapped in cloth and burlap. Muskets with fixed bayonets were slung carelessly over drooping shoulders or balanced in frozen hands. Tattered uniforms bore a dusting of snowflakes and sleet. Gray infantry caps sported half an inch of ice on the crowns and bills, worn by men too tired to remove them. But far more tragic than any sight he found on his ride past Hood's crawling columns were the faces he saw, the sad defeated eyes and sunken cheeks of men near starvation, frozen by hours of endless marching in weather so brutal that it required all the energy these soldiers possessed to move forward now into ice-laden winds. Seeing them as they were, Jon knew this war was over. Men so close to starvation and freezing to death could not fight even one more battle. Hood's brigades were defeated, and Jon knew there was no fight left in them.

And for all the suffering he saw among these infantrymen, it was magnified beyond measure for those who were wounded. He began to notice a strange sound coming from the columns, a low moaning noise like the distant murmur of bullfrogs after a spring rain that could be heard above the continual coughing plaguing most of the troops. He listened, and when he heard it more clearly, his heart was torn by it. Cries from the walking wounded and groans coming from the ambulances became a ghastly chorus of suffering that he knew he would never forget.

He located a shell-pocked ambulance that he remembered as the last place he saw Nurse Brooks. At the back of the wagon he leaned out of his saddle to part a canvas curtain keeping out bad weather. "Nurse Brooks?" he inquired, wrinkling his nose when an odor like rotting fish wafted from inside, the scent of gangrene and dysentery and urine.

"Yes, Doctor?" a muffled woman's voice replied. Clara came to the opening with a cloth over her nose and mouth to keep out the smell as best she could. She had no color in her face, which became more evident when contrasted by her dark-blue dress.

"I'm advising you to leave the wagon as soon as we start to move. Walk across the bridge with the infantry."

Her brow pinched. "May I ask why, Dr. Cross?"

Jon felt too tired to fully explain about the bridge. "Just do as I ask, Nurse Brooks." He reined away from the ambulance to begin a search for Lorena Blaire.

Farther down the line, parked beneath a towering gnarled oak with bare limbs, he found an ambulance and Nurse Blaire instructing Goodie Carrothers over final resting places for two bodies. A shoeless corpse was already covered by a thin layer of snow and sleet. Goodie placed a blanket-clad body beside the first, doing it as gently as though the soldier was merely asleep.

"We can't spare his blanket," he heard Lorena say. "Please give it to one of the men inside."

Goodie was removing the blanket as Jon rode up. Apparently Lorena had seen him from the corner of her eye for she turned at the waist. When she looked at him, when her dark eyes met his, no words were needed to express the agony he saw in her face. Her suffering was so evident that in an instant, before he thought better of it, he was dismounting to rush to her side and put his arms around her. But as soon as his feet touched the

frozen ground he regained control over his emotions, reminding himself that he hardly knew her well enough for such a show
of affection. He stood in front of his horse holding the reins, forcing his gaze away from Lorena to the pair of bodies. "I see we've
lost two more," he said quietly.

"They died during the night," she told him, her voice thin
and somehow distant, removed.

He remembered the reason for his visit. "As soon as these
columns start moving again, I want you to walk up front with
the infantrymen. These wagons may be too heavy to cross that
bridge without breaking through."

"But what of the men inside, Doctor?"

"It's a calculated risk undertaken by our commanding officers. Floating wagons across takes too much time. Perhaps the
bridge will hold."

"Some of them might be able to walk if it isn't too far, or they
could be carried on litters."

Because he was tired, his patience was short. His tone was
harsh when he told her, "We can't save them all, Nurse Blaire.
There aren't enough litters, nor enough able-bodied men to
carry them. Now, do as I've instructed and cross the bridge with
the infantrymen when the order is given to move." He turned
abruptly for his horse and mounted.

She was staring at him and the look she gave him was as cold
as the weather. "And what if I refuse?" she asked, folding her
arms across her chest. "Will you have me hanged? Or put before
a firing squad?"

Jon sighed in resignation, slumping forward in the saddle as
a rush of icy wind swept past the ambulance. "No, Nurse Blaire,
I will not order your execution. I was only thinking of your safe
passage across a dangerous bridge. If you insist upon riding in
this wagon, then do so. I'm too tired to argue with you."

Goodie shuffled away from the tree. "Do like the cap'n say,
Miz Blaire. I kin stay with the wagon an' toss out the piss pots
if need be. You ain't gonna be no help to them boys inside if a
bridge fall down, anyways."

Lorena looked at Goodie. Jon saw tears form quickly on her cheeks. She stood on her tiptoes and kissed Goodie lightly near his oversized left ear; then she turned her back on Jon and went back into the ambulance without saying a word.

Jon spoke softly to Goodie. "See that she walks across with the infantry. Carry her, if you have to. That bridge was weakened by Union shelling and it may not hold."

Goodie smiled. "I kin do it, Cap'n, but she ain't gonna be none too happy 'bout it, mos' likely."

Jon rode back toward the Cumberland with his hat brim tilted to keep out wind and ice, wondering if he would ever understand a woman's nature. He was sure of one thing as he neared the river: Lorena Blaire was not a Union spy.

11

Her shoulders hunched, she leaned into the wind with Clara walking beside her. Old timbers creaked somewhere below them in damaged bridge supports as columns of soldiers marched across a narrow section where splintered planking surrounded a hole made by a mortar shell. Men stumbled or slipped where ice formed on sections of the bridge. Thirty feet below, the Cumberland River—swollen by days of heavy rain fall—swept past the bridge with a quiet hiss and the dark promise of death for anyone who fell into its inky waters. Sleet and snow continued to fall, and now the wind had begun a howling sound akin to the baying of hounds. Men walking on frozen feet limped in front of them. Some collapsed, lifted and helped the rest of the way by others who suffered less from the cold or minor wounds.

Clara spoke. "I don't understand why you're so angry. He is only concerned for our safety, Lorena, dear. It was chivalrous of him, to show how much he cares for our well-being, and yet you behave as though he is guilty of an affront. For goodness sake, all he asked is that we walk across this bridge."

Lorena kept her head bowed into the wind. "It was his manner I object to. The decision should have been ours to walk or ride in ambulances with the wounded. He has a profound arrogance that I despise, believing he can order us around like slaves. I resent his tone, his manner. He ordered me to walk. We were not given any choice in the matter."

Clara took a breath of crisp, cold air. "I, for one, am most thankful to be away from the terrible smells for a while. I have vomited so often that my sides hurt, I've been unable to keep anything down for days, and I have wept so many tears that I may never be able to shed another. This war is the most inhumane event anyone can imagine. Willard told me it was a noble effort to set men free from slavery, but I see nothing very noble about what is happening here. Men are being slaughtered like sheep, and hardly a one understands what he is fighting for. The dying men cry out for their wives and children, begging God to free them from pain, or they ask for their mothers as if they were children themselves. When I return to Boston, I intend to inform Willard of his mistake . . . there is no nobility in any of part this, not so much as a smidgen."

Lorena remembered David Cobb. "A good many of them are only children. The boy from Texas was fourteen. His friend was even younger, just thirteen. If these Southerners feel they must fight a war against the government, they should wage it with men, not schoolboys." Crossing a patch of ice, she thought about all the deaths she had witnessed. "We were promised our actions could be very helpful bringing this war to an end. This is what we should remember when so much suffering is all around us. The letters I sent Mistress Wheeler may shorten the war and thereby save many thousands of lives. We must continue to believe that, no matter how these Confederates attempt to influence us toward their evil cause. We may be saving lives, Clara, and we simply must trust in the Lord that it will happen soon."

Clara gave Lorena a sideways look. "Or it may cost us our

own lives if Major Canfield becomes too suspicious. We shouldn't talk about it again . . . what we're doing. I know he heard us that night. I could tell by the look on his face."

"You're imagining things, Clara. No one suspects us."

The Barnum Cotton Company warehouse contained row upon row of blanketed bodies. Smudgepots burning coal oil gave off meager heat while black smoke thickened near the ceiling, a dark pall of oily clouds floating above the wounded, smelling of kerosene that helped lessen the stench of gangrene and offal somewhat. Amputated limbs were carried from the building as quickly as possible as more surguries were being performed, yet the smell of decaying flesh and smoke soon made Lorena queasy. Carrying steaming pails of hot water from boiling cauldrons outside, she grew dizzy and for a moment stopped to rest near one of the doors, holding on to the doorframe with both hands until the feeling passed.

"I simply cannot allow myself to faint again," she said in a hoarse whisper, taking deep breaths of cold night air. "I am made of sterner stuff. . . ."

She felt a hand touch her shoulder. When she turned around, she found Jonathan watching her with concern.

"Are you feeling all right?" he asked gently. His surgeon's apron was covered with blood and pus. His arms were stained dark red up to his elbows, and there were tiny flecks of dried blood on his face and neck.

"A bit lightheaded," she replied, "but I'll be fine in just a moment or two. It must be the smoke."

"You're tired," he said. "We're all near the point of total exhaustion. Find a place to lie down. I sent Goodie to bring us something to eat. Food will help, along with some rest."

"It is not necessary to pamper me, Dr. Cross. I am quite capable of performing my duties. . . ." As the words left her mouth she was surrounded by darkness, as though someone had snuffed out a candle. She felt herself falling until a pair of strong arms encircled her waist. Barely conscious, she knew she was being carried somewhere, and she struggled against it. A feathery voice from far away said, "Lie still, pretty lady. A few hours of sleep will do you a world of good."

She gave in to the darkness and slept.

Hazy images came and went. A face, then nothing. Now a dim light. She couldn't keep her eyes open until a damp cloth passed across her forehead, along her cheeks. A voice, soft, calm, and reassuring, spoke.

"You're awake. As soon as you feel able, you should take a few spoonfuls of this soup."

The same face was there again. A pair of blue eyes, so deep and clear that they resembled pools of water, stared down at her. She was in a room with papered walls, lying in a bed, covered to her chin by a patchwork quilt. Jonathan Cross sat on the edge of the bed with a pan of water, wiping her face gently with a cool cloth. An oil lamp burned low on a washstand near the bed. When her wandering gaze returned to him, he smiled.

"You fainted," he said. "It was smoke from our smudgepots, I feel certain, along with a generalized weakness suffered by all of us after a punishing march in inclement weather. I had Goodie bring you some soup. When you feel you are able to sit up, take some of it so your strength will return."

"Where am I?" she asked, still groggy, unable to clear her thoughts.

"At a small boardinghouse across from the hospital. You needn't worry about it. You'll be fine here until you feel well enough to return to the hospital. I made arrangements with Mrs. Peabody for you and Nurse Brooks to lodge with her. You'll be more comfortable."

Lorena raised her head off a down-filled pillow for a better look at her surroundings. She was in a tiny bedroom. A window near her bed framed by lacy curtains was frosted over, yet she was able to tell it was dark outside. Slowly, her mind cleared. "I remember feeling faint," she said, turning from the windowpane. In a rush of unwanted emotion she began to cry, despite a desperate wish to control herself in front of Jonathan. "I only wanted a breath of fresh air," she whimpered, falling back on her pillow when a flood of tears streamed down her cheeks. She covered her eyes with her hands. Quite suddenly it was all too much for her to bear, the burden of caring for dying soldiers; the smell of death everywhere; grim scenes on operating tables so bloody and terrible, they left her feeling numb; amputated limbs lying in a grisly heap near the tables; and endless, piercing screams from men who had no painkiller. All at once she felt overwhelmed by events, her responsibilities. Weeping, unable to stem a flow of tears, she let herself go, giving in to it the way she had when David Cobb died. A cry of anguish came from deep within her, a sound she didn't recognize as her own voice.

"Miss Blaire," Jonathan said quietly.

She felt his hands on her shoulders. He lifted her off the mattress, then his arms closed around her. He drew her against him gently and held her while she cried. For a few moments she wept with her face pressed to the front of his gray tunic, her body wracked by tiny tremors.

"I'm so sorry," she sobbed, clutching the lapels of his coat fiercely, trying her best to regain control of herself, humiliated by this sudden outburst. "I don't know what's come over me. I can't seem to stop all this foolish crying."

He held her in an embrace that was comforting but not at all presumptuous. "It's really quite natural to be overcome by what we've been through. To shed tears over it. I myself have wept. On countless nights I look up at the stars wondering why I'm here and why God allows this to happen. Both sides in this war have been reduced to savagery befitting wild animals. We are killing each other without regard for our humanity, as if the ability to reason has been temporarily suspended while we engage in warfare. I could never have imagined such cruelty, so much total disregard for human life and suffering. Our generals order one senseless attack after another without considering the toll in human lives. Hood must be utterly mad, although I've been warned to keep this opinion to myself or face a court-martial. By all accounts we lost over five thousand men at Franklin, and more are dying from their wounds every day. It's incomprehensible, yet we continue to be told of preparations for another offensive when reinforcements arrive. It's madness."

Lorena's tremors stopped as did her tears, for there was something about what Jonathan was saying that touched her. He wasn't echoing Confederate sentiment, not what she'd been told were Southerners' reasons for fighting a war. He talked about compassion for dead and dying soldiers, not the right to own slaves or states' rights. He called this war madness, which it most certainly was, and he told her he'd wept over it. Drying her eyes, she drew away from him to search his face, although he continued to keep his arms around her.

"That's better," he told her, smiling again. "Your tears are quite understandable. You needn't apologize for crying under conditions such as these. I doubt that at any time in history has anyone been a witness to so much death and suffering. None of us can be expected to experience it without feeling the horror of it at the very core of our being. You are to be commended for what you've done for so many desperately needy men, but you can't be expected to continue your duties without food and rest."

The anger she felt earlier over being ordered to walk across the bridge melted away. Feeling his arms around her now made her forget everything else for the moment. "You're nothing like I expected you to be," she said, comforted by his presence and his gentle embrace. "You have a tender heart and genuine feelings for your patients. One might think a surgeon under these circumstances would become callous."

His smile faded yet he continued to look into her eyes. "I suppose in some ways I am hardened to it, at least on the surface when there is so much to be done. But inside, in what's left of my soul, if such a thing exists, I still grieve. We save so few of them while the rest die horrible deaths. No one can watch it without feeling helpless."

"I truly do understand, Doctor." As she said this, she was aware of a subtle change in the way she was feeling with his arms around her. More than being comforted, she began to notice how good it felt to be held by this ruggedly handsome man. His chin was again unshaven, mottled with beard stubble, and his blonde curls dangled in neglected strands over his forehead and down his neck to his broad shoulders. He was the kind of man she'd never been attracted to before—untidy in appearance, almost wild in the way he ignored his looks as though he didn't care what others thought of him. And now, being so close as he held her against his chest in soft lamplight, her attraction grew stronger. For the moment she didn't think of him as a Confederate, an enemy, only as a man for whom she felt the beginnings of desire.

As if he could read her thoughts, he bent down and kissed her lightly on her forehead. "Eat some of the soup before it gets cold," he said, his voice barely above a whisper. "Then I want you to rest for a few hours."

His kiss, while only a gesture of kindness, sent a shiver down her spine. He mistook it for a sign that she was cold and lifted the quilt up around her shoulders. But when he saw the look in her eyes he hesitated with his face only a few inches from hers.

"Forgive my boldness, Miss Blaire, but you are one of the most beautiful women I have ever known. Under less stressful circumstances I would be sorely tempted to court you, with your consent." He grinned boyishly. "While I'm not experienced as a suitor, I would try to make up for my shortcomings in other ways. It is most unfortunate that we have to meet in the midst of this terrible war."

Lorena smiled over his awkwardness. Could a man with his charm and good looks truly lack experience as a suitor? "I'm flattered, Dr. Cross." Though she knew it was an unladylike gesture, she lifted her chin and gave him a kiss on the lips, only the lightest of touches before she pulled away. Embarrassed, she quickly looked askance. "I shouldn't have done that and I can't explain what came over me!" she said, cheeks filling with color. For a moment she'd completely forgotten about Paul.

"I'm glad you did," he told her. "I won't soon forget it, I promise you."

She reached for the bowl of broth on the bedside table and pretended to ignore him, all the while wondering what had driven her to kiss a man who was almost a perfect stranger.

12

He left Peabody's Boardinghouse in a blinding snowstorm to cross the road for a short visit to the hospital before finding a place to lie down, barely noticing the weather. Remembering the sweet kiss Lorena had given him and the way it felt to hold her in his arms, he was only dimly aware of the cold or the deepening snowdrifts around him. When she brushed her lips against his, he'd come close to returning her kiss with a more forceful show of affection, but a lack of courage on his part kept him from doing so, fearing she might reject him. He was quite sure he had not mistaken the look in her eyes as he held her, nor had he misjudged a hint that she felt something for him, too. But when he had an opportunity to say things a woman might wish to hear, and even suggest that they begin a courtship, his courage failed him dismally. He'd allowed a special moment to pass without taking advantage of it, leaving him to wonder if he would be given one more chance.

She's so very beautiful, he thought, trudging over to the

makeshift hospital at Barnum's, his boots crunching through the accumulated snow and ice where gusts of wind had formed drifts. His mind was on Lorena Blaire, not on a cotton warehouse full of sick and dying men nor on the lack of sleep that had numbed his legs to a point where he scarcely knew he was walking. Those few stolen moments away from the hospital with Lorena had lifted his mood to such a level that he'd almost forgotten about what awaited him inside. But when he entered one of the doors, he was immediately reminded of his duties, greeted by the sights and sounds and smells. All across the warehouse floor rows of wounded and sick soldiers lay in varying degrees of misery. Moans echoed back and forth amid a chorus of wet coughs. Occasionally, someone cried out in pain or started sobbing, calling a loved one's name. Oily smoke from smudgepots hovered near the rafters, making his eyes water and burning his nostrils.

He found Major Canfield at one of the operating tables with his bone saw grinding. Jon marveled at how a man Canfield's age was able to continue performing surgeries without sleep. The major was past fifty, and yet he could remain standing for hours while the younger doctors, Jon and Buel Green, often needed to rest. Canfield was sawing off a gangrenous foot as two orderlies held an unconscious soldier on the table. Another big cotton warehouse across the town square had been established as a hospital under the direction of Dr. Roberts and Dr. Green, which left Dr. Canfield as the sole physician on duty at Barnum's.

The major was sweating profusely when Jon walked up to don a clean surgeon's apron, deciding against asking for a few hours of sleep after having been away too long while attending to Lorena. Canfield looked up from his amputation. "You are badly needed here, Dr. Cross. There is no time to waste pampering weak-spirited women. I was told you carried Nurse Blaire in her swoon to a boardinghouse. Fainting nurses have no place in this army. If she can't hold together at the sight of blood, then send her home. Your medical skills are needed by seriously sick and injured men, not swooning women."

Jon tied his apron strings, bristling over Canfield's remark while reminding himself of the major's rank. "It wasn't only the sight of blood, Major. Simple fatigue caused her to collapse. I fully expect Nurse Blair to return to her duties in a matter of hours. Both women have been through a most trying ordeal riding in the ambulances, changing bandages, administering what opiates we have. In my opinion, they've given everything they can."

Canfield's stern expression deepened. "I pray they haven't also given away our destination to Union commanders, Captain. I lack the same high confidence you place in those women. There's something about them. . . ." He went back to work with his bone saw without finishing what he started to say.

Gritting his teeth, Jon walked off to find a pair of medical corps orderlies to help him begin surgeries at a vacant operating table. Canfield's attitude toward Lorena and Clara made no sense and it was getting under his skin. Why had a mere mention of a letter written to an aunt in Virginia convinced the major that their nurses were Union spies?

He found two privates in blood-splattered uniforms passing buckets of soup among the wounded. "Come with me," Jon ordered. "Find two wounded men who can walk, and have them offer soup to the others. We have dozens of amputations to be performed."

On leaden legs he made his way to the operating table, only to find it caked with dried blood and pus. His instruments had not been washed, nor had sponges been cleansed. A small amount of potassium iodide and a vial of silver nitrate was hardly enough to cauterize more than a few open wounds or amputations. Septicemia was so rampant among old wounds that no amount of cauterizing agent was enough. A bottle of pure bromine that could be applied by a glass pipette and a smaller vial of morphine sulfate with a lone syringe sat in a wooden apothecary case. It was so little in the way of medicine, considering the task awaiting him.

For a moment he closed his eyes, steeling himself for the next few hours of brutal surgery; then he went off to find a man whose life he might be able to save. Through one of the doorways he noticed the sky brightening with dawn. He'd been without any meaningful sleep now for three days, dozing briefly in his saddle during their hasty retreat from Franklin.

To put his mind on more pleasant thoughts he recalled what it was like to hold Lorena in his arms, to feel her soft lips if even for a fleeting moment. He wondered if he might be falling in love with her.

Snow mixed with ice fell on Nashville all morning, worsening the plight of men without boots and coats. Soldiers wrapped in thin blankets huddled around smoky bonfires across the city. Half-starved mules and horses were given most of Nashville's limited supply of hay and grain. Scarce food was prepared at mess tents. A few local families offered frozen men shelter in their homes and barns, but most soldiers suffered greatly in the cold, living in tents or in makeshift lean-tos made of canvas and wood scraps. Jon saw these gloomy conditions from various hospital doors when he stepped out briefly to get away from foul smells inside and to clear his head of oil smoke. As the noon hour approached, orderlies from mess tents brought food for harried surgeons who barely found time to eat. Jon went outside to sit on a pair of snowy warehouse steps to have his lunch in spite of a chilly wind and spits of snow, taking deep breaths of wonderfully fresh air. Salt pork, black-eyed peas, and cornbread made him feel somewhat better, although his arms shook with fatigue and his eyelids grew heavier and heavier. As he was finishing his meal, he saw Lorena emerge from Mrs. Peabody's wrapped in a shawl. He stood up before she crossed the street.

"How do you feel?" he asked when she was close enough to hear his question.

She climbed the steps but wouldn't look at him, and he was puzzled by the way she avoided eye contact.

"I'm feeling much better, thank you," she replied in a flat voice, keeping her head down as she hurried inside the hospital.

His heart sank. Why had she ignored him? Was it the kiss she had given him that embarrassed her now? Or something he may have said, his admission of being tempted to court her if there were more favorable circumstances. He'd been thinking about her all morning, even as he sawed off mangled, gangrenous limbs or treated bullet wounds, probing infected tissue for balls of lead. The memory of her kiss helped take his mind off the grim reality of what he was doing. But when she hurried up the steps a moment ago, she made it quite plain she had little she wanted to say to him. Why had her feelings toward him changed so suddenly?

I hope she doesn't regret what happened last night, he said to himself. Near the point of complete exhaustion, he tossed his empty tin plate aside and gazed across the rooftops of Nashville, lost in thought for the moment. While preparing for his medical education there had never been time for love affairs. He admitted to being shy around women. When he met a woman, it seemed he could never think of just the right things to say, how to act, always feeling awkward in her presence. He had never learned how to waltz properly—it was as if he'd been born with two left feet. Most of his adult life had been spent in pursuit of an education and then a medical degree, and in the process he'd neglected to learn a gentleman's etiquette, he supposed. Had he said something too brazen to Lorena that offended her? She was, quite clearly, a woman of refinement. Had he chosen the wrong words?

He sighed and turned to the hospital door, prepared for a long afternoon of surgery. His supply of morphine sulfate was depleted, and Major Canfield had informed him there was none available anywhere in Nashville. He knew he should be accustomed to sawing off a screaming man's arm or leg by now. . . .

When he entered the warehouse, he saw Lorena attending to a wounded soldier, applying fresh bandages to the stump of his left leg. Forcing his gaze in another direction, Jon returned to his operating table and spoke to Goodie Carrothers.

"Wash off as much of the blood as you can, Goodie. Soak my

sponges in hot water and rinse my instruments. Then ask Major Canfield if he has any silver nitrate solution he can spare. My vial is empty."

He donned his surgeon's apron, casting a glance across rows of blanketed bodies. Hundreds of men occupied small spaces on Barnum's warehouse floor, and the number was growing by the hour as infected wounds among those who had been able to walk became gangrenous. Jon wondered if there would be a man left in Hood's Brigades without a missing limb after the bloody assault on Union lines at Franklin.

Darkness came to Nashville with no letting up of the winter storm. Bonfires flared across the city, at street corners and between rows of field tents. Firewood was growing scarce, and as a substitute soldiers were tearing down barns and sheds to burn planks to keep warm. A general mood of discontent had swelled among thousands of starving, frozen infantrymen. No word had come regarding supplies from Richmond, or promised reinforcements. Hungry soldiers began looting stores. Bands of angry men roamed Nashville's streets looking for food and clothing and wood for dwindling fires. Hood's officers rode patrols, seeking to end the looting. Chaos threatened to undermine officers' authority as more and more soldiers took to the streets. Desertion was at an all-time high, a wounded cavalry officer told him while the doctor removed a lead fragment from the colonel's swollen right arm. Men were fleeing into the Tennessee woods with what they could carry in the way of food and clothing looted from Nashville homes and stores, too many for exhausted sentries and cavalry patrols to halt. Hood's army was dwindling. Dr. Roberts had informed Canfield that General Hood was in a wild rage over desertions and Richmond's failure to send him reinforcements and supplies—and most of all a lack of discipline among his troops. He kept demanding morphine and laudanum until he achieved a calm state bordering on stupor, according to Roberts.

Jon stood outside Barnum's warehouse on a loading platform, watching fires flicker on hilltops around Nashville. If a Union army found them here now, it would disastrous. The city had no fortifications, resting in a narrow river valley surrounded by low mountains. Union artillery would have a field day dropping shells from those hillsides into an unprotected town. Hood's soldiers would be blown to pieces in a matter of hours. Retreating to Nashville had made no sense, unless this was a prearranged rendezvous with Bedford Forrest's troops Jon knew nothing about.

He took a pint bottle of home-brewed whiskey from a pocket inside his tunic and drank deeply. He'd requested a few hours of sleep from Major Canfield when it seemed the most needy men had been attended to. Canfield himself had finally gone to his tent for rest. Jon found he was barely able to stand after so many hours at an operating table, his knees trembling so badly he had to support himself against the table while performing the last of his surgeries.

He drank again, preparing to go down the steps to a room he had hired at Peabody's, when he heard quite footsteps behind him.

"I wanted to apologize, Dr. Cross, for the way I behaved last night. I don't know what possessed me. It was never my intention to mislead you or behave in an unladylike fashion. I can't explain it properly, not even to myself."

When he turned around, he discovered Lorena standing close to him. A few stray locks of hair fell across her forehead where a hairpin had come loose. In lamplight spilling from the hospital door she looked more beautiful than ever, if that was possible. "If you wish to apologize for crying, it is not necessary. I have freely admitted to shedding tears myself over this bloody war. I assure you no apology is expected, Nurse Blaire."

She seemed a bit uncertain, looking past him, then back to his face. "It wasn't that, Doctor. In a moment of recklessness I gave you a kiss. . . ."

He corked his pint and pocketed it while staring into her eyes. She had virtually ignored him throughout the day, and now she was trying to explain. Although he was desperately tired, he summoned a smile and the courage to say things he might not say otherwise. "It may not have been recklessness," he said gently as he took a half step closer to her, gazing down upon her face while feeling his heart begin to race. "Consider the possibility that it may have seemed the natural thing to do. Granted, these are difficult times and all of us are near our wit's end. I must confess I am most attracted to you, Nurse Blaire. You are blessed with a rare beauty of spirit as well as being a truly beautiful woman. What man could resist being attracted to someone like you? If I seem too brash, then forgive me a man's weakness for a woman who fills my heart with desire. I shall always remember the kiss you gave me, whether it was merely an impulse you now regret or perhaps something you felt at the moment. I find that I'm unable to keep thoughts of you from my mind, day or night. If I sound foolish, then I've no choice but to seem a fool in your eyes. But you can be sure of one thing—my words and actions are sincere."

"Dr. Cross, you mustn't say—"

Before she could finish he reached for her, taking her by the shoulders. Bending down, he planted a kiss on her mouth and let it linger a moment before pulling away. "Good night, Nurse Blaire," he said softly, releasing her when he felt her stiffen in his grasp. "You must grant me my own moment of recklessness tonight. I hope I haven't offended you."

He turned and went down the steps, crossing a snowy street to the boardinghouse without looking back, nor did he have any regrets for what he'd said or done.

13

She stood on the loading platform, ignoring an icy wind and the brush of snowflakes against her face, long after Jonathan was out of sight behind Mrs. Peabody's front door. Her thoughts were so utterly confusing that she couldn't sort one from another for a few minutes—feelings she was unable to readily identify. Guilt mingled with a curious sense of longing to have his arms around her again, to feel his kiss. She thought of Paul. They had often talked of marriage, but there had been no engagement, no actual mention of betrothal. Paul had told her the war made banking a risky enterprise with heavy drains on the bank's reserves; thus it was best to wait until the war ended before they made marriage plans or began an engagement. Baltimore might even be a dangerous place to live, should a Rebel band invade Maryland, he had explained. It was better to wait until this Southern rebellion was crushed, as everyone knew it would be, before he and Lorena planned for the future. She loved Paul. He was a gentleman. She felt contentment in his presence. Why, then, was she permitting this rogue Confederate surgeon to invade her thoughts and nightly dreams? What was it about Jonathan that made her momentarily forget her feelings for Paul?

Yet it was there, as undeniable as any emotion she'd ever experienced, an attraction to Jonathan that was growing as time passed. What sort of woman was she, that she could love Paul and be attracted to another man? Was this war turning her into some common strumpet with no regard for pledges of love made to a sincere suitor with forthright intent whom she had left behind in Baltimore? What a frightening discovery it would be to learn that she was capable of betraying Paul's trust. She simply could not let it happen—and yet it *was* happening, beyond her control. Making this admission, she became angry with herself. Why was it that she was unable to close her mind and heart to Jonathan? What had come over her?

It was all so confusing. In defense of her growing feelings toward Jonathan, he was a sincere man with great compassion for his patients despite inhumane treatments he was forced to perform as a physician without proper medicines or facilities. He was not a Confederate by any definition she knew about—he owned no slaves nor did he voice opinions favoring it, making it all the more difficult to consider him an enemy. Since joining Hood's army she hadn't met a single soldier who was a slave owner or anyone with a clear understanding of states' rights, which only made her wonder what this war was truly about. War issues aside, Hood's men were not unlike men from Maryland or New York or Massachusetts if one disregarded differences in speech, the slow Southern drawl so common to Texans and Tennesseans. To Lorena, the only discernable difference was the color of their uniforms when one considered them individually, as men rather than soldiers. And if this were the case, it made this war all the more senseless. It had all seemed so clear when Dorothea Dix explained it as necessary to end a civil rebellion over the right to own black slaves. But the Confederates who were dying here were, as far as she knew, poor men who didn't own slaves nor care a whit about the rights of states to govern themselves.

Shivering now from the cold, she turned and went back inside to prepare clean bandages, more confused than ever over feelings she had for Jonathan Cross. There was no choice but to admit she was drawn to him in ways she'd never experienced with a man. Far worse was the guilt, knowing these feelings were a betrayal of a kind man in Baltimore whom she professed to love and hoped to marry.

She was tearing strips of bedding into bandages when suddenly her hands froze, color draining from her face. Not only had she betrayed her beloved Paul, but with a coded letter to Gaines's Mill she was betraying Jonathan to the Union Army. Her letter to Bertha Wheeler would bring about an attack upon Nashville.

"My dear God," she whispered, knotting her fingers into the cloth, "what have I done?"

Looking down at her hands, she wished with all her heart she hadn't written that letter, hadn't agreed to be a part of this spying mission for General Grant. If only she had stayed with Dorothea and the Sanitary Commission rather than risk everything, including her own life, by coming to Tennessee. In the beginning it had seemed so courageous, the right thing to do for the sake of her country—preserving the Union, Grant and Dorothea had said. In less than a week she had discovered none of that would be quite so simple.

Goodie found her attending to a wounded boy's arm. He came through the hospital with obvious reluctance as though he was fearful to say what was on his mind. "I got some news fer you an' it ain't real good. Doc Green said to tell you Miss Clara got a case of the typhus. She got the fever an' them red pox is sproutin' all over her face. Real sudden-like, she sat down an' didn't seem inclined to care to git up. Doc said you'd want to know. . . ." He looked down at his shoes, waiting for her reaction.

"I'll have her taken to the boardinghouse across the street at once," Lorena said, quickly tying off a bandage strip. "Has Dr. Green given her quinine?"

Goodie shrugged. "He give her some powders. Can't say jus' what it was."

"Please carry her to Peabody's Boardinghouse. I'll meet you there." She stood up, wiping her hands on her dress. "And please hurry, Goodie."

Goodie shuffled off toward one of the hospital doors without saying anything. Lorena hurried over to the apothecary case for a bottle of quinine with her stomach churning. Clara could very easily die from typhus. Her fever might last for days, and if she suffered as most did, her ordeal would be difficult, even fatal.

Concealing quinine under her shawl, Lorena ran from the hospital without regard for her other duties, thinking only of Clara and a disease that might claim the life of her dearest friend.

By lamplight, she bathed Clara's face and neck and chest with water while her friend slept. Dark red spots had appeared on her cheeks and the rest of her body. Her skin was hot, flushed by fever, and no matter how often Lorena bathed her, nothing seemed to lessen an increase in her body temperature. Small doses of quinine and a pinch of morphia showed no effect whatsoever. Beyond the frosted bedroom window, dawn brightened the eastern sky. Sometime during the night it had stopped snowing, and now a bitter cold blanketed Nashville, worsened by wind. Lorena could imagine the soldiers' suffering outside. Almost a foot of snow and sleet had fallen on the city since their arrival. Men without shoes or boots would be stricken with frostbite. Denied sufficient apparel and food, Hood's army was not capable of fighting in this weather. As Lorena was bathing Clara, she wondered how General Hood could avoid coming to the inevitable conclusion that surrender was his only reasonable choice.

A soft knock on the door startled her. "Come in," she said, closing the front of Clara's nightdress.

Beatrice Peabody came in with a bowl of steaming broth and

a cup of hot tea. "I brought this soup for the young nurse and a cup of tea for you." Beatrice was a plump woman near sixty with a friendly manner, willingly taking as many Confederate boarders as she could since Hood's army had arrived. She looked down at Clara before she put the bowl and cup on a bedside table. "I've seen plenty of cases of the typhus before. If her fever doesn't break soon, she'll drop off into what my grandma called the death sleep. You won't be able to wake her up no matter how hard you try, and there's a strong likelihood she will die from it. Grandma's old remedy was a potion made of hot whiskey, lemon juice, and honey. If I had any lemons I'd make her some, but it's the wrong time of year for lemons. I suppose we could try it without the lemon juice. After she drinks it, you'll have to cover her up with all the quilts I can spare and hope she breaks into a sweat."

"I've given her quinine," Lorena explained, "which is what the doctors give our men with typhus."

Beatrice gave her a doubtful look. "Doctors don't know all there is to know about everything, my dear. My whiskey and honey potion won't hurt her, and it could save her life."

"But Clara has never allowed so much as a drop of whiskey to touch her lips. She was taught it's not proper for a lady to partake of distilled spirits. If she found out I gave her some while she was ill, she'd never forgive me."

Mrs. Peabody leaned over the bed, examining Clara's face in lantern light. "If it was me, I'd rather ask her forgiveness than let her die. Those pox will only get worse. I have precious little faith in quinine as a cure for anything other than the gout."

Lorena struggled with her conscience. "Very well, please do make some of your potion. Clara has been my dearest friend, and I must do whatever I can to help her."

Beatrice started for the door. "Come with me to fetch some extra quilts. Pile them on her, and see that she stays covered as soon as she's drunk all of grandma's remedy. I'll warm up a cup of whiskey and sweeten it with honey right away."

Minutes later Mrs. Peabody returned to the room with a

china cup of foul-smelling liquid. Lorena lifted Clara's head and said in a quiet voice, "You must drink all of this, Clara. Drink every drop."

Clara's eyes opened, but only slightly. Obediently, as if in a trance, she swallowed the potion until the cup was empty; then she went back to sleep while Lorena covered her with thick quilts. Beatrice nodded approval and left, almost bumping into Jonathan Cross in the poorly lit hallway.

Jonathan entered Clara's bedroom and closed the door behind him. "How is she?" He came to the bed, his face freshly shaven, dressed in a clean shirt and an officer's tunic. "Dr. Green just informed me of her condition. It's very clearly a case of typhus. She was given quinine and morphia at the hospital."

Lorena swallowed uncomfortably, wondering what he might say about Beatrice's whiskey potion. "Mrs. Peabody made her a cup of warm whiskey and honey. She insists it helps break a fever."

To her surprise, Jonathan agreed. "It's an old-time cure for fevers, and quite often it works well. Keep her covered as tightly as you can. She'll sleep for a while." He looked into Lorena's eyes. "You look tired," he said with a kindness she truly felt.

"I'm okay, although I'm terribly worried about Clara. So many have died from typhus. . . ." She sat on the edge of the bed smoothing wrinkles from her nurse's gown self-consciously until he spoke.

"I'll drop in on her from time to time, as often as I can. It may be several hours, even days, before her fever breaks. A sweat is a sure sign of a cure. No one knows what causes these typhus outbreaks, but given proper care, she stands a good chance of pulling through."

"Thank you, Doctor, for your concern."

He grinned. "Please call me Jon. Surely we've known each other long enough to dispense with formalities."

She knew she was blushing. "If you wish."

"I do wish it, and I also wish we could find time to get to know each other better. While that may sound a bit too forward,

I've decided to take the risk. Some things in life are worthy of risk taking. Getting to know you would be worth a considerable amount of risk on my part. 'Recklessness,' I believe you called it earlier."

She wasn't sure what to say. A part of her wanted to agree while another argued against it. "I suppose I need some time to think. I have a beau. His name is Paul."

Jonathan seemed briefly nonplussed; then he gathered himself and nodded politely. "This Paul is a very lucky man, whoever he may be." Turning on his heel, he started for the door.

Moved by some force she didn't fully understand, Lorena got off the bed quickly to catch his arm before he left the bedroom. He felt her touch and hesitated, facing her.

"I think I'd like getting to know you better," she said, a slight nervousness creeping into her voice, "if you'll only give me time to consider what I'd be doing to Paul. I've always been so sure of the way I felt about him, until . . ."

His slow grin returned. "That's all I ask. Please give me the chance to show you who I am, the man I really am inside. All you have seen of me is what this army and this war demands of me. Grant me the opportunity to show you another side, and if you are willing, allow me to find out who you are, the things you care about, what makes you happy, what makes you sad." Again, before she could protest or resist, he bent down and kissed her lips so gently that she barely felt his touch. "I must get back to the hospital," he said, reaching for the doorknob, walking out so suddenly that there was no time for her to speak to him.

A moment later she shut the door and leaned against it with her eyes closed, remembering his kiss and the softspoken words he said to her. Now, more than ever, she knew she was falling in love with him.

14

Byron Willoughby was shown to General Grant's office by two soldiers. Snow fell on Washington in swirling sheets, deepening accumulations to a point where carriage traffic was light. Most people were staying home during the worst of a blustery winter snowstorm blanketing the East Coast. Willoughby had driven through drifts so deep that his carriage horse felt the crack of the whip over most of a difficult journey from Twin Forks. The message Byron carried was too important to wait for more moderate weather, and he made the trip with blankets draped around him and warm gloves protecting his hands. He had been instructed not to trust telegraph operators with any intelligence information on John Hood or Jubal Early. Men with Southern sympathies could be anywhere, and if Hood and Early were to be surrounded and joined in battle, no leaks as to their whereabouts should be risked. Thus it fell to Byron to drive through a blizzard to deliver personally any information his spies had gathered. No one other than Allan Pinkerton, head of the

Federal Secret Service, Chief of Staff John Rawlins, or Ulysses Grant, was to be told anything about Hood or Early if they were located.

Byron entered General Grant's office with his bowler hat in his hands. Grant was seated at his desk, making preparations to leave for Petersburg to direct the assault against Lee's fortifications himself. The stump of a cigar remained clenched between Grant's teeth, and a bottle of bourbon sat near his elbow, half its contents missing.

"Good evening, General. A team of nurses has relayed the location of John Bell Hood. I came as quickly as I could, even though this weather slowed me down considerably. As we agreed, nothing was entrusted to a telegraph."

John Rawlins came out of his chair, tossing aside maps of Confederate trenches and gun placements around Petersburg. "At last, a stroke of good luck," he said, giving Grant a sideways glance filled with satisfaction. "Pray tell us, where the hell is Hood?"

"Nashville," Byron replied, taking a leather-bound chair he was offered when General Grant pointed with the tip of his cigar. "He went the most unlikely direction under cover of a rainstorm—due north. The man is most certainly insane, or he does not know that General Thomas is at this very moment headed for the Cumberland River with eighty thousand men and enough heavy artillery to blast Nashville from the face of the earth."

Rawlins nodded thoughtfully. "I suggested Nashville as his possible objective," he said, reminding Grant of his prediction a few days ago.

Grant drew on his cigar. "Then, by God, this time we've got him. We're most grateful for your fortitude driving through this impossible snowstorm, Willoughby." He looked to Rawlins. "Send wires and dispatches to George Thomas immediately. Instruct him to surround Nashville and blow the city to pieces. Hood must be soundly defeated, his damnable Texans whipped decisively. Tell George no quarter is to be given. Pound Hood into submission and destroy every artillery piece and wagon he has. Prisoners are to be marched to Camp Morton in Indianapolis. If John Hood is among them, I want him delivered to Washington under the heaviest guard possible. Inform George that haste is of the essence now, for we know how quickly Hood can disappear."

Rawlins opened one of his maps slowly, a map of northeastern Tennessee. "According to our latest dispatch, Thomas is probably within two days of Nashville under forced march, unless weather slows him down. After such a battering at Franklin, it's unlikely Hood could evacuate before we can surround him. Should we trust this information to telegraph wires?"

"There may not be time to do otherwise, John. A dangerous thorn will be removed from our side if George can get in place rapidly," Grant was quick to add, pouring himself a drink. "With Hood rendered harmless, we can concentrate on Lee and Early. Lee clearly plans to spend the winter at Petersburg, leaving Early as our last renegade hellion to track down. I plan to throw enough mortar shells into Petersburg before Christmas to give Lee and his Virginians a case of the rigors. Sherman is burning his way across Georgia, leaving nothing but empty ground behind him. Gentlemen, we are poised on the very brink of winning this war. By early spring there won't be enough Confederates in the field to call themselves an army. With Hood out of the way and Lee surrounded, I fully expect the Confederacy to crumble before the first buttercups are in bloom."

"You may be somewhat optimistic, General," Rawlins remarked as he studied his map of mountains and roads above Nashville. "I do share your enthusiasm over finally locating Hood, however."

Grant frowned thoughtfully. "Who would have believed those women would be the instrument of Hood's destruction. I doubted their abilities from the start, I must confess. Inform Mistress Dix of their success. Perhaps if God and human nature are in harmony elsewhere, the other two nurses will tell us where Early is hiding. Written commendations are to be given to the two in Tennessee . . . I fear I've forgotten their names just now.

They have handed us John Hood on a silver platter. It was always his tempestuousness that would do him in, I felt sure. Like a good fighting cock with a broken wing, he went north to prepare for an assault rather than quitting the field in dishonor. He meant to peck at us from another direction, only this time, he miscalculated our strength and our resolve." He glanced across the desk at Byron. "Forgive my poor manners, Willoughby. Pour yourself a drink. You must be frozen to the bone."

Byron got up to take a glass from the sideboard. "If I may say so, General, those nurses have proven themselves to be most worthy as informants. Two letters came, one merely told us that they arrived without difficulty, the other advising that Nashville was Hood's destination." He poured himself a brandy with hands still trembling from the cold. "One of my informants with Bedford Forrest was discovered and sent to Belle Isle Prison, I learned last week, thus we have no way of knowing where Forrest is now. No word has come from the two nurses we sent to Early. I hope the worst has not befallen them."

Rawlins began scribbling a message on a piece of stationery when he said, "Perhaps they have been unable to locate him. It was fortunate that the other two found out Hood's plans so quickly. We know Early moves erratically, without apparent purpose. He was never as brazen as Hood, seeking confrontations."

"Hood's bold nature is now his undoing," Grant said. "I am delighted. I'll inform the President immediately." He aimed his glowing cigar tip at Byron. "Keep me informed. I intend to be at Petersburg by the end of the week to direct our shelling. If there are any further developments, advise General Rawlins and he will send word to me."

Byron quickly downed his brandy when General Grant stood up to don his coat. Grant spoke to Rawlins. "Come with me, John, and bring your maps. We'll inform Mr. Lincoln that, at long last, the devil from Texas has been found."

Byron put on his bowler and shook hands with both men, then let himself out. Rawlins gave his dispatch to a guard posted at the door. "Have this sent to General George Thomas by the most rapid means available. You are to hand it to Colonel Cox personally with those instructions. Have it wired to Kentucky, to Fort Donelson if no lines are down."

Grant and Rawlins started for the capitol and its unfinished dome, marching through drifts of snow, Rawlins carrying several maps of eastern Tennessee and southern Virginia under his coat.

The President's office was dark, reflecting his perpetual gloom over a continuing war despite optimism and bold promises made by his military commanders. Lincoln sat at his desk staring through a window at the snow while his private secretary, John Hay, told him of a meeting between Horace Greeley, editor of the *New York Tribune,* and Canadian-based Confederate commissioners to discuss a failed offer of armistice without a reunion of states or the emancipation asked for by President Lincoln. The Confederates wanted Lincoln blasted in the newspapers for repudiating an armistice, calling him a warmonger. Hay had just given the President a bleak casualty report. Since the war began the Army of the Potomac alone had suffered sixty-five thousand dead.

"Our losses are dreadful," Lincoln agreed, his deep voice as somber as his mood. His joy over winning reelection had been short-lived. "We simply must have an honorable peace with a reunion of this nation and an emancipation of Negroes. Otherwise, so many lost lives become meaningless. They leave me no choice but to push for an unconditional victory. They accuse me of being iron willed and inflexible in this regard. I suppose I am. Grant assures me he can end this war soon. I pray he can. At least he knows how to fight."

"Some are still calling General Grant a butcher," Hay said, thumbing through a sheaf of papers, reports of casualties from other Union commanders. Grant's losses were among the highest in the Union Army. Hay put them away in his briefcase when he heard muffled voices outside the office.

The President seemed not to hear his remark about General Grant, staring blankly at a pane of glass encrusted with melting ice that gave a view of the city.

Boyd Pierce, a presidential aide, rapped twice and stuck his head around the door. "Generals Grant and Rawlins asking to see you, Mr. President."

Lincoln turned from the window. "Show them in," he said as he drew his lanky frame from his chair, appearing to be almost too tired to stand.

Grant and Rawlins came in. Grant hurried over to shake hands with the President first. "We have good news," Grant said as Rawlins took Lincoln's hand. "You may remember Byron Willoughby of our Federal Secret Service, Allan Pinkerton's hand-picked assistant. He just arrived with word from two of our spies that John Bell Hood has retreated to Nashville. George Thomas is two days away with eighty thousand men. Nashville lies unprotected in a river valley of the Cumberland. Thomas has more than three hundred of our best pieces of artillery. Within two or three days George will begin shelling Nashville. Hood is reported to have less than fifteen thousand soldiers. Our victory is virtually assured."

Lincoln's shoulders seemed to droop. "What of the citizenry in Nashville? There could be so many civilian casualties. The press will have a field day with us if we kill women and children to get at Hood."

Grant tugged at his coat sleeves. "We simply cannot let Hood escape us now, Mr. President. Shelling Nashville is the only way to force him to surrender, in my view. After he feels enough fire-power from all sides to make the ground shake underneath his boots, only a madman would continue to fight."

The President nodded silently.

Rawlins said, "With Lee ensconced at Petersburg, widening his circle of trenches, Hood and Jubal Early represent the only Rebel armies of any size moving freely about the country. If we crush Hood, and with Sherman's successes in Georgia, we might expect a full Confederate surrender before winter is out. I have maps to show you where General Thomas is now and a map of the area around Nashville."

Lincoln sighed. "I don't need to see your maps, gentlemen, or hear about your battle plan. This country sorely needs an end to war—the killing has to stop." He looked at Grant with deep sorrow in his eyes. "Do what you must. *Harper's Weekly* delights in telling this nation how many men have been killed during my presidency, yet if we do not press forward to win this war, those who lost their lives did so for naught. Make whatever plans you deem necessary and proceed with them."

"Removing Hood from the battlefield is a key element to our strategy, Mr. President," Grant said earnestly. "With General Lee under siege at Petersburg, it can't last much longer. Phil Sheridan controls the Shenandoah Valley. Sherman's march through Georgia hardly meets any resistance now. Victory is within our grasp, and it begins with defeating Hood."

"I hope your optimism is warranted," Lincoln said. "In the beginning we all believed this Southern rebellion could only last a few months. Men whose military expertise everyone respected assured me the Confederacy could not organize nor equip an army of substance. As we now know, we were wrong in this belief. No one counted on the military genius of men like Robert E. Lee or Stonewall Jackson or James Longstreet or half a dozen more. They took a handful of men and exacted a heavy toll on our armies before we realized what brilliant strategists they were." Here the President paused, gazing out his window. "As to General Hood, you'll forgive me if I postpone my celebration over the victory you say is within our grasp until you report his defeat or surrender. I remember well George McClellan telling me that John Bell Hood is a will-o'-the-wisp with a sharp saber and the courage of a lion. Let us hope we have the lion cornered this time."

Rawlins cleared his throat. "Instructions are on the way to General Thomas at this hour. With reasonable weather, Thomas can surround Nashville in three days. Hood's defeat will give us the entire state of Tennessee. General Sherman controls Georgia. As soon as Lee can be blasted from his trenches, we'll have Virginia and the Confederate capital. They'll have nothing left."

"I'm leaving now for Petersburg," Grant said, "to direct the assault on Lee. General Rawlins will keep you informed as to our progress on all fronts while I'm in Virginia."

Lincoln nodded again, still watching the snowy scene beyond his window. John Hay seemed to sense the President's distraction and said, "If that is all, gentlemen, President Lincoln is very tired. His son, Tad, has come down with whooping cough. He and Mary were up with him most of the night."

Rawlins remembered that the Lincolns had lost a son, Willie, only a few years earlier, to bilious fever. "Sorry to hear of it," he said, backing away from the President's desk.

"We wish him a speedy recovery," Grant said, turning for the door. "General Rawlins will inform you of all developments. A good day to you, Mr. President."

Lincoln barely acknowledged their departure, a faraway look in his eye as he watched more snow fall on Washington.

15

Whenever he could, Jonathan Cross dashed across the street to check on Clara Brooks's fever as another bitterly cold day worsened conditions for all of Hood's soldiers. Cases of frostbite were on the rise, as were cases of pneumonia. A third hospital was being established at an abandoned railroad depot—no trains were running to Nashville now after Union shelling and a fire had destroyed the town's only railroad bridge. Another hospital was needed to house men with more serious illness. Buel Green was the physician in charge of this new facility, adding to the responsibilities of doctors treating wounded at the cotton warehouses. Jon was so weary by the middle of the afternoon that it seemed he performed procedures in a daze, barely aware of what he was doing, numbed by fatigue and the cold weather despite heat from smudgepots inside Barnum's. Smoke had grown so thick near the ceiling that it appeared a stormcloud was building indoors. But as a tonic for his weariness he thought of Lorena, looking forward to seeing her the next time he went to Mrs. Peabody's to check on Clara, remembering to wash blood from his hands and face before he crossed to the boardinghouse as if his visits were social rather than professional calls.

As nightfall approached, a new threat began to build above a group of hills to the north and west. Another snowstorm was on its way. A bank of dark clouds advanced toward Nashville, driven by ever increasing gusts of wind. Men who were already suffering from the cold would soon feel the bite of snowflakes. Firewood and coal were in short supply, while kerosene for smudgepots and oil lamps dwindled.

As lanterns were being lit inside Barnum's, Jon completed a row of stitches holding a flap of skin over the stump of a young soldier's lower leg. Major Canfield walked over, his surgeon's apron smeared with dried blood.

"For now, most of our serious cases have been attended to," he said, glancing around the warehouse, fatigue making his voice so thick he sounded hoarse. "I finished an inspection. Three men were deceased, and I had them removed, making room for three more should the need arise . . . which I'm quite sure it will."

Jon put his needle and thread aside. "I have no more silver nitrate or morphine. Only a small amount of bromine. The supply of laudanum was depleted yesterday. Without medicines I fear we are reduced to spectator's roles in so many of these cases."

"It can't be helped," Canfield sighed. "Dr. Roberts has informed me that when he attended to General Hood today, Hood is talking about pulling us out of Nashville soon."

Jon washed his hands in a pail of tepid water. "These men can't be moved, Major. More than half are on the brink of death the way it is. Moving them would certainly cause many to die of exposure. Another storm will hit us within the hour."

"It's already snowing again," Canfield said, with a look out one warehouse door. "I agree our mortality rate will be high if we are ordered to move."

"How is General Hood's mental condition? Did Hiram make any mention of it?"

"He is said to weep continually now, frustrated over failure in Richmond to send supplies and reinforcements. His aides are so terrified of him that they remain outside until he summons them."

Jon said nothing more about Hood's mental deterioration, for he knew Canfield believed Hood's senses would return. He dried his hands on a small piece of clean cloth. "If there are no more pressing matters, I'll look in on our sick nurse, Clara Brooks," he said, sleeving into his coat.

The major frowned. "A case of typhus, I believe you said it was."

"It appears serious. Her fever mounts and she is delirious when she awakens. I've noted an inordinately high incidence of pox. Quinine seems to have no effect on her fever."

"Quinine is best suited for malaria, as you know. After I have some rest I'll look in on her. By the way, have they asked to send any more letters?"

"None I'm aware of, Major. With all due respect, I do not share your suspicions that they could be spies. They are both so young—too young, it would seem, to be versed in such matters."

"I may have been wrong. Time will tell. I want to be informed if they deliver a letter to our couriers. Get some sleep. I'll look in on Nurse Brooks tomorrow. I've seen cases where a small dose of cayenne pepper will break fevers."

Canfield walked off with his shoulders drooping, looking as tired as Jon felt. Jon went to a warehouse door opposite the boardinghouse, noting that it had indeed begun to snow again. He crossed the street, seeing broken windows in many storefronts where looting soldiers had taken what they wanted. Hood's army was on the verge of total insurrection unless supplies reached Nashville soon. Men stood in groups around fires, trying to stay warm along every roadway, soldiers without sufficient shelter from another building snowstorm. An order to move out from General Hood might light a fuse igniting riots among so many disgruntled men.

He entered Clara's room quietly. A lantern was turned down

to a pinpoint of light on the table beside her bed. Lorena sat in a rocking chair next to the window, and when she saw him she got up and came over to his side.

"She's sleeping now," Lorena whispered. "I've been bathing her with cool cloths to help bring her fever down, yet nothing seems to work."

"It takes time for typhus to run its course. Be patient. I know she's your friend and you're concerned, but there's nothing more we can do for her now." He turned from the bed to look at Lorena. In soft light her face was like smooth ivory. Her eyes sparkled, reflecting the lantern's glow. "I know it's cold outside, but would you go for a walk with me? We can talk and, despite the weather, a snowflake can be a pretty sight."

"Perhaps I shouldn't," she protested, glancing over to Clara as if to say she was needed here.

"Miss Brooks will be fine for a few minutes. She's in a deep sleep. We won't be long."

Lorena's slow smile made his heart quicken.

"Only a short walk," she agreed, taking her long woolen coat from the foot of Clara's bed.

He helped her into her coat and opened the door, feeling a rush of excitement that made him forget how tired he was. As she walked past him, he noticed a fragrance about her that might have been perfume.

Strolling past groups of soldiers gathered around bonfires, they said nothing to each other for several minutes. Snow fell in irregular spits when winds gusted, then died. He took her by the arm and she offered no complaint nor did she look at him as he escorted her around soldiers who stared at them when they walked by.

Passing a dark livery stable away from watchful eyes, Jon stopped where a stable wall protected them from icy winds. "I thought of you often today," he told her, hoping his admission wasn't too bold. "I don't seem to be able to help myself. My thoughts return to you at the most unexpected times. I have not forgotten that you asked for time to think about me and a beau you have back home, yet I felt I needed to tell you that I do think of you quite regularly. In fact, I find I'm unable to think of anything else lately." He knew his speech was awkward, clumsy, lacking a gentleman's flair for the right words but he'd said them anyway, for they came from deep within his heart.

"You shouldn't be thinking of me," she said, "not when you have so many patients who need your attention." She searched his face, looking, he supposed, for signs he was telling the truth.

He held on to her arm gently, unwilling to let go or continue their walk until he'd said what was on his mind. "I told you, I can't seem to control it. No matter how hard I try to concentrate on my duties, my thoughts keep returning to you. I wonder at times if you'll think me an utter fool, should I tell you of my preoccupation. I'm taking a chance that you'll understand how a man can find a woman so attractive that he loses all semblance of reason."

She laughed, although there was no ridicule in it. "I am flattered, kind sir, that I can be such a powerful distraction."

"You are. I must confess I've never been so distracted from my work before. I hope you won't be put off. . . ."

She smiled so warmly that he almost kissed her, until he reminded himself that he must control himself.

"I'm not put off. I suppose I am putting off a decision as to . . . my loyalties. I love Paul. He's a good man, decent, from a good family. I feel it's wrong to consider another man's attention while I've pledged my love to Paul. It would be dishonest."

"I understand. Your honesty is forthright and commendable. I only wish there was some way to convince you that I am a good man, a decent man, all things considered, although I may lack the good breeding you say Paul has. My father is a rather uncomplicated cotton farmer. I grew up on the Brazos River where breeding is given less regard than men who keep their word, dealing with others fairly, paying their just debts in a timely fashion. The Cross family would never be considered bluebloods by any real measurement."

"Your father owns slaves," she said, more a question than a statement.

He was a bit puzzled by her remark. "This isn't considered a crime in Texas. Thomas Jefferson and George Washington owned slaves. In case you've forgotten, that's what this war is about, to decide whether Negroes are property or human beings with the right to decide for themselves where they live and work."

"I only wondered how you felt about it."

He looked up at clouds dropping snow around them. "I don't know how I feel, honestly. I guess the answer lies in determining the nature of Negroes as I suggested to you before: Are they human, or something less? I only have my own experience by which to judge them. My father's slaves are simple, hardworking people. As a child I felt closer to my black nanny than I did my own mother. Ida saw to my every need. I loved her dearly until the day she died. I still recall how she cared for me with great fondness. But the issue over her freedom to go elsewhere if she wanted was never discussed. She was like a part of our family. She never wanted to leave us, of that I'm quite sure."

Lorena moved ever so slightly closer to him, and now he could smell lilacs—a perfume, he supposed.

"If only it weren't for Paul," she said in a softer voice as she looked into his eyes. "If we were to decide to begin . . . a courtship I would have to write him a letter explaining why my feelings had changed toward him, if I knew how to express it. I wouldn't want to hurt him."

Jon thought about the conversation Major Canfield had overheard regarding a letter to Virginia, but this was neither the time nor the place to ask Lorena about it. He was heartened to think she might be considering a courtship at all. "It would make me very happy, should you decide in my favor." He grinned. "My manners need a bit of polish, and I can't always think of the right things to say." Swallowing, he made up his mind to take a chance. "I feel that sometimes, actions say things better than words." He bent down and kissed her very gently, hoping with all his heart that she wouldn't take offense and pull away.

She allowed his lips to remain against hers for a few brief seconds, and to Jon, they seemed an eternity. She did not resist as she had before, stiffening while he held her. The soft patter of falling snow around them was like sweet music accompanying the beat of his heart until finally Lorena pressed a dainty hand to his chest and drew back.

His mind raced to find something to say that wouldn't seem too bold. "I think I'm falling in love with you," he confessed, blurting it out without thinking when nothing else came to mind. It was the truth yet perhaps he shouldn't have said it so soon.

"Oh, Jon," she whispered, "I am so afraid that I may also have fallen in love with you. I know it's a most shameful thing to do to Paul. I feel so guilty every time I think of you instead of the man I'd planned to marry. I didn't want this to happen—I truly did not."

When he heard her admit to having similar feelings, he wanted to embrace her, but he held his emotions in check. "Quite possibly we were destined to meet. No one knows what the fates have in store for us. It fills my heart with joy to know that you may also love me."

She tilted her head slightly. "I'll call it the beginnings of love. We're little more than strangers."

"But the mutual attraction is there. We can begin to get to know each other. We share the same feelings."

Her brow furrowed. "I won't be pushed. I must have time to think."

"I give you my oath that I will not push you. As best I can, I'll keep a gentleman's distance until you've made up your mind."

"Are you a man of your word?"

"I am."

She glanced around them, making sure they were alone at the front of the livery; then she slowly put her arms around his neck and drew his face close to hers, parting her lips invitingly with her eyes closed.

He kissed her tenderly, being careful not to crush her with

the power of his embrace, while his heart soared. For a few precious moments she allowed him to hold her against him with his
mouth covering hers. He felt, as well as heard, her sigh in his
arms.

"I love you, Jon," she said, in a voice so soft he scarcely heard
her, taking her arms from his neck. "Now I must go be with
Clara."

16

Lorena stood with her face to the window, paying little heed to bonfires burning beyond the glass or the shadows of men around them. For several hours she'd been thinking of Jonathan and what he had said to her about his feelings, telling her that he loved her, that he thought of her often. Remembering their kisses, she felt warm inside and an excitement she'd never known with Paul. When Jonathan put his arms around her, holding her wonderfully close, there was something so different and special about it that she couldn't compare the experience to her courtship with Paul in any manner. Paul's embrace was comforting, while Jonathan's filled her with something deliciously thrilling, an inner glow that was in some ways almost wicked, forbidden, although not in a bad or sinful way. There was a passion between them they both felt. It defied description. No man had ever made her feel the way she did when Jonathan embraced her, when he kissed her. Even the soft sound of his voice awakened some part of her she had never known existed as if his words touched an inner chamber of her heart she had been guarding from Paul. She was certain now that she loved Jonathan Cross— she had no doubt about it, no fear that it may only be a girlish infatuation with a handsome man based solely on his good looks.

Her breath frosted the window. She couldn't keep her mind from Jonathan's tenderness. She hadn't wanted this to happen, yet it had, and now she faced a terrible moment of truth. The letter she had written to Mistress Wheeler would bring certain disaster to the man she loved. If she admitted to what she'd done, that she was a spy for the Union Army advising General Grant of General Hood's whereabouts, Jonathan's feelings for her would most surely change, and that would be the end of their love affair. Beyond that, if he did his duty, he must expose her and Clara as enemy informants to his commanding officers. She and Clara would be sent away to a Confederate prison, or even hanged.

"Whatever shall I do?" she whispered, pressing her forehead to the windowpane, resisting an urge to cry. Crying would not solve her dilemma. Honesty would end all hope of a relationship with Jonathan. Her silence could get him killed. The longer she thought about what she'd done, the more perplexing her situation seemed. Neither course of action was acceptable. Saying nothing might easily earn Jonathan a death sentence during a Union attack on Nashville, or at best a prison term in a Union prison camp. Telling him the truth would end the love he felt for her when he learned she betrayed him. How could she allow a man she loved to run the risk of dying or going to prison by remaining silent? But was she willing to lose his love by admitting to her role as a spy?

"I only did what Dorothea and General Grant asked me to do," she said, watching snowflakes land against the window glass, then slowly begin to melt. The joy she experienced earlier while she was in Jonathan's arms had also melted away, and in its place was a cold realization that what she'd done would destroy any feelings he had for her if he learned the truth. Keeping silent was the only solution, the only way she might avoid losing the love developing between them. When the Union attack came, as she knew it would, Jonathan's fate was in God's hands.

Clara stirred beneath her bedcovers, taking Lorena's attention from the window. She crossed to the bed and sat beside Clara, preparing a damp cloth for her forehead.

"Our soldiers are coming," Clara mumbled, her eyes closed as she dreamed in a light, fevered sleep. "We . . . told . . . them . . . where to find us."

"You mustn't say that, Clara!" Lorena scolded, awakened to a new fear—that Clara might expose them if Jonathan or anyone else overheard her. "Please wake up and listen to me! You can't talk about what we've done, not even in your sleep!" Her heart was drumming and her hands trembled badly. "What if Major Canfield happened to hear you?"

Clara's eyes remained shut. "They are . . . coming to save us."

"Clara!" Lorena cried, shaking her friend's shoulders. "You must wake up!"

Clara's eyelids parted, becoming slits. She tried to focus on Lorena's face. "Who called . . . me?"

"Please listen to me, Clara. You were dreaming about what we did, and you were talking in your sleep. You mustn't think of it at all. Forget about the letter. Can you hear me?"

"Is that you, Lorena, dear?"

"Yes, it's me. I want you to wake up for a moment."

"I feel so cold. Are the soldiers coming to take us home?"

"Please don't talk about it. If Captain Cross or that awful Major Canfield should happen to overhear you, we'll be arrested. You have to stop dreaming about it. Do not allow yourself to think of it at all. You simply have to put it out of your mind or we will be discovered."

"I suppose I was . . . dreaming." At that, Clara began to cry. "I want to go home. I'm so terribly sick. I want to sleep in my own bed and see my own doctor. I need to see Willard and mother and my home again. I can't stand any more of this bloody war or these Confederate savages we are forced to endure. Please take me away from here, Lorena. Take me back home at once or

I know I'll surely die in this dreadful place, away from my mother and father and dear, sweet Willard and my friends in Baltimore. I beg you to take me home immediately."

"It can't be done," Lorena told her quietly, passing a cool rag over Clara's fevered brow. "We must be brave and strong until our soldiers arrive. And until that time comes you mustn't talk about it or think of it any longer. Push it out of your thoughts entirely. Think of Willard, of his promotion at the college, anything else."

"I want to go home," Clara sobbed, tears running down her now pockmarked cheeks in tiny rivulets. "Tennessee is a terrible place, and this room is so frightfully cold."

"It's your fever. Dr. Cross visits you frequently to see how you are. You'll get the best care they can give you. These are most trying circumstances for everyone."

She rubbed her eyes with the back of her hand. "Am I going to die from it?" she asked.

"You have typhus, my dear. The fever has to run its course and then you'll feel better."

For a moment Clara was silent while staring at the ceiling. "When our soldiers come to save us, I can go home," she whimpered in a small voice, on the verge of more tears.

"Please don't let those thoughts enter your mind or we'll be discovered. You were talking in your sleep. If you wish to see Willard and home again, you simply must stop thinking about what we've done. Close your mind to it completely."

"I'll try, and I'm going to pray that God won't let me die of typhus in this miserable place."

"You're a strong-willed woman, Clara. You can will yourself to overcome it if only you'll try. Be strong, and be patient. I know things will work out for the best very soon."

Despite Lorena's assurances, Clara started to cry. She wept while the wet cloth passed over her face, sobbing fitfully until at last, she drifted off to sleep.

Lorena returned to the dark window. She sat in her rocking chair listening to snow patter softly against the windowpane and

Clara's regular breathing. A new threat to their safety loomed with a worsening of Clara's fever. If she talked in her sleep while Jonathan or anyone else was present, their chances of escaping discovery were slight.

Remembering back to that night they met with Ulysses Grant and Dorothea Dix, Lorena thought how easy it would have been to decline the offer to serve their country this way. She had been the first nurse to accept, followed by Bessie Higgins and Ruth Ann Waldrop. Clara was the only one to have doubts, yet she agreed in the end, probably because they were best friends and Lorena had consented to undertake this dangerous mission.

Another recollection of that night seemed curious now, for when she told Paul about it, that she was leaving for Tennessee to the war front, he'd simply said the choice was hers. Strange, coming from a man who professed to love her. Why hadn't he asked her to stay in Baltimore where they could be together?

A huge snowflake landed on the windowpane, its pattern vivid in light from the lantern. As it began to melt, Lorena was unable to watch it dissolve, fearing that like this snowflake, a developing love between her and Jonathan might quickly dissolve if he accidentally learned of her treachery from Clara.

17

General George Henry Thomas was proud of his nicknames. His courageous battlefield performance had won him the monicker "Rock of Chickamauga," while officers of equal rank called him "Pap" for his fatherly appearance, a graying beard, and a gentle manner that belied his cunning and resolve in battle. He sat in his command tent on a cold night, his Army of the Cumberland bogged down by snow on the second day of December only a few miles from the Tennessee border in Kentucky. By lantern light he and Colonel John Menem pored over maps of the region. Palming tin cups of coffee laced with brandy, Thomas aimed a blunt finger at a point on the map.

"From Franklin he could have gone most any place. I am of the opinion he retreated west or southwest. Our scouts and the field reports from divisions at Franklin say Hood may have done what no one expected, scattering his forces to regroup elsewhere when he's been resupplied. There is no solid trace of him other than bodies of his dead left behind all over eastern Tennessee.

He's a wily veteran, crazy as a loon, some say. In this snow we're down to a crawl looking for him. It would appear the gods favor him with inclement weather so his trail is hidden."

Colonel Menem frowned at one map. "He wouldn't go directly to Nashville. The city has no defenses and no working railroad. We can rule out Nashville, I think. Pulling back toward Memphis is one possibility. Supplies could reach him on the Mississippi River if Richmond slips small barges past our blockade."

Thomas disagreed. "Memphis is too far for a crippled army in weather like this. He must have thousands of sick and wounded to slow him down. I say he's much closer, but I've no idea where to look."

"No scouting details have found any trace of him. It's as though he has sprouted wings and disappeared from the face of the earth."

Snow whispered against the tent roof and sides while Thomas continued to study his maps. "Centerville is a strong possibility and it's closer," he said gravely, stroking his beard. "If it continues to snow, we may never find him until he resurfaces with fresh troops and supplies. Centerville is southwest. Hood may decide to use the Tennessee River to run supplies to him there."

"It could take us two weeks to reach Centerville at the rate we're traveling. Our caissons bog down in every snowdrift, and in places our wagons are unable to move at all without doubling the teams of mules."

Thomas leaned back on his folding canvas stool to stare up at the lantern. "It's no small trick, moving almost one hundred thousand men and supplies under the best circumstances, John. I worry that we'll be snowbound here for some time. General Grant wants results from us, and I'll be damned if I intend to sit here while Hood slips away. I've been charged with the responsibility of finding him and smashing him. At first light I want you to send our best scouts to Franklin, including those three Delaware Indians. Have them dig through every rubbish heap and snowdrift with a teaspoon if necessary until they've found some trace of Hood. Have scouts question the citizenry along the way. We may find a Union sympathizer who saw them pass by."

"Locals aren't going to cooperate, General. We've tried to question them before, and it's as though they've all gone deaf and blind."

"Ask anyway. I'm counting on luck as well as determination to find those Texans. We'll leave nothing to chance. As my old grandpa used to say, I'd rather be lucky than good anytime. Lady Luck is a fickle bitch, but she may be on our side now. Hood got his ass whipped badly at Franklin. Maybe his luck has run out."

Colonel Menem rolled up one of his maps as the sound of hoofbeats neared the tent. A voice shouted, "I've got a dispatch for General Thomas from General Rawlins in Washington!"

Thomas rolled his eyes. "John Rawlins has sent us a Christmas greeting. I'd sooner have a visit from my mother-in-law."

A sentry drew back a tent flap to admit a courier in a heavy coat dusted with snow. The young soldier's cheeks were red from the cold. He opened a leather dispatch case and handed a letter to General Thomas. "From Fort Donelson, sir," he stammered, lips a deep purple, his teeth rattling when he spoke. "A wire from General John Rawlins identified as 'most urgent.' "

"Most urgent," Thomas muttered, opening an envelope bearing the seal of command at Fort Donelson in Kentucky, certain that it contained nothing of real importance. Few dispatches from John Rawlins amounted to more than time-wasting requests for field reports, and as of now there was nothing to report beyond weather so foul no man could move in it and a growing list of frustrations trying to find Confederates to engage in battle.

But when Thomas read the short message, his expression was quick to change. "Hood is presently in Nashville," he said to Colonel Menem. "At long last, a chance to fight the mighty Hood on a battlefield. Nashville is perfect. No fortresses or any breastworks of consequence. The Cumberland River is an open door to the city from two directions. We'll overrun them in a matter of hours. With cannons placed on high ground around Nashville, I can shell the place to sawdust in a single day. I will have the intractable John Hood mewing like a motherless kitten if he stays put long enough for us to get there. Pass the order down at once to move out. We'll march day and night if we have to, but I will have Hood's balls in my grasp within three days unless fortune is against us." He addressed the shivering courier. "Please convey my gratitude to General Burke at Fort Donelson and ask that he send a wire to Chief of Staff Rawlins that we are proceeding at top speed for Nashville within the hour." Thomas turned to John Menem. "Waste no time preparing our columns for forced march. I want this army moving in an hour. Any man jack not ready to move at the appointed hour is to be summarily shot and left behind as food for the wolves for refusing to obey a direct order."

Colonel Menem saluted and wheeled from the tent. The cry went quickly down mile after mile of tents where George Thomas's Army of the Cumberland was camped for the night: "Move out! Be ready to march in one hour!" More than eighty thousand men began to scramble from tents to move toward Nashville in the dark during a blinding snowstorm. A First Sergeant from Ohio shouted to his men, "We've found Mr. Hood and his terrible Texans! Roll out of those goddamn blankets and let's give him a taste of Yankee lead!"

As the pink-faced courier from Fort Donelson departed, George Thomas came slowly to his feet. He walked to the tent flap and clasped his hands behind his back to watch preparations being made for a night march toward Nashville. John Bell Hood, one of the South's most courageous generals, had by all accounts made a serious mistake, choosing Nashville for a destination. Under the worst of weather conditions Nashville was three days away. By the grace of God and with only an ounce of luck, the Army of the Cumberland would blast Hood's Brigades to smithereens before the week was out.

*　　*　　*

Appalachian Mountain roads rose and fell sharply, making it all the more difficult for wagons and caissons to navigate when snow was piled two feet deep in places where wind created drifts. Columns of foot soldiers marched over mountains and across valleys like a monstrous snake stretching for miles. Extra teams of mules were required to haul the heaviest wagons over steep climbs. As dawn came to northern Tennessee the Army of the Cumberland began its slow, methodical advance on Nashville with George Thomas at the front of his divisions. Snow continued to fall, worsening the plight of soldiers marching through it as temperatures fell to near twenty degrees. Infantrymen with heavy coats and bulky backpacks slogged across packed snow behind cannons and a division of ammunition wagons destined to reach Nashville first so shelling could begin as soon as possible. Scouts rode ahead to report road conditions and the slim chance that Thomas's columns might encounter a few Rebel patrols. As the troops passed through mountain villages, residents came out on porches or stood below leafless oak trees and snow-clad pines to watch the endless Union force marching south, the largest army ever to enter this region of Tennessee. Thomas knew word of their arrival was sure to reach Hood ahead of them. However, if he pressed forward without pausing for more than a few hours of rest, he was certain Hood's Confederates could not withdraw in time to escape him.

Colonel Menem rode out to meet a scout detail returning at midmorning. Thomas hurried his bay gelding forward to hear the news himself firsthand. As he rode closer, he noticed his scouts held a pair of prisoners at gunpoint, two men who appeared to be staggering through more than a foot of snow covering the roadway. Falling snowflakes prevented him from identifying them until he was a few yards away. Both men were Confederates, infantrymen by their billed caps.

"We found a couple of Reb deserters," the captain of scouts announced, pointing to the two shivering men. One was wrapped in a blanket. The other had no boots, just strips of canvas tied around his feet, and a coat with so many holes in it that one might guess its previous owner surely died of shrapnel wounds.

Thomas stepped down from his saddle to approach the prisoners. Both men were trembling so violently from the cold that he was immediately sorry for them. He spoke to the captain. "Take these soldiers to the side of the road and build a fire. Have you questioned them?"

"Yessir. They're from Hood's Third Infantry. Deserted four days ago because there was nothing to eat. One of 'em is carrying a frozen roasted chicken—you can see he's been gnawing on it for quite a spell and he won't give it up. He said we'd have to shoot him before he'd hand it over."

Moved to more compassion by the soldiers' sad condition, Thomas said, "Have someone bring them rations. I want to question them myself. Take them over to those trees and get a fire going so they won't die from exposure." He took another step toward his prisoners, addressing the man with no boots. "You will be given the best treatment possible as prisoners of war, but I want you to answer my questions truthfully. Is Hood still in Nashville?"

The Confederate nodded, keeping his face to the ground as he stamped his feet to warm them. Columns of Union cavalry rode by when the first Cumberland divisions reached the spot where Thomas met with his scouts. A scout gathered dry limbs and pinecones to get a fire started near the edge of the road, clearing a place in the snow. With pistols pointed at them, the prisoners were taken from the roadway when heavy field cannons rolled to the top of a ridge where the road started downhill.

Thomas noted that the prisoner who gripped the frozen carcass of a half eaten chicken underneath his blanket was young, less than twenty, and his eyes were sunken, dull, as if he might not be in good health or totally aware of his surroundings.

"How many men are with Hood now?" he asked, directing this question to the youth.

"I . . . ain't exactly . . . sure, sir. We lost six thousand down at Franklin, somebody said. Them bodies was layin' so deep that we had to jump over piles of 'em to make a charge up them hills."

The other prisoner spoke, although his teeth were chattering and his words were hard to hear. "We was told . . . there . . . wasn't but twelve thousand . . . of us. Half of 'em are so sick they can't fight nobody. Got no powder . . . or shot, neither. No . . . medicine fer them that's sick . . . or wounded. Me an' Clay ain't had nothin' to eat since we got there 'cept for peas an' soup. A bunch has deserted . . . like us. We was cold an' starvin'."

Flames started to lick up the piled pinecones and limbs at the foot of the tree, crackling, giving off smoke. Both Confederate prisoners hobbled over to the fire, shivering. The soldier named Clay began to cough, a wet sound coming from his lungs.

Thomas spoke to the other prisoner. "Will General Hood stay in Nashville, or does he plan to leave?"

"Gen'l Hood don't tell nobody what he aims to do, but most of his men are too weak to go no place else right now. We got so much sickness that there ain't no way they can march. Got no food or much of nothin' else. Me an' Harley decided this war is over fer us. I'm done fightin'. If you'll only let us go home, we ain't gonna fight no more. You got our word on that."

Thomas turned to Colonel Menem. "Have someone see that these men are properly fed and clothed. Put them in one of the supply wagons until they're strong enough to walk. If this is the kind of army we face at Nashville, I suspect it will be the short-est battle of the war. These poor creatures are starving and frozen beyond any capacity to fight." He gave two of his scouts a look of irritation. "Put those revolvers away. Anyone can see these men are too weak to run off."

Climbing back atop his bay, Thomas considered his won-derful good fortune. Hood's brigades had dwindled to twelve thousand men who had nothing to eat and no gunpowder. The pounding they'd taken at Franklin cost them dearly. Now Hood had chosen the most unlikely place in Tennessee to lick his wounds, a city he couldn't defend.

Thomas glanced up at dark clouds dumping snow across forested mountains, thinking even the foulest weather could not prevent him from getting to Nashville in time, after what they'd learned from the two deserters. Hood's weakened Confederates would not attempt a further retreat in this blizzard. Thomas knew Lady Luck and Mother Nature were with him now.

18

President Lincoln sat in a chair beside his son's bed in an up-stairs bedroom of the White House, listening to Tad's dif-ficult breathing. Lawrence Collins, one of Washington's most regarded physicians, closed his medical bag.

"I've given him camphor chest rubs and gum weed syrup to end the coughing spells, Mr. President. There isn't much more we can do. Steam frequently breaks up congestion. Pots of steam-ing water under a bedsheet placed over his face may help some. Time is the best cure. Whooping cough must run its course. He's a strong lad."

Mary Todd Lincoln stood facing a bedroom window. She seldom mentioned Willie now, their older son whose death had given her weeping fits lasting almost a year. But when Tad's health was threatened, she had lapsed into silent depression as though expecting the loss of another son.

"I'll have servants prepare boiling water," Lincoln said in his continual monotone. He turned to Mary. "Mother, if you'll speak to the women in the kitchen about it . . ." He was known to frequently call her Mother when their children were present, and since Tad's illness she rarely left the boy's bedside.

Dr. Collins walked to the door. "I'll look in on him later in the evening," he said, letting himself out.

The President was concerned when Mary didn't leave to make arrangements for boiling water. "Did you hear me, Mother? Tad needs pots of steam. Shall I see to it myself?"

Still there was no answer. He got up and came over to the window to see what Mary was staring at so intently. On a street corner stood an imposing brick building with snow-capped roof and smoking chimneys, holding Mary's attention. Ever since Willie died, Lincoln often found her staring at this mental hospital. "Mother, do you see that large building yonder?" he asked gently, placing his hand on the small of her back. "Try to control your grief over Willie or it will drive you mad and we may have to send you there. Tad needs pails of steaming water. Please attend to it and do your best to forget about Willie."

Mary turned. "Willie's death was divine punishment for having been too wrapped up in the world, too devoted to our own political advancement. God has punished us, and He may do so again by taking Tad from us. I feel it is this war. So many good men are dying every day—"

"General Grant has assured me it will be over soon. He has Lee bottled up in Virginia. He's a fighter, not a politician."

Mary's expression darkened. "Grant is a butcher and not fit to be at the head of an army. He loses two men for the enemy's one. He has no management, no regard for human life. I could lead an army as well myself."

"Now, now, Mother. Grant is a capable military man. I have the utmost confidence in him. Please ask the servants to prepare boiling water for Tad. God does not want another son from us as divine punishment for a war we did not initiate. A house divided against itself cannot stand, nor do I expect the house to fall. Grant will give us a victory and we shall be united again. Ours is a just war, which must be fought to its end. See to Tad's hot water now and put aside your grief."

She left the window and went downstairs, leaving Lincoln to ponder just how close his wife was to outright madness. No one had grieved more deeply than he over Willie's death, but as the years passed he thought of it less. Mary had never truly gotten over it.

He looked at the mental hospital himself for a moment or two before returning to Tad's bedside. The boy was asleep, resting as peacefully as anyone could expect. Settling into his chair, the President closed his eyes, chin resting on his chest, dozing.

It was after dark, close to midnight, when an aide brought a message from Chief of Staff John Rawlins:

> General Thomas and Army of the Cumberland are advancing on Nashville. We expect Hood's unconditional surrender within three or four days. General Grant has been advised en route to Petersburg. Prospects for ending the war have never looked better.

Lincoln dropped the message on his lap. In the darkness of Tad's bedroom he allowed himself a private moment of hope. If a peace could be achieved before spring, his second term would then be devoted to reconstructing a war-torn country. After so many years of death and despair, the prospect seemed brighter than any he might have hoped for.

19

He recalled how sweet her words seemed when she had said, "I love you, Jon" in front of the stable, and the wonderful feeling as she put her arms around him before she kissed him. Something inside him awakened that night, emotions so intense he could find no way to describe them, for no words were sufficient to express a boundless joy nor desire so overpowering that he could think of nothing else.

While treating sick and wounded that next morning he had felt removed from the soldiers' suffering, a detachment, as if someone else were performing his grisly duties. He still felt the same compassion for his patients, he believed, yet something had changed. His heart no longer ached for each injured man in quite the same personal way as though somehow he had rid himself of feeling responsible for their pain because there was no medicine. In the past, he had been burdened with a sense of guilt for lacking the skill and understanding to effect cures or save bullet-torn limbs. But today there was no guilt. In its place was what he might have called acceptance of his role as a physician without knowledge of ways most disease spreads or surgical treatments that could mend an arm or a leg mangled by lead balls. He was resigned to simply doing his best under the worst circumstances with the training and experience he had.

By noon the last of his reddish-brown bromine was gone when he filled a glass pipette to treat a wound. He went back to his apothecary case and took stock of what little was left. A small vial of nitric acid that sometimes appeared to retard the spread of gangrene and erysipelas remained. A jar of creosote, a bottle of digitalis, ammonia water—almost nothing useful for treatment of wounds. He sighed and shook his head, glancing around him at row upon row of wounded men. Dr. Green had told him this morning of an outbreak of scurvy among men at the railroad depot, and there was no dried fruit to be found in Nashville, thus no way to halt the increases in swollen, bleeding gums and anemia. Conditions among Hood's men were deteriorating rather than improving. Food was so scarce that armed citizens were protecting staples they had from foraging bands of hungry soldiers. No one could keep track of the desertion rate. Jon found himself hoping that Hood could be convinced it was pointless to continue and disband the remnants of his army.

He walked out on the warehouse loading dock to get a breath of fresh air. It had stopped snowing just before dawn, yet skies were still gray and threatening. Gazing across Nashville toward the river, Jon thought about Lorena again. He knew without doubt that he loved her dearly, and although he had given his word not to push her, he longed for another chance to hold her in his arms and tell her of his love. Remembering her kiss, a tiny fluttering occurred in his chest, like the whispering wings of a moth near a candle's flame.

"I love you," he said softly as he looked across the road to Peabody's Boardinghouse, thinking of Lorena sitting at Clara's bedside. Unconsciously he smiled, until a sound coming from the east distracted him. Teams of horses and mules were pulling a winding column of limbers and field cannons into the hills above

Nashville, splitting into groups moving in different directions at the outskirts of town. Jon knew at once what this meant, that Hood was preparing to defend the city. He wondered if word had arrived of an approaching Union force.

"Another battle," he said to himself sadly, thinking of so many frozen, starving men who would be put to the test should a fight occur. How could any man in possession of his full senses ask these soldiers to enter another battle? he wondered. Hood was most certainly insane or blind to the truth that his army was not in any shape to fight again.

The rattle of caissons and harness chains brought people and soldiers from houses and tents across Nashville. Most stared at the cannons silently, for, like Jon, they knew what these maneuvers indicated—a battle was forthcoming, anticipated. Dr. Roberts had been wrong to believe General Hood wanted to pull out of the city. A battle to hold Nashville looked certain now.

From the direction of one livery, columns of cavalry rode out of corrals and stables in pairs, following cannons to the east at a trot. What had been only a guess seemed sure: Hood intended to hold his ground rather than retreat further.

"It's madness," Jon observed, saying it quietly even though he stood alone on the platform. "We'll all be killed." In the same instant he thought of Lorena, of her safety. If a pitched battle reached Nashville's streets, which it surely would when Hood's starving army was beaten back, Lorena's life would be in grave danger.

He decided quickly to search for a basement or a root cellar where she and Clara could hide in the event Nashville was overrun by Union troops. A mound of snow covering a trapdoor to one side of the boardinghouse might be the answer. He left the platform and hurried across the street without his coat. Pausing at the snow mound to inspect it, he felt satisfied the door led down to a basement. He walked around to the back of the boardinghouse and knocked on the kitchen door. Beatrice Peabody answered his knock with a small caliber pistol in her hands.

"I'm so sorry, Doctor, but so many ruffians have come to beg for food scraps and they won't go away without . . . persuasion," she said, standing back to admit him. "Why, you've come without your coat and it's freezing out there."

He came in, smelling wonderful smells. A pot bubbled softly on a woodstove. "Something smells delicious, Mrs. Peabody. I've a favor to ask—your cellar may be the safest place for our two nurses in the event Nashville comes under attack. I see cannons rolling into the hills just now, and that may mean a Union force has been sighted. Would you allow our women to hide down there if a battle starts?"

"Of course, Doctor, but you should take a lantern down first to clean out cobwebs an' such. Make a pallet on the floor for the sick girl. Take that lantern over yonder, and a broom. The key to the padlock is on that windowsill."

"Thank you, Mrs. Peabody. I suggest you join them if you hear cannon fire." He picked up the lantern, key, and broom.

"Nonsense," Beatrice said sternly. "This is my house, and I won't tolerate having it shot to pieces. I'll stand on my front porch with my shotgun and pistol to dare the first bluebelly who tries to shoot out a window or burn me out. I may be a feeble old woman, but I can still shoot straight." She pointed to the stove. "When you get finished in the cellar, come have a bowl of my potato soup. Best in Tennessee."

"Thank you kindly, ma'am," he said, going up a darkened hall to tell Lorena and Clara about the basement. "I can't wait for a taste of that soup."

When he entered Clara's bedroom, Lorena was wiping her brow with damp cloth. Lorena looked up and smiled.

"Come with me," he told her quietly. "Soldiers are moving to the hills around Nashville, and we may be coming under attack. I want to show you a cellar where you and Clara will hide if any shooting starts."

Lorena's face quickly lost its color. "Under attack?" she gasped. Tears immediately flooded her eyes. She got off the bed and ran to him, flinging her arms around his neck. "Oh Jonathan! I . . ." Her voice trailed off.

"Don't worry. You'll be safe down there," he said, closing his arms around her waist despite the items he carried. "Come with me, and bring a quilt for a pallet so Clara can lie down. I will carry her down should any shelling begin."

"I have . . . something I must tell you," she whispered, tears wetting her face.

"There may not be time. You can tell me later, while I'm cleaning out cobwebs. Please hurry." He put lantern and broom in one hand and took her by the arm, somewhat puzzled by what it was she wanted to tell him. Could it be an admission that she loved him unconditionally? Had her feelings for Paul changed? He dared not hope for so much so soon. She could also be about to tell him she loved Paul.

Walking out the front door, he saw Major Canfield along with Captain Hiram Roberts hurrying up the street, their boots caked with snow. He handed Lorena the broom and lantern before going down slippery front steps to speak to the major.

"Why are the field guns and cavalry moving?" he asked.

Canfield glanced over his shoulder to the hills where cannons and horsemen were being deployed. "Simply a precautionary measure in case Yankees find us."

Jon briefly studied the hills himself. "Then no attack is imminent?"

The major shook his head. "A field exercise as well as a precaution, Captain."

"The two of you were walking so fast, I feared we might be on the verge of being attacked."

"We're hurrying because we were summoned to General Hood's headquarters at the Marshal House. We're both hoping it will be to hear good news, that supplies will reach us soon."

Jon felt his shoulders droop. "I was preparing a shelter for our nurses in the basement. I'm quite relieved to know this was only an exercise. I sincerely hope the general isn't thinking of moving us elsewhere, Major."

"It's his decision to make, not ours," Canfield remarked, giving Lorena a look as he said it. "How is the other nurse?"

"I see no change," Jon replied.

The major grunted, nodded once, and then led Dr. Roberts away toward a mansion overlooking the Cumberland known as the Marshal House, where General Hood was a guest of a Nashville family while bad weather made living in tents a sufferance.

Jon turned to Lorena. "We'll prepare the cellar, anyway, in case it's needed." He took her arm and helped her down the front steps to the snow-covered trapdoor at one side of the house. Sweeping snow away, he unlocked the door and started carefully down stone stairs before he halted to light their lantern.

At the bottom of the stairs was a small, musty cellar lined with burlap sacks of potatos and corn. He hung the lantern on a nail. "What was it you wanted to tell me?" he asked, watching her in lamplight with high hopes in his heart. His hopes might be dashed completely if she meant to tell him she truly loved Paul.

Although her tears had dried, there was still anguish in her face. For a time she stood before him, silent, as if she had to make a most difficult decision. "I suppose," she began quietly, "I wanted to tell you . . . that people aren't always who they seem. I may not be . . . the woman you think I am. How would you feel if you learned I'm not only a nurse, that I was someone else, that I may not have told you everything about me?"

He spread his hands in a helpless gesture. "I know enough to know that I love you. You see, I've never really been in love before. I never knew or dreamed I had feelings so deep, or that a woman could enter my heart and change the way I felt about every part of my existence. My work, my life, my future plans have all changed because of you, Lorena. What else is there to know? My only hope is that you'll feel the same way, given time."

Her eyes grew wet again. "Oh Jon," she sighed, coming into his arms, nestling her face against his chest.

He embraced her, fearing she meant to tell him her feelings had changed, that she didn't love him, couldn't love him because of Paul. But what did she mean when she said people might not be who they seem, or that she hadn't told him everything about her? His heart told him nothing else mattered beyond having her love. "I don't care who other people are, or whatever it is you may not have told me about yourself. I only know that I love you, that you fill me with happiness. If there is more, it can wait until this damnable war is over. We can talk about it then."

Her hands clutched the front of his shirt and he felt them trembling. A quiet sob came from her throat; then she was silent until she lifted her face, blinking away tears.

"I do love you so, Jonathan," she said. "Forgive my crying spells. I lack the courage to explain them to you."

"There's no need to explain anything now." He kissed her, tightening his arms around her. She returned his kiss ever so gently, and he forgot everything else. They stood, embracing each other in the dank cellar for several minutes, his mouth covering hers, while off in the distance the rumble of iron-rimmed wheels faded to silence. For the first time in his life Jon knew what it was like to fall in love, and he had fallen so deeply in love with Lorena Blaire that nothing else in his existence was of any consequence. At last he understood why some men behaved foolishly in order to win a woman's heart. A great mystery had been revealed to him: Love was more than a word, and discovering this made the war and all its hardships seem easier to bear.

20

Lorena sat beside Clara as night came to Nashville, darkening their bedroom window. Clara's fever showed no signs of lessening, nor was she awake for more than a few minutes at a time when she was fed soup or Mrs. Peabody's honey-sweetened whiskey. She was often delirious, mumbling things that made no apparent sense, but she made no more mention of soldiers coming or of letters written to Mistress Wheeler. Her face and upper body were covered with bright red pox resembling measles, and her skin was so warm to the touch that Lorena feared the worst. Patients sometimes died of typhus, although it was not regarded as being a serious illness from which there was no chance of recovery. Like other fevers common to battlefield conditions, it usually ran its course until the fever broke, according to Jonathan, yet Clara's continued longer than Lorena felt it should, without any indication of improvement. At the nursing academy run by Dorothea Dix, they had been instructed to give cooling alcohol baths whenever possible, or cool water applications when no alcohol was available, to patients with fevers. But no matter what was done for Clara, she failed to respond to her treatments.

When Clara had eaten the last of her potato soup, she dropped off to sleep. Lorena went to the window, watching fires burn in Nashville's streets while thinking of Jonathan. She harbored no doubts now that she loved him dearly—he was the gentlest man she had ever known, so sincere, and it was like a dagger piercing her heart knowing she'd sent a letter betraying him to the Union Army. She had almost confessed her guilt in the basement while she was alone with him today. A part of her wanted to tell him of her betrayal and another, her selfish side, kept her silent. She wanted his love, his embrace. She couldn't bring herself to admit what she'd done, although her conscience cried out to tell the man she loved that a Union force was on its way to Nashville. It had never been her nature to cry before she came to this war when events or circumstance confounded her, but now, despite her resolve to be strong, she came close to weeping, thinking of what might happen to her beloved Jonathan. Strange, she thought, that in such a short a time she could call another man her beloved—they'd known each other less than two weeks, yet she was sure she loved him more than she had ever loved Paul.

And what of Paul? How would she ever write a letter to him describing what had happened? Where could she find the words to tell him how she'd fallen in love with a Confederate surgeon from Texas? None of it made any sense, not even to her, when viewed in the light of harsh reality. Without so much as a respectable period of courtship, she had fallen deeply in love with an enemy soldier, a man she'd been sent to Tennessee to destroy by an act of espionage.

She sat down in the rocker and drew a comforter over her lap while staring absently out the window. It had begun to seem she was destined to sit at this window for all eternity, debating her conscience.

*   *   *

A light rap on the door hours later startled her. She got up and opened it, finding Jonathan in the hallway.

"How is Clara?" he asked, stepping into the room upon her silent invitation. He wore a clean shirt and his best officer's tunic, one without worn places at the elbows or frayed sleeve hems. He closed the door behind him.

"She's sleeping. She ate Mrs. Peabody's soup and drank a cup of sweetened whiskey, but I swear it seems she doesn't know where she is, as though she's in a stupor."

"A symptom of high fever in some cases. A person's mind can retreat to a dark corner of the brain we know nothing about when pain or discomfort becomes too intense. I suppose it's a way of escaping it temporarily." He walked over to the bed and adjusted the lantern for better light. When he touched Clara's forehead his expression turned grave. "Her fever is very high, I'm afraid, but she seems to be resting comfortably. We're doing all we can for her."

"I bathe her regularly with cool water."

Jonathan turned, giving her an understanding smile. "I'm sure it's a difficult time for you, as well." Reaching inside his coat, he took out a pint bottle of amber liquid. "A gift from Mrs. Peabody, a peach brandy she made. It's very sweet, and it might lift your spirits."

"I've told you I don't partake of strong drink."

"It won't harm you, I promise. And if you feel up to it, we can go for another short walk. It's a chilly night, but it isn't snowing now." He pulled out the cork and offered her the pint.

She took the bottle of peach brandy, sniffed it, and drank a very small amount, feeling a bit naughty. While the sweet liquor burned somewhat going down her throat, it did taste nice. Long ago she'd tried a secret sip of her grandfather's whiskey and found that it was so unpleasant she never wanted another—besides the obvious fact that drunkenness was the very lowest form of behavior.

"A short walk sounds good," she agreed, reaching for her coat. The walk was only an excuse for the two of them to be alone, and she was certain he knew this as well as she.

Leaving the boardinghouse, they walked arm in arm, avoiding groups of soldiers whenever they could in order to reach the livery stable. Snow packed by thousands of feet made a crunching noise as they strolled down quiet side streets. Jonathan looked up at the sky. "We're all hoping it won't snow again. These men are miserable enough the way it is."

Lorena felt gentle pressure from his arm; then suddenly her hand was clasped in his. She smiled playfully. "I am tempted to say you presume too much, Dr. Cross, taking my hand without my permission."

"Once again my recklessness comes to the fore when I'm in your presence. I find I'm almost out of control, beyond reason or even good judgment." He laughed. "It's the price you must pay for being both charming and beautiful."

She halted suddenly at the mouth of a dark alley when she heard his remark. "I sincerely hope it is more than a physical attraction explaining your interest in me."

"A great deal more. You have an inner beauty, a beauty of spirit, which I discovered when you took such pity on the young men under your care. The boy—I believe his name was Cobb—received much more than nursing from you, as did so many others. This is beauty coming from the heart, from within, and it is every bit as beautiful as your lovely face and your sparkling eyes. While I will freely admit I'm fascinated by your physical charms, I'm equally drawn to your compassion, your dedication to caring for our wounded in a very personal way—ways the youngest of them need so desperately during their first experiences away from home in a terrifying war."

What he said to her filled her with a rush of emotion. His sensitivity to her feelings for wounded soldiers reached that same hidden chamber of her heart that she had kept from Paul, not knowing it existed. She gripped his hand, reading his face, his eyes. "It's the compassion and dedication I find most appealing in *you*, Jonathan. You're a handsome man and a gentleman, but those are characteristics found elsewhere. What I find unique about you is how much you truly care for your patients, not only their injuries but also their feelings. You are a dedicated doctor, a very kind person, and so much more. . . ."

He reached for her and she did not resist, allowing him to wrap his arms around her. "I love you with all my heart, Lorena," he said, his voice so soft and tender. "We find ourselves in a bloody war that prevents us from becoming acquainted in a more traditional way. You may have doubts that I could be so certain of the love I feel for you because we've known each other such a short time. I can only assure you that I know my own heart, know how deep my feelings are. You warned me that you wouldn't allow me to push you toward a decision, and I'm doing my best to honor your request; however, I felt I had to tell you that my love is genuine and sincere, not mere words intended to deceive you."

"I believe you," she said very quietly, feeling the warmth of his embrace while an inner voice cried out that it was she who had deceived him in a far more sinister way. Yet she knew she did not have the courage to tell him. The more deeply she fell in love with him, the surer she became that she could never admit to what she'd done. "When I came here, the very last thing I wanted was to fall in love. I honestly believed I loved Paul. I was not prepared to love another, nor could I have thought it would be possible. I'm not a silly schoolgirl who falls in and out of love on a whim. I believe in commitments, in giving myself to the man I love unconditionally. That's why I asked you not to push me, Jonathan. I want to be sure of you and the way I feel."

"I understand. I simply wanted you to know what was in my heart. I wasn't pressing you for an answer. For now it's quite enough to know you feel the beginnings of love for me. I hope that, given time, it will grow."

"I do love you," she whispered, staring into his eyes. "I hadn't wanted to. . . ."

He kissed her more passionately than ever before, muscles in his arms turning to iron around her waist. She gave in to it and returned the pressure of his mouth with hers. A sensation spread from her chest down the length of her body, a tingling warmth of a kind she'd never known before, reaching her fingertips and her toes. She allowed his lips to remain, not wanting the wonderful feeling to end even though she knew her behavior was unbecoming a woman of good moral character.

Their kiss ended abruptly when sounds made by a carriage came from one end of the street. A liver chestnut harness horse drew a canopied buggy at a trot toward them, snow flying from its wheels. A small carriage lantern cast a pale yellow glow over ruts cut deep into packed snowfall where the horse made its way at an unusually fast pace. When the driver pulled alongside them, a deep voice from the back seat ordered him to stop.

A uniformed man leaned out from under the canopy—a bearded face with cold, expressionless eyes giving him a fierce countenance—whom Jonathan recognized immediately, bringing him to full attention whereupon he saluted. Lorena had never seen this officer before.

"Captain Cross, isn't it?" he asked, his tone gruff to the point of being irritating. "You're one of my surgeons, I believe. Why aren't you attending to our wounded?"

"Just out for a short walk, General. A breath of air. We have virtually no medicines, as you know, sir."

The general gave Lorena a cold look of appraisal. "This is one of our new nurses, I presume?"

"Yes sir. This is Nurse Lorena Blaire."

Lorena bowed politely, disliking the general's manner, the way he asked questions. She was sure this man was the infamous target of General Grant's spy mission, John Bell Hood.

"It appeared the two of you were kissing," he added, leaving no doubts about his disapproval. "Surely you have other duties."

Jonathan seemed momentarily perplexed. "We took a little

time for ourselves, General, only a few minutes."

Hood examined Lorena again—she didn't like the way his eyes roamed over her.

"Women have no place in an army camp," he said. "I'll inform Major Canfield they are to be dismissed and sent home." Hood turned to his driver. "Move on!" The carriage jolted forward at the crack of a buggy whip.

Lorena stood close beside Jonathan as the carriage rolled away to a street corner, where it turned and went out of sight. For a time neither of them spoke. Finally Jonathan sighed heavily and caught her arm.

"This was my fault," he said. "I'm very sorry to have put you in such an embarrassing position. Worst of all, I'm so sorry that you will be sent away. General Hood is rumored to be on the edge of madness, existing on opiates."

"I don't like him at all," Lorena said. "He may be mad, but he is also harsh and quite rude. More than that, he is insolent to insist women have no place with an army. Wounded soldiers do need nurses. I have a very low opinion of General Hood upon our first meeting."

Jonathan was staring at her. "I don't know how I'll exist without you, without seeing you." He glanced to the corner where Hood's carriage turned. "It isn't fair to condemn you for being away from your duties for a short time." Reaching for her hand, he said, "I'll resign my commission. I won't let Hood or anyone else keep us apart. I love you, Lorena, and if you'll have me, I vow to leave this army and take you with me."

When she heard this, she experienced joy so intense that she felt something inside her release the heavy burden of guilt she bore since she'd fallen in love with Jonathan. If they left Nashville before Union troops arrived, no harm would befall him. She would never have to reveal her treachery. She looked into his eyes, at the same time remembering her dear friend, Clara. "If I agreed to leave with you, we'd have to take Clara with us until she is fully recovered from her illness."

Jonathan took her in his arms again. "I'll speak to Major Canfield at once about resigning my commission. We'll take Clara in the buggy you drove to Franklin when you arrived, making her as comfortable as we can. Driving west, we'd stand a good chance of escaping any fighting. This war can't last much longer, and when it's over we can start new lives anywhere you wish."

"I wanted more time to think."

"Because of General Hood's order there isn't much time."

In her heart she wanted to say yes even though it would be frightfully immoral conduct to leave with a man she'd only known a couple of weeks. She wondered if, for once in her life, she ought to listen to her heart rather than her head.

"I'll give you my answer in the morning," she said. She was quite certain she'd be unable to sleep until she arrived at her decision.

21

They walked the streets of Nashville for over an hour, arm in arm, hardly speaking. Jon was thinking about leaving the army, not an altogether unhappy prospect if Lorena agreed to go with him. He could go back to Fort Worth and set up his medical practice. In a war-torn economy he could expect scant returns from his enterprise, yet it would hardly be any worse than not being paid by the Confederate government for over a year. When he escorted Lorena back to the boardinghouse, he was certain he would resign from the medical corps rather than lose the woman at his side.

As they came down a dark hallway, he heard voices in Clara's room and saw light coming from a crack below the door. He felt Lorena's arm stiffen when she heard someone inside. As they entered the bedroom, Major Canfield and Colonel Buford Jackson turned away from Clara's bed. Jon remembered that Colonel Jackson commanded a brigade of Hood's cavalry and was one of his closest confidants. But it was the look on Major Canfield's face that stopped Jon before he crossed the room, for he could tell something was terribly wrong. A lantern burning brightly on a nightstand showed Clara was awake, eyes fixed dully on her bedroom window.

"What is it, Major?" he asked, wondering why Canfield turned his steely gaze to Lorena.

When the major spoke, he bit down on each word as though they had a terrible taste. "It would appear these two women are Union spies, Captain Cross! Nurse Brooks has just informed the Colonel and myself that Yankee soldiers are coming to rescue them. They wrote letters to a woman in Gaines's Mill, Virginia, advising her of our location so that a Union army could be dispatched before we were able to move. According to Miss Brooks, we should expect an enemy attack at any moment."

"There has to be some mistake. . . ." Jon couldn't finish what he was saying, stunned to silence. Lorena let go of his arm and took a half step back.

Canfield wagged his head. "At first I thought it might be a delirium from her fever, until I questioned her further. I came by to see how she was doing and found her alone, mumbling something about soldiers coming to rescue them. But even in her near delirious state she told me everything. I sent for the Colonel so he could witness what I heard and report it to General Hood. These women are spies, Captain. They were sent by Ulysses Grant himself to spy on us. Two more women are with Jubal Early. I'm quite sure there is no mistake. She gave us details."

Jon turned to Lorena and found her crying silently. "Is it true?" he asked, almost unable to speak. Was it possible that a caring, sensitive nurse like her could also be a Union spy?

When she wouldn't answer him, he knew the truth. Devastated, unable to fully grasp what he'd just learned, he felt his stomach twist into knots. "I can't believe it of you," he said haltingly, watching quiet sobs wrack Lorena's small body. She couldn't look at him.

Clara stirred below her bedcovers. She moaned softly and cast a wavering glance around the room until she saw Lorena. "I want to go home," she whimpered. "When are . . . the soldiers coming for us?"

Lorena rushed to her bedside—she took Clara's hand and held it to her breast. "I don't know," she stammered. "Oh, my dear Clara, why did you tell them about those letters?"

It was as if Clara couldn't hear her. "I want to go home at once," she mumbled. "I . . . don't want to die in Tennessee."

Major Canfield snapped, "You may well die in a Confederate prison, Miss Brooks, along with your nurse conspirator. When we tell General Hood what we learned I predict you will both be sent to prison for a very long time."

Jon still found it impossible to believe Lorena had deceived him. "It's too incredible," he said, speaking to Major Canfield. "They're only a couple of girls."

"I warned you that I overheard something suspicious when we were at Franklin. Some instinct told me these women were more than young nurses. It seems now that my instincts were correct."

Colonel Jackson, a hard-twisted cavalryman with a deep scar on his left cheek, addressed Canfield. "I'll have men place them under arrest here, guarding the door and window until General Hood hears what has transpired. When the general decides what's to be done with them, I'll have them taken under guard wherever he sends them, but we've a far more pressing problem, James. A Union army is headed our way. We have no munitions to speak of. Our horses and mules are in such poor condition we can't run far. We have but once choice, I fear—defend Nashville against attack. And this city is quite indefensible, as you must already know. We will be overrun by a force of any significance. Our losses most certainly will exceed those at Franklin if we are engaged."

"We have no medicaments whatsoever, Colonel. Unless we are resupplied quickly, the suffering and deaths will be too horrible to contemplate. Our medical corps is virtually unable to do even fundamental procedures now. If we are engaged in a battle of any consequence, my surgeons will be quite helpless."

Jackson nodded, giving Clara and Lorena a withering stare as he turned for the bedroom door. "One might speculate that these two women may bring about the defeat of our Texas brigades and what is left of the Army of Tennessee. What Sherman and Grant could not accomplish might well come about at the hands of a pair of nurses. I'll speak to General Hood immediately, after placing guards at this room."

Canfield nodded. "Please give General Hood my most sincere apologies for what has happened. I suppose I should have questioned these women closely myself before they were allowed to be part of my corps. I merely took them at their word when they showed letters of introduction from a Virginia nursing academy. At the time I was grateful for their help. Even when my suspicions were aroused I did nothing about them."

Jackson went to the door. He looked at Jon. "Can we trust this man, Major? You said he was keeping company with the nurse named Blaire."

The major didn't hesitate when he said, "Yes, Captain Cross is completely trustworthy. He has given years of service to our brigades. I'm sure it was happenstance when he became involved with the woman. He's an excellent doctor and a highly skilled field surgeon. I've no doubts whatsoever about his loyalties to the Confederacy."

Jackson turned back to Lorena. "She might be called pretty. There's a prison in Memphis, Camp Ford, where she can be interrogated by one of the best officers we have at breaking down all resistance to questioning. We need to know how extensive a network Grant has of women spies portraying themselves as nurses. Grant may have female spies with Lee and Forrest. If this woman knows, she'll tell everything to Major Von Bulen. He's a mercenary from Austria—and he knows how to conduct a thorough interrogation."

"Torture?" Jon asked incredulously. "Surely he won't exact torture upon a woman. . . ."

Colonel Jackson smiled without mirth. "Von Bulen gets us

results, Captain. We don't particularly care how he does it."
Jackson swung the door open and stalked out, his boots sounding down the hallway.

Jon faced Lorena. "Tell me it isn't true, that it's all a sad mistake. What was in the letters you wrote?"

Clinging to Clara's limp hand, Lorena collected herself. "I
only wrote that we were going to Nashville."

Surrounded by a feeling of unreality, wondering how he
could have misjudged her so badly, he asked, "The letters were
forwarded to General Grant?"

"We weren't told, only that we should write our destination
to a woman at Gaines's Mill as soon as it was known."

Major Canfield was listening closely, watching Lorena as she
answered Jon's questions, though he said nothing for the moment.

"How could you do this to us, to me?" Jon asked. "You said
you loved me. We will be destroyed when those Yankees arrive.
So many more men will lose their lives."

She left the bed and stood before him, her chin quivering as
she spoke. "I wrote the letters before my emotions took control
of my heart, Jonathan. When I discovered that I loved you, it was
too late to change what I'd done. I could only pray that somehow you might escape unharmed. We were told by Mistress Dix
and General Grant that our actions could end this war and halt
the senseless killing. We all believed it was our duty to our country."

Canfield approached Jon with a stern look on his face. "I want
you to return to the hospital, Captain, to begin preparations for
what will surely be a bloodbath. Have orderlies begin making
bandages from anything they can find. I order you not to visit
these women again. Colonel Jackson will see to their confinement
and transfer to prison as soon as General Hood makes his decision."

Feeling helpless, Jon merely nodded, but as he was preparing to leave, he heard Lorena's voice.

"I'm so terribly sorry, Jonathan. I only did what they asked me to do. I hadn't wanted to fall in love with you but I did, and by that time nothing could be changed."

Her explanation seemed too shallow and he ignored her, leaving without looking at her. Learning she was indeed, as the major had suspected almost from the beginning, a Union spy, left him feeling empty, drained, numbed by a chilling confession spoken from her own lips. Only minutes ago they had spoken of their love for each other, planning to leave Nashville together to begin new lives as their love deepened. Now there was no love between them at all, only regrets—and his pain when he was informed of her deception.

He walked across the same snow-packed road where earlier he and Lorena had strolled arm in arm, passing two cavalrymen guarding the front door of the boardinghouse. Bitter tears formed in his eyes as he climbed steps into Barnum's, where he had to begin all manner of preparations for an attack on Nashville that was sure to bring about the highest casualties in the history of Hood's brigades.

He went looking for Goodie Carrothers.

Dawn came windy and cold. Leaden skies held promise of more snow. Goodie and a skinny orderly named Don Suggins piled strips of cloth at operating tables before carrying pails of watery soup among the sick and wounded. Greasy smoke from smudge-pots caused everyone's eyes to water inside Barnum's, yet they were the only source of badly needed heat in a cavernous building where fevered men were suffering. Jon saw to preparations in a state of despair while doing his best to forget about Lorena, her treachery, and how much he loved her. When he thought about her, his heart ached to see her again and hold her in his arms—until he was reminded of what she'd done whenever he caught brief glimpses of guards posted at Mrs. Peabody's front door.

An hour past daybreak he went outside for a breath of air and to gather his jumbled thoughts. Now and then he glanced to hill-tops east of Nashville, the direction from which he believed a Union attack would come. Goodie brought him a tin cup of tepid potato soup.

"Ain't no more sheets for bandages," Goodie said, stuffing his oversized hands in his pants pockets. "We done got all there is in Nashville. Heard somebody say them bluebellies is comin' real soon, maybe today."

"Nobody's sure, Goodie. There's no sense worrying about it until they get here."

"I ain't all that worried, Cap'n, but I knows we ain't got enough bandages. Soup pots are near 'bout empty too. Mess ain't got hardly any black-eyed peas left. Won't be much to eat. That soup ain't much more'n salty water."

"Do the best you can," Jon told him in a somber voice, for he knew Goodie was worried despite his denial. "We'll make it just fine. See to the chamber pots if you haven't already."

Goodie disappeared into the warehouse. Jon's gaze wandered across the street. For the past couple of hours he'd given more thought to what Lorena had said last night, that she'd only done her duty to her country. Her country happened to be north of a line called Mason-Dixon, an imaginary line separating slave-owning states from those opposed to it. It had been the same country until the twelfth of April in 1861, when General Beauregard fired on a fort in South Carolina. Was her loyalty to those Union states enough cause for him to totally disregard his feelings toward her? Or was her loyalty more like his, a nationalism he had never truly felt because he didn't really understand the issues. It had occurred to him more and more as the war dragged on that few men understood why they were fighting beyond living in a particular region that was either Confederate or Union. He found he couldn't think of Lorena as an enemy—she was simply a nurse on another side of a debate over slaves and states' rights because she happened to live in the North.

Staring across the road, he pondered matters. What sort of man would allow politics to change the way he felt about someone who had given him the only real love he had ever known? Or had she also deceived him when she told him she loved him? How could he ever be sure of her affection after something like this?

He decided a few moments later to talk to her, to give her a chance to tell him privately about her feelings, both then and now. He'd been ordered not to see her again, but he had questions needing answers, and before Colonel Jackson took her away to prison, he wanted to hear what she had to say.

Remembering the time they had spent in Mrs. Peabody's cellar, he questioned what she had meant when she told him people aren't always what they seem. Had she been about to tell him she was a spy for the Union? Could guilt explain the tears she had shed, which she told him she had lacked the courage to explain?

22

General Thomas halted his lead columns upon the crest of a snowy valley to give his scouts time to ride back with reports of what lay ahead. Another snowstorm darkened early-morning skies to the northwest. According to maps, they were very close to the city of Nashville, less than a day of marching time under favorable weather conditions. He'd pushed his army relentlessly day and night, punishing animals and men to the fullest, determined to arrive before Hood slipped away. Off to the south he could see the Cumberland River, a black ribbon of water twisting among snow-encrusted hills.

He turned in the saddle to Colonel Menem. "Take a battalion of cavalry and seven batteries of light artillery. Circle the town by a northern route and set up gun emplacements west along the river to cut him off. Get there as quickly as you can before Hood tries to run that direction. Slower moving guns and ammunition wagons will be behind you, accompanied by infantry. Colonel Stevens will deploy cannons and mortars to the north. Our main body will attack from the east while Major Ryan floats field guns across the river to block a southern escape route, shelling what bridges they have to prevent a mass exodus over the Cumberland by bridge. You'll be reinforced as soon as bigger guns and infantry arrive. I don't want the elusive Mr. Hood to slip past any gaps in our perimeter. This time, Hood won't be allowed to run."

Menem's face screwed into a frown. "I don't expect Hood to run, General. He'll fight us with everything he has. We can look for a difficult time of it. However, with our overwhelming numbers and firepower, he can't hold out very long. I have one concern, sir, as to the citizens. When we begin dropping shells into Nashville, there will be high casualties among the civilian population. You'll be criticized."

"A necessary byproduct of war, Colonel. I intend to offer Hood a chance to surrender. If he chooses to fight, he faces as much responsibility as I shall. I'm following orders. I'll let General Grant explain it to the newspapers and to Congress."

Moving across the valley, a scout detail headed for Thomas's waiting columns at a steady trot. A dozen men pushed steadily through accumulated snow blanketing the valley floor.

"Hood knows we're coming by now," Thomas remarked. "I feel sure he has begun fortifying the city as best he can."

Colonel Menem offered no opinion on the subject. He spoke to one of his lieutenants. "Order the Sixth Cavalry and seven batteries from the Ninth Artillery to move forward. We are turning west across this valley to encircle Nashville from the west, and I want everyone moving as rapidly as possible. Inform company commanders speed is of the essence now."

The lieutenant saluted smartly and wheeled his horse. Word was shouted down the line for the Sixth Cavalry and guns from the Ninth to swing out for a move to the front. A murmur spread down lines of weary soldiers. Marching would soon result in a fight.

It was several minutes before Thomas's scouts returned to the top of the valley. A sergeant saluted and addressed him.

"They've got cannons spread out across the hills, sir. Men are crawling around like ants. There's just one remaining bridge across the river, and it's blown all to hell but still usable. It was easy to see they're gettin' ready for us."

Thomas was puzzled. "Does it look like they're forming up to withdraw their main force while a few cannons try to keep us at bay?"

"No sir, there is no indication of any wagons being loaded nor any sign of a pullout. They're building fortifications where roads lead into town . . . piles of furniture and wooden crates, just about anything they can find. It was kinda hard to tell through my field glasses, but it sure looks like they mean to stay put."

Colonel Menem said, "I felt sure Hood wouldn't run. He'll be like a cornered animal, fighting hard to save his skin."

"He's a badly wounded animal," Thomas observed as men from the Sixth trotted toward the front, several thousand cavalrymen who were for the most part seasoned battle veterans. "Get behind him from the west and dig in. When you hear us shelling, fire into the city at will. I want them pounded, John. Rattle every door and window, but avoid shelling private homes as much as you can."

Menem saluted and rode back to his advancing battalions as Thomas gave the order to march. In two mighty columns the Army of the Cumberland divided at Old Hickory Creek to begin forming a circle around Nashville on the fourth day of December. A few tiny snowflakes began to fall.

23

Heavy snow came on mighty gusts of wind, obscuring all but dim outlines of buildings lining the street as Lorena followed two soldiers carrying Clara on a canvas litter from her room to the front of Peabody's. An old two-seat carriage waited by the steps, its wheels missing a few spokes, a canvas canopy crowned by several inches of snow. Colonel Jackson stood on the porch giving instructions for placing Clara in the rear seat, wrapped in quilts. A soldier sat in the driver's seat, hunched against the wind wearing a tattered greatcoat. Trunks containing Lorena's and Clara's belongings had been lashed to the back. A cavalryman waited nearby atop a shivering brown horse with a rifle in his hands. Two gray-clad guards escorted Lorena to the buggy . . . one offered his arm to assist her inside. She sat beside Clara and covered her as best she could before buttoning her own coat.

Colonel Jackson came down the steps and spoke to Lorena in a rasping voice. "These men will take you to Camp Ford. They have been instructed to see to your comfort as best they can. However, if you try to escape, they have orders to bind your hands and feet—and should you attempt another escape, you will be shot. I trust you understand."

Jackson's piercing stare bored holes through her. "I understand," she said.

The colonel hooked his thumbs in his pistol belt. "I suggest you cooperate fully with Major Von Bulen, Miss Blaire. Since you have refused to answer all our questions, we must take other measures to get at the truth and punish you for your crimes."

"I've told you everything I know," she stammered, chilled to the bone by snow-laden winds. Colonel Jackson and General Hood's personal aide had questioned her for several hours today, and she told them all she knew about Grant's plan to send four nurses into the Confederate camps of Hood and Early, her letters sent to Bertha Wheeler written in code.

Then came the most terrifying moment of all, when another visitor arrived. General Hood, hobbling on a wooden leg, one arm dangling at his side, came over to her with a look of pure hatred on his face. She was so frightened, she had to steady herself when her knees began to tremble. He reeked of liquor, she remembered, and his eyes were like glowing embers in a fire when he shouted, "You traitorous bitch! Because of you my men will be asked to bleed again! The blood of brave men will be on your hands!" He lowered his voice. "Major Von Bulen will see to it that you regret your mistake. Before he finishes with you, you will confess everything and beg God Almighty for His forgiveness." He glared at her, then left the room, limping down the hall until a door slammed behind him. Lorena had never felt a presence like his, one so sinister that had he not spoken a word she still would have feared him.

Colonel Jackson nodded to the driver. A slap of his reins sent the team of buggy horses lunging forward. Lorena, cradling Clara's head in her lap, was thrown against the back of the seat. As they drove away, she turned around for a last look at the hospital, wishing with all her heart that she could have had a few moments alone with Jonathan before they took her.

Through a curtain of snowflakes she saw someone run out on a loading dock at Barnum's, and she knew at once who he was. A man in shirtsleeves wearing a bloody surgeon's apron waved farewell. Before he was out of sight, she lifted a hand and whispered a soft "Good-bye, Jonathan." Then snowfall obscured the platform and the man she loved entirely. She wasn't going to allow herself to cry, she vowed. Not now. Not until she was alone.

Bringing up the rear, a lone cavalryman trotted his horse a few yards behind the carriage, slumping in his saddle with his hat tilted into the wind, his coat collar turned up against the cold. The carriage rolled down empty streets . . . all night, soldiers had gone into the hills around Nashville preparing defenses, barricading roads into the city, building breastworks where artillery took up firing positions. Now the town appeared deserted, save for a few citizens scurrying about with foodstuffs and firewood as word of an impending attack spread. While the buggy drove across Nashville, Lorena held Clara to her breast, watching men and women and children gathering anything they could find before the battle began. Peering out at them from below the canopy, she imagined the terror they must feel, and she knew this was happening because of her letter. Not until now did she truly realize what her letter might do to the lives of innocent people who had no part in this war. Cannon fire would destroy homes, killing entire families. When fighting reached the streets, rifle balls could strike anyone. Bodies would be piled everywhere as they had been between battle lines at Franklin. All because of the letter she'd written to Gaines's Mill. And the man she loved was here to face the bullets and cannons she'd directed to Nashville. It was as if she had unknowingly ordered his execution.

At the edge of town their carriage halted where a group of soldiers guarded a barricade of empty wagons, overturned tables, furniture of every description.

"Let us pass!" the driver shouted. "We're on orders from

General Hood, taking these women to Camp Ford at Memphis!"

A bearded soldier approached the buggy. He looked at Clara and Lorena, cradling a long musket in the crook of his arm. Snow covered the bill and crown of his hat. "These are the two women who betrayed us to the Yanks," he remarked. He examined Lorena closely. "I was brought up to show respect fer a lady, ma'am," he said, as an edge crept into his voice, "but you sure as hell ain't no lady or you'd never done what you did to us." Slitting his eyelids, he spat on her and wheeled away. "Let 'em through!" he shouted to a pair of guards blocking the road.

Dozens of haggard-faced Confederates watched the carriage roll through an opening in the barricade. Lorena couldn't look at them, bowing her head until Nashville fell away behind the buggy. She wiped the soldier's spittle from her coat with her sleeve as the urge to cry welled strong inside her. So many humiliating events had befallen her within the past few hours that another merely added to a dulling of her senses. She and Clara were on their way to a Confederate prison, exposed as spies, threatened with a fate too terrible to contemplate. Her beloved Jonathan was likely to be killed, and she would never have the chance to fully explain why she had agreed to act as a spy for the good of her country, or so she believed then. What she had not known at the time was that Confederates she came to know in Tennessee were also her countrymen. She and the other nurses had been deceived into believing they were helping to end something evil, a black-hearted enemy so vile that the Union couldn't survive unless it was destroyed. Instead, she found boys like David Cobb and so many others who were enemies only because they lived in the South and a man like Jonathan Cross who was kind and full of compassion, hardly the remorseless slave owner she had been led to believe all Southerners were.

Fighting back deepening anguish, she gazed down at Clara as the carriage jolted over hidden bumps beneath the snow. Clara, weakened by typhus, could die from exposure in this weather. Her closest friend might lose her life because of this secret mission to track down an army of Confederates, and Lorena was very much to blame for having been first to volunteer, drawing Clara into a web of conspiracy for which neither one of them was suited. They were not spies—they had trained to become nurses. Why, oh, why, she wondered, had she agreed to something so dangerous? And now it appeared everything would come to a bitter end in a Confederate prison.

Occasional swirls of snow swept beneath the canopy on gusts of wind. Lorena wiped snowflakes from Clara's sleeping face and wept silently, grieving for Jonathan and Clara and the mistake she had made that night in Dorothea's office when General Grant came to the academy seeking volunteers.

The carriage rolled steadily westward. Now and then their driver glanced back over his shoulder. When he looked at her, the *way* he looked at her, she felt something dark, something menacing about him. He wasn't like the others, those young men she had cared for at the hospital. His beard-stubbled face was hard, heavy browed, threatening—she might have called his expression fierce. This soldier was very different in ways she couldn't quite define . . . and the looks he gave her were unsettling.

24

The first mortar blast sounded from the east while Jonathan Cross was attending to a soldier with a gangrenous hip. A whistling noise followed the distant explosion; then a second roar thundered in the skies above Barnum's. Seconds later the bellow of cannons grew to a single sound, coming from every direction, drowning out a chorus of shouts from soldiers manning fortifications around the city. Hammering mortar fire continued without cessation for several minutes. From various parts of town Jon could hear the crash of cannonballs landing against brick and mortar, wooden walls and roofs, and the splatter of grapeshot shattering windows across the city. The assault on Nashville had begun. Word came that Union commanders had offered General Hood an unconditional surrender, which he refused. In his heart Jon was sure the battle would be over soon. Union soldiers would overwhelm their meager defenses in a matter of hours after Yankee artillery blasted its way through thin barricades. He motioned for Goodie to remove the soldier from his operating table as the pounding of mortars continued.

Major Canfield strode in from the snowstorm, shedding his coat. He approached Jon's table. "Be prepared to make choices!" he shouted, to be heard above the thundering guns. "Stop as much bleeding as you can when you feel a patient can be saved. If the damage is too severe don't waste your time with it. These will be difficult decisions, Captain, however under the circumstances they must be made."

A knot was forming in Jon's belly, listening to the slam of heavy shells landing all around them, feeling the earth tremble underneath his feet. He nodded in acknowledgment of Canfield's order. But even as battle sounds swelled his mind was on Lorena, and he asked, "Were the nurses sent to Memphis?"

Canfield grunted. "Prison is more than they deserve. It is only due to the benevolence of General Hood that they were not executed on the spot." He hurried off toward his operating table while rolling up his sleeves, putting on a clean apron.

Jon took his instruments from his medical bag and laid them out on a piece of cloth, still thinking of Lorena and a Confederate prison run by an Austrian mercenary whose specialty was interrogation. Would Von Bulen torture her? Jon couldn't allow himself to think about it—somehow he had to push it from his mind.

Suddenly an explosion rocked the south wall of the warehouse amid the sounds of breaking glass and splintering wood. Through an open doorway Jon saw the front of Peabody's Boardinghouse erupt. Pieces of planking and shingles flew skyward, tossed into the air as though weightless, mingling with swirling snowflakes in odd patterns of color. It felt as if the wall of Barnum's had convulsed, bending inward yet still intact. Screams and yells came from across the road before the blast ended. While bits of wood fell to the ground, a chimney crumbled, bricks landing with a muffled thud in the snow, some sliding down what was left of the slanted roof before falling into the road. Jon was frozen by fear, realizing how close he had been to a deadly round from a Union artillery piece. For a moment he stood there watching the front of Peabody's disintegrate—the porch roof collapsed. He saw it fall and still he didn't move. Had Lorena been inside she would have been seriously injured or killed.

Then he saw a sight that sent him running for the warehouse door. Beatrice Peabody, her dress covered with blood, staggered from her front door with a shotgun, stumbling over parts of the porch roof blocking her path. Her face was bloody and she seemed in a daze, but when she came to the edge of rubble where the roof had fallen, she stopped and raised the shotgun to her shoulder. A veil of snowflakes surrounded her. She cried, "Damn you Yankee bastards!" and fired into the air, reeling backward when the kick from her shotgun struck her. She fell, toppling off her porch into the snow. Coatless, Jon ran down slippery steps and raced across the road, kneeling when he reached the woman, ignoring the rumble of cannons in the distance, the clap of canisters exploding among gray storm clouds above him, and the thud of heavy cannonballs crashing to the earth.

A deep gash in her scalp bled profusely. She tried to sit up on her own until he got his arm around her.

"My house," she mumbled, dazed by her wound and falling off the porch.

"Let me take you to the hospital," he told her, helping her to stand. "You've got a nasty cut on top of your head. You need a bandage to stop the bleeding."

"They ruined my house!" Beatrice cried, turning to look at gaping holes in her roof and front wall. "This house is all I've got. . . ."

He led her gently toward Barnum's. A whistling canister of grapeshot exploded somewhere above them, followed by a rain of hot lead balls dropping with a quiet hiss into the snow a few yards down the street. The woman stumbled, off balance until he steadied her. "You can rebuild a house, Mrs. Peabody, but you can't survive unless I stop that bleeding. I expect this battle will be over quickly. We can't hold them back for long, I fear, and with luck your house won't be hit again." He glanced over his shoulder. "Was anyone else hurt when the shell landed?"

"Preacher Johnson," she replied weakly, like she was about to cry. "He was callin' to me from under a big pile of lumber in the parlor, only I couldn't think of nothin' besides shootin' at those bluebellies who ruined my house. My other boarders ran out the back door."

"I'll send someone over to help him," Jon told her, assisting her up the steps. To the east, noise from pounding mortars increased. A bell tower atop a brick church near the railroad depot exploded in a shower of red clay . . . the bell sounded once before it fell, clanging on the church floor a second time while bricks cascaded off the roof.

Goodie and several orderlies from the medical corps carried wounded on bloody litters toward the hospital, leaving trails of blood in the snow. Jon escorted Mrs. Peabody to his table and tied strips of cloth around her head wound as quickly as he could before the litters arrived. There was no medicine, and he knew the soldiers he treated today would suffer to the limits of human endurance. Once again he would be forced to close his mind to screams of agony while doing what he could to save lives.

"Go down into your cellar," he told Beatrice when her bandages were tied. "It'll be the safest place until this is over. I'll have Goodie help you across the road and see about the preacher."

She looked at him with tears in her eyes. "This is a stupid war, Doctor. My very own nephew in Kentucky is a Yankee soldier. He could be one of them who's shootin' at us right now. If that ain't stupid, nothin' is. Nobody knows what this war is about. It's about politicians and rich folks, only they aren't the ones gettin' their houses shot to pieces."

"I agree, Mrs. Peabody." He motioned for Goodie. "Now, go down into your cellar and don't come out until the shooting stops."

Goodie and another orderly placed a groaning soldier on Jon's operating table. The infantryman's belly was torn open, revealing his liver, pancreas, and coils of intestine. He would die in a matter of hours, perhaps in minutes. "Take this woman across the street and put her in her cellar, Goodie, and see if you can help a man trapped inside. Please hurry."

Goodie took Mrs. Peabody's arm and led her away. Jon looked into the wounded soldier's stomach and shook his head. He spoke to Private Suggins. "Take this man away. I can't help him. See if you can find a place where he'll be warm." He felt as if he were choking on words when he pronounced this case hopeless.

More litter bearers hurried into the hospital, carrying men from fortifications in the hills. Most were covered by blankets under a layer of snowflakes, and where their wounds bled, a mixture of blood and melting ice left a crimson stain telling Jon about the seriousness of their injuries. Extremities could be bandaged, stemming blood flow and providing the best chance for survival. Men with belly and chest wounds needed surgery—he had to choose the ones he thought he might save and allow the others to die. Of all the battles he'd witnessed as a surgeon with Hood, this would be one he would never forget, deciding in God-like fashion who lived and who must perish. Filled with sorrow beyond measure, he began an inspection of newly arrived wounded, searching for those who might benefit from a tourniquet and bandages, perhaps a bone splint and stitches, the only things he could provide without a painkiller or cauterizing agents.

A shell slammed into the east wall of Barnum's, shattering heavy planking like kindling wood, causing beams and rafters to creak all across the warehouse. A lead ball thudded to the floor, giving off steam, narrowly avoiding a row of wounded men from the battle at Franklin who had been moved near outer walls to make room for arriving casualties. The noise startled Jon as he was tying bandages and a splint to a screaming soldier's lower leg. Smoke from smudgepots burned his eyes, making it harder to see much of the gaping hole in the hospital wall other than gray sky beyond it and a few snowflakes. An orderly holding his patient to the table hunkered down and said, "Damn that was close, Doc. Sure do hope one don't come through that roof over our heads."

Jon tied off the last strip of cloth, vaguely aware of some change in faraway battle sounds—they seemed to grow louder.

He said, "Take this man to a pallet." From the corner of his eye he saw Goodie coming through the south warehouse door with a limp figure in his arms. An elderly man in a bloodstained white shirt and torn trousers was carried unconscious to his operating table. When Goodie put him down, he said, "Don't know what's wrong with him, Cap'n. He was under this great big pile of timber. You can see he ain't dead 'cause he's still breathin', but he won't wake up."

Jon quickly examined the old man's chest. Superficial cuts were bleeding. A large bruise on one side of his head explained his loss of consciousness. "It doesn't look serious, Goodie, so find a place to put him on a pallet for now." A team of orderlies came toward him, carrying a canvas sling dribbling blood over the warehouse floor. On the litter a young soldier had had his cheek blown away, distorting his face so it appeared he wore a perpetual one-sided grin. Several teeth were missing where the ball went through, probably a wound from a canister of shot or maybe, even worse, a rifle ball, which meant fighting was at close quarters now. The boy was hoisted onto Jon's table. Without cauterizing agents, he had nothing to stop the blood flow. Wrapping bandages around a wound such as this could hardly be called treatment by a physician, yet it was Jon's only remedy at hand. He felt utterly useless as he began tying strips of bedsheet around the soldier's head, ignoring the boy's soft groans, unable to look into a pair of pleading eyes begging for an end to his pain.

A thunderous explosion rocked Barnum's roof. A cannonball fell, striking one of the smudgepots, knocking it on its side as coal oil spilled and ignited. Flames leaped from a spreading pool of oil, crackling, then roaring when an inferno sprang to life in a corner of the building. Wounded men screamed. Some managed to crawl away from the blaze before they became engulfed by flames. Jon grabbed a bleeding pail from beneath his operating table and ran for the fire, watching in horror when a blanketed soldier became a human torch, a fiery apparition scrambling blindly for a doorway with his entire body ablaze. Diving out into the snow, the man began to roll in an effort to smother the flames. Three wounded men stumbled outside with blankets to help extinguish the fire before Jon got there.

Injured soldiers who could stand were beating flames at the overturned smudgepot with blankets, reminding Jon that any liquid would only cause an oil fire to spread. He took a blanket from a sleeping man and began beating the edges of the fire while all around him, from every corner of Barnum's, men shouted and cried for help. Goodie arrived with two blankets and commenced rapid strokes over the flames with both hands, pounding out portions of fire faster than anyone else. Major Canfield came with a piece of bloody canvas from a litter, beating back flames approaching a warehouse wall. A thick pall of black oil smoke rose from what remained of the fire until, at last, it was smothered. Panting, exhausted, and badly frightened men stood around the overturned smudgepot for a moment catching their breath.

"It's out," Canfield said, finally turning away to hurry back to his operating table.

Jon heard a series of screams outside. Gasping, inhaling smoke making his lungs burn, he went to the door where he found men piling snow over the burned soldier in his smoldering blanket—his cries so shrill they sent chills down Jon's spine. "Bring him inside!" he shouted, listening to the drum of cannon fire in increasing salvos. Union forces were bringing in more field guns to surround Nashville. If this shelling continued, there wouldn't be a building left standing beside the Cumberland River.

Coughing smoke from his lungs, Jon went back inside to finish bandaging the boy's cheek. When he passed a doorway with a view of the river, he saw a strange sight, one he couldn't explain, as a contingent of Confederate cavalry crossed over what was left of the remaining bridge into Nashville, the same weakened bridge he had crossed when they arrived. Hundreds of mounted soldiers trotted their horses through windswept sheets of snow to reach the south bank of the river, where they turned west, away from the brunt of Union shelling. Unless General Hood was planning to flank Union guns with cavalry, this exodus could be a mass desertion. Frowning, Jon returned to his table and bandaging, puzzling over what he had just seen.

A mercantile beside Barnum's took a shell through its front window. Breaking glass and snapping timbers alerted everyone to how close the ball had come to the hospital. Exploding canisters echoed back and forth more frequently now, proof that more Union guns were in place. Jon finished wrapping the soldier's jaw and grimaced, knowing he'd done virtually nothing that might save his life. "Take him to a pallet, Goodie," he said as injured men who could walk carried the burn victim to the operating table as quickly as they could—another case where lack of medicines rendered Jon all but useless for there was almost nothing he could do without ointments and salves.

Once, while the battle raged, he turned to a doorway with a view west, thinking of Lorena. It was best, he decided, that she was elsewhere today, even bound for prison. The unrelenting fury of this Union attack was certain to claim so many lives that few would survive it, quite possibly not even himself.

25

Dawn's pale-gray light came through windows at Marshal House on the Cumberland. Huge snowflakes pattered against window panes and melted almost at once with heat from roaring fireplaces in the study and front parlor. Glass lamps on mantlepieces shed golden light on assembled officers gathered around a long mahogany table in the study. At the head of the table, John Bell Hood sat in a high-backed chair staring at his withered arm while Dr. Roberts gave him an injection of morphine. Silence in the room grew heavy, lengthening. No one dared say a word after General Hood's fiery outburst moments earlier. Now he sat as though in a stupor, heavy lidded, watching a second injection flow into his atrophied bicep.

A sap knot popped in the fireplace, and the sound seemed to awaken Hood from his trance. He looked up, blinking, licking a trace of saliva from whiskers sprouting off his lower lip. He gave his officers a blank, lifeless gaze. The silence continued half a minute more while Hood appeared to collect his thoughts. To some, the walls still echoed with his previous tirade, the shrill resonance of his bellowing, pounding his fist on the polished table until he had fallen back in his chair, spent, ordering Dr. Roberts to inject him again.

Colonel Wilson Simmons was sure he was staring into the eyes of a deranged madman.

Colonel Philip Work shuddered inwardly. He couldn't quite grasp what he was seeing. A great man, a true military genius, had been reduced to slobbering fits and tears. His accusations against his field commanders were groundless. No one could fight under these conditions, denied food and ammunition and clothing to ward off the elements. Nashville had become a Confederate death camp. The cause was lost, and Hood would not concede their untenable position. His heart could not accept defeat, no matter how desperate conditions became.

Buford Jackson watched the needle enter Hood's arm dispassionately, expressionless. After the disaster at Franklin, he felt nothing. He had no feelings left, no emotional reserve, no more compassion. War had become an almost monotonous recitation of principle. Lives were given for a cause, for a principle men had sworn allegiance to. General Hood had given his oath to that cause, to defend it at all costs. No man could be asked to give more than he had—a leg and an arm, years of pain, isolation from his family and friends, total dedication to winning that robbed him of sleep, driving him to the brink of lunacy. The injections were simply another price to be paid, a price he paid in the name of the cause. And now the treachery of two Yankee nurses would do what Union generals like Pope and Sherman and McClellan could not. It had taken a Judas from within to corner Hood's brigades, with the arrival of General George Thomas and an army stretching more than thirty miles along Tennessee back roads.

Hood's stare wandered to a window. "It's snowing," he said in a faraway voice, as though he hadn't noticed the weather until now. "How nice it will be to have a white Christmas. It's a shame we can't give the men a fine turkey dinner. Plum pudding would be such a treat. . . ."

Colonel Simmons gave the other officers a quick glance. "If I may interrupt, General. The Union force will be at our doorstep within the hour. What are your orders?"

Hood focused on Simmons. "My orders? My orders have always been to fight the enemy with unrestrained fury. To hurl your men into battle and show no quarter. When have my orders been otherwise?"

Simmons turned red. "There is no ammunition, sir. No shot or gunpowder with which to sustain an attack or even a reasonable defense of the city."

Hood seemed bewildered. "A reasonable defense? Pray tell, what is a reasonable defense?"

Simmons's embarrassment only deepened. "One that stands some reasonable chance of success. . . ."

Tears formed in Hood's eyes again. "Would you have me call for the surrender of God's legions? I lack the capacity to ask our proud men to lay down their arms before tyranny. How can any man who fears God surrender His army? It isn't in me. I can't do it, no matter how dire our circumstances may seem. In the final accounting, every man must face his Maker, and in this life I must answer to our President. I refuse to inform President Davis of our capitulation to an army of Negro-loving Unionists. I shall not yield to Abe Lincoln's mercenaries." Using the table for support, Hood came slowly to his feet, swaying to maintain his balance. "Neither will I go to God with anything less than one last charge into the teeth of the enemy! If there is no shot, let us give them a taste of steel bayonets!" Now he turned his hard stare on the other officers. "I can do no less. We have been betrayed by two wenches from Grant's alliance with Satan. They must use women to achieve their ends no differently than the Philistines. We were seduced by Samson's mistresses posing as nurses. Would you have us surrender to them?"

For a moment there was silence as Hood glared around the table. No one was willing to speak.

"Then prepare your brigades for a defense of Nashville!" he cried, eyes growing round, spittle running into his beard.

Colonel Simmons spread his palms. "We have deployed cannon batteries around the city, sir. The Union troops are advancing on us from the northeast, although we expect them to throw a circle around us. If they overrun our positions in the hills, nothing will be able to stop them from shelling the heart of Nashville. We will be shot to oblivion."

Tears streamed down Hood's cheeks. He looked from one man to the next as if he expected someone to provide a solution. "I hear nothing from the rest of you to sway Colonel Simmons's belief that the city will fall. . . ." His voice was breaking. He paused when he came to Colonel Jackson. "Have you nothing to say, dear friend?"

Jackson's eyes fell. The scar on his cheek became a darker violet. "We have asked these men for everything they have, sir. Even the deepest wells may run dry. Richmond refuses to resupply us or send reinforcements. A lion must be fed." He looked up now, and when he spoke he was hard to hear with anguish clotting his throat. "Nashville will fall. Nothing can prevent it."

Hood visibly winced. He lowered his head. "Then have my horse saddled at once. I find I am unable to watch this sad day unfold. I have led these men in their finest hour, and my heart will not allow me to see an end come to the Texas brigades." He directed a glassy-eyed look at Wilson Simmons. "I shall notify Richmond of my resignation from the Confederate Army. I cannot lead men who are unwilling to follow. Colonel Simmons, I place you in command of these united brigades. With all my heart, I urge to you fight the enemy to the last man. Nothing less will be expected of you. I urge you . . . do not fail our brave President or our wives and children."

Sheets of wind-driven snow accompanied them to the railroad bridge, shrouding them from peering eyes across most of Nashville as they rode starving, spavined horses to the crossing. The rattle of hooves on bridge planks was muffled by an accumulation of snowflakes. Colonel Buford Jackson led his mounted troop over the bridge. A lean figure wrapped in a heavy great-coat sat his bay horse in peculiar fashion, slumped over the saddle, shoulders drooping.

At the end of the bridge Jackson turned his troop west, past houses with snow-covered rooftops where groups of shivering men stood around meager fires, clinging to empty muskets. A few gave General Hood a respectful salute, while others merely watched as their leader rode by with his face to the ground.

Jackson followed a rutted lane running beside the Cumberland with his men riding in pairs, leaving Nashville's buildings and the bridge hidden by falling snow behind them. In a stand of snow-laden trees south of the road, they encountered a Confederate gun battery with its cannon muzzles aimed west to protect an advance upon the town from that direction. A fire flickered near one of the caissons where freezing soldiers fed flames with planks from the caisson's flooring. Jackson's mounted troop rode past them in silence, soon vanishing into a curtain of snow.

Where the road began climbing away from the river, Colonel Jackson signaled a halt when they heard a distant explosion from the east.

"It has begun," he told the general quietly.

Hood's body was wracked by sobs.

26

A different kind of commotion in the streets drew Jonathan Cross's full attention away from a patient with a mangled arm. Soldiers were running, shouting to each other, falling back from fortifications on the eastern edge of Nashville. Just as quickly, cannon fire slowed to an occasional shot. A chorus of yells came from every direction. Roads passing the hospital were crowded with men in retreat from the east. Many were limping; some held wounded arms to their sides or clasped their hands over belly wounds. Hood's battle lines had been broken, yet the retreat westward would only take them into the teeth of gun batteries to the west. What was sure to follow was a full-scale charge into the city by Union infantry and cavalry. Jon hurriedly wrapped a bandage around a splint holding his patient's arm in place. Before he was able to finish, Major Canfield walked over, his apron and sleeves smeared with blood. He wasn't looking at Jon—his attention was on what was happening in the streets as soldiers retreated past hospital doors.

"The cannons have stopped," he said, as though he was only now aware of an end to the shelling. "Our brigades have been routed. Look at them . . . they're running like scared rabbits. I never thought I'd see the day when our proud men turned tail to run from a fight in total disgrace. General Hood will have every last one of them court-martialed. We've been under siege only a few hours, and they've already given up."

Jon heard disbelief in Canfield's voice, and he was bewildered by it. "They're only trying to stay alive, Major. Those Yankees must have us badly outnumbered. Our soldiers simply can't hold them back or survive continuous bombardment indefinitely. We're being shelled to pieces. How can any man expect them to stand and fight when a fight can't possibly be won? We've got so many wounded now, there's no room for them inside our hospitals."

The major gave Jon a look. "Our Texans have a proud tradition, which you've obviously forgotten, Captain. Courage on the battlefield has made General Hood's reputation. These men aren't retreating—they're deserting. Just look at them. . . ."

Streets near the warehouse were choked with fleeing men. A few of the wounded hobbled to Barnum's doors to watch. It was a sorrowful sight, Jon agreed, but quite understandable despite the major's belief in the courage demanded of them by their commander. "I believe in tradition, Major, but I also understand how men can be pushed beyond their limits. Our soldiers are cold and hungry and most have little ammunition. The way they are now, they simply aren't equipped to put up a fight." He thought about the consequences when Confederates fled the city. "What shall we do? Remain with our wounded or leave with the others? We'll be taken prisoner if we stay."

Canfield adopted a stern expression. "General Hood has not ordered us to withdraw from the field—I'm quite certain of that. We await our orders, Captain, as always."

The major's stubbornness would result in certain imprisonment for everyone who stayed. Jon found it an odd coincidence that Lorena was bound for a Confederate prison while he was sure to wind up in a Union prison camp for the duration of the war unless some miracle saved Canfield's medical corps from being captured. "Should we send someone to General Hood to ask what our orders are?" he wondered aloud.

"Perhaps," Canfield replied tersely, his frown deepening as hoards of soldiers in gray crowded the streets. "However, we can't move our wounded under these conditions. Our ambulances could not navigate roads full of deserting cowards." The crackle of distant musket fire ended the major's remarks. He turned an ear toward the sounds and listened.

"They've ordered a charge, Major. I expect we'll see Union cavalry and infantry any moment now."

Canfield wouldn't be budged from his belief in his commanding officer. "The general will order a counterattack. All is not lost." He continued to watch scenes beyond the doors, of men pushing and shoving in their haste to escape a Union assault they could hear moving in behind them.

Jon stood silently to watch the retreat, and in some small way he was almost grateful. Surrender and imprisonment would bring an end to so much suffering, so much dying. It was a thought he couldn't share with Major Canfield, of course, but nonetheless he felt the time had come for Hood's army to stop fighting with empty guns, empty bellies, and shoeless feet.

Two orderlies managed to make their way through the throng with a litter. Private Suggins swung the front of his litter toward Jon upon entering the hospital, hurrying as fast as he could. Before the stretcher arrived, Jon glanced at the wounded man they carried, and when he did, he almost cried aloud when he saw Goodie lying between the poles. Blood pooled around Goodie's neck and chest, and it appeared he was no longer breathing.

"What happened?" Jon asked, hurrying over as Goodie was lifted to his operating table.

"He took a ball through his throat," Suggins replied, "as we was carryin' another man back here. Them Yanks are comin' like a swarm of blue ants, Cap'n. Never saw so many—must be thousands of 'em." He gazed sorrowfully down at Goodie. "Looks like that ball went plumb through his neck. He got shot from behind by one of them yellow sonsabitches."

Jon examined the front of the wound before gently turning Goodie's head. A large exit hole at the base of his skull oozed fresh blood, although too slowly for heart action. He found no pulse in Goodie's neck. "He's dead," Jon whispered, saying it to himself, grieving quietly over the loss of a friend, a big, good-natured giant who had always performed his duties without question.

"I figured he was dead," Suggins said. "He got shot from behind like I said, didn't he?"

"He was shot from the front," Jon sighed, turning away, for he was unable to look at the body any longer.

At that moment Dr. Roberts entered a side door of Barnum's with a worried expression wrinkling his face. He strode over to Major Canfield. "General Hood has departed the city in a rage. He told his aides he refused to command an army of cowards who would not obey orders. He left with a mounted escort a half hour ago across the bridge yonder, leaving Colonel Simmons in command. Simmons is beside himself . . . he doesn't know what to do. Nashville is surrounded. General Hood said he will inform Richmond of his resignation. He ranted almost endlessly until I gave him the last of my morphine. I believe Colonel Simmons will surrender immediately. We'll be prisoners of war."

Canfield's face changed. "General Hood intends to resign?"

Roberts nodded, glancing out one door. "He felt he had no army left. As you can see, he may have been entirely correct in that assumption."

"I find it hard to believe John Bell Hood would ever quit a battlefield in dishonor," Canfield remarked, watching the roads full of retreating Confederates. "Without General Hood, we face certain defeat now. We are doomed."

Jon did not express his private belief that they had been doomed after the beating they took at Franklin. "What should we do, Major?" he asked.

The major straightened his spine. "As doctors, we are bound by oath to help our patients, gentlemen. Let us see to that task until the outcome is decided. If the Union commanders are honorable men, they will give us medicines and allow us to treat our wounded." Suddenly, as if he had just remembered something, Canfield turned to Jon. "We have those nurses to thank for this crushing defeat, Captain. With traitors in our midst, we stood no chance whatsoever of recovering sufficiently or being resupplied before we were engaged. You were so smitten with Miss Blaire that you were unable to believe in her capacity for treachery. I hope now you understand your trust was badly misplaced."

The rattle of musket fire very close to the hospital saved Jon from further discussion of Lorena and Clara. He looked past a door at a surreal scene: hundreds of Confederates clogged every roadway on the east side of Nashville, running for their lives from a hail of rifle balls fired steadily into their rear. In a snowstorm, the grisly drama took on a strange quality, somehow out of place where buildings and streets were covered in white by the stroke of nature's paintbrush.

He thought he heard someone sobbing nearby. Private Suggins stood next to Goodie holding the dead soldier's wrist, crying uncontrollably as if he only now understood his friend was gone. Then another sound came from the east, a rumbling of pounding hooves announcing a cavalry charge. Falling snow prevented Jon from seeing any horsemen for the moment, but the noise continued, unmistakable to an experienced soldier. "This is it," he said quietly, his voice lost to other sounds, the pop of guns, yells from retreating Confederates, drumming hoofbeats.

"It's their cavalry," Dr. Thomas remarked, watching through the same doors as Jon and the major. "May God have mercy on our souls."

Canfield's face lost its color. "Without our general, these men have lost their will to fight."

Thomas shook his head. "It isn't willpower they've lost, in my opinion. They have no gunpowder or shot. No general on earth can command a weaponless fighting force. If anyone is to blame, it is President Davis. Richmond never sent us promised supplies or any ammunition. Men cannot fight on sheer willpower alone."

Now the lighter chatter of pistols came from the east, and with it a chorus of cries and screams from wounded men. Canfield said, "They intend to shoot us down to the last man."

Jon noticed some of the less seriously wounded inside the warehouse gathering blankets and whatever they could find to flee along with the others. Men with bandaged arms and legs managed to stand and hurry outside when the pistol shots grew louder. A few with amputated legs were assisted by companions into the road where they joined masses of retreating Confederate infantrymen. And then from the west a barrage of cannon fire resumed, meant to drive Hood's soldiers back from any escape route westward.

"It's over," Major Canfield said when he heard mortar blasts blocking off a retreat. He hung his head, staring at his blood-stained boots. "This army has been reduced to nothing but sheep. We'll all be slaughtered unless Colonel Simmons surrenders at once. Our men haven't fired a shot to turn back the assault. He has no other choice. . . ."

"Our soldiers have no way to shoot back!" Thomas countered, his face to a hospital door where cavalrymen in blue uniforms could be seen through falling snow firing into the rear of retreating men in gray. "Their guns are empty!"

Jon saw Confederates stumble to a halt and raise their arms in surrender near the Union cavalrymen. More and more of Hood's men lifted their arms and stopped running, dropping their weapons into the snow. And with their surrender, an end came to seemingly endless pistol fire from Union troops, with only a few scattered shots here and there, then silence. Off to the west, cannons still beat out a thumping rhythm of heavy blasts until, at last, all shelling abruptly stopped. Then an eerie silence spread across Nashville, a quiet so stark and complete that Jon wondered if he might have gone suddenly deaf as a stone.

Major Canfield looked up from the floor. "Let us see to our

wounded, gentlemen. We are doctors. Let the soldiers negoti-
ate terms of our surrender while we attempt to save what lives
we can here."

Jon turned to Private Suggins. "Help me find a place to put
Goodie," he said gently. "We'll see to his burial after we have
done what we can for the others."

They lifted Goodie's heavy body and carried it to an empty
space near the rear wall. Outside, at the eastern outskirts of
Nashville, he glimpsed Union cavalrymen with drawn pistols riding slowly among surrendered Confederates. Through thick
snowfall he saw hundreds more blue-clad cavalry as they advanced into Nashville's crowded streets, aiming rifles and
sidearms at Hood's defeated men. At last, he thought, no more
blood will be shed by Texas brigades. For them this war was over,
and Jon believed that most would count it a blessing.

He found a wounded artilleryman from the Army of Tennessee lying on a blood-soaked blanket beside a smudgepot. His
forearm was shattered, and two fingers were missing from his
hand. The blond boy's face was twisted with pain, tears streaming down his pale cheeks while he held his injured arm across his
chest. Jon knelt down beside him. "I can put a splint on your
arm and sew back some skin where you lost fingers, but we have
no painkiller. There's nothing I can do for pain right now. Sorry."

The soldier nodded. "It hurts so bad I can't hardly stand no
more of it, only please don't cut my arm off. I'd as soon be dead
as havin' only one arm."

"I'll do the best I can," Jon promised, motioning for his medical bag.

The distant thud of a lone mortar sounded from the west, and
when he heard it, he glanced to a warehouse door, listening to
the whistle of an airborne canister overhead. The noise grew
louder. A second later he was knocked off his feet by a thunderous roar. Timbers from the hospital roof exploded into bits of
kindling as he fell onto his back, watching sections of the roof
tumble down on him. He tried to shield his face with his hands
when huge pieces of planking dropped to the floor. Something

struck his head. He heard men shouting and saw a ball of fire erupt near one of the smudgepots just before his vision blurred. A heavy weight fell across his chest, crushing him; then he felt his ribs crack. An involuntary scream rushed from his lips, hearing his own cry as though it belonged to someone else, someone lying below him as he experienced the sensation of floating away from his body into a world of total darkness.

27

General Thomas rode slowly through Nashville with a company of hand-picked cavalrymen, surveying scenes of devastation made by his gun batteries. Crumbled bricks where a store once stood, houses without roofs or gaping holes in clapboard walls, hundreds of shattered windows, a church with a missing steeple. His guns and artillerymen had performed magnificently, blasting Hood and his weakened army into submission in five short hours. He was surprised to learn Hood had abandoned his soldiers when the battle was clearly lost, and somewhat disappointed. He had privately hoped to deliver John Bell Hood to Washington personally, handing him over to General Grant as a Christmas present. Hood's escape only supported a widespread belief that he was mad as a hatter after too many debilitating wounds. Morphine was said to make slaves of men, robbing them of the ability to reason. Hood had once been a brilliant tactician. Allowing himself to be trapped in Nashville was the mark of a military leader without his full senses—or a man who simply couldn't run any farther. The officer Hood left in charge, a Colonel Woodrow Simmons, had been only too glad to agree to an unconditional surrender.

Near the center of town they came upon a shell-pocked cotton warehouse, now obviously a hospital with rows of blanketed men lying on the floor. A fire still smoldered in a corner of the building below a giant hole in its roof clearly made by a mortar, a tragic but understandable occurrence when artillerymen fired into a city they knew nothing about. Thomas signaled a halt, noting that at last it had stopped snowing. Columns of Rebel prisoners marched slowly past the warehouse under heavy guard. Thomas saw how ragged they all seemed, hardly a one with sufficient clothing or serviceable boots to keep them from freezing. He turned to Colonel Menem. "It's a sad sight, the condition of these poor men. One wonders how they survived. They look half starved and completely dispirited. I must confess that seeing them now makes this a bit of a shallow victory. Hood's mighty Texans are a pitiful sight. General Grant spent many a sleepless night worrying about where they would show up next. He could have slept soundly. These men posed no real threat to anyone. I'd be hard-pressed to call this an army."

"Our orders say we are to take all prisoners up to Indiana, Camp Morton at Indianapolis," the colonel remembered. "These starving bastards aren't capable of walking that far. Most have no shoes, tying rags to their feet."

As Thomas was pondering a march with shoeless prisoners, he saw one of his officers emerge from the hospital. A captain came quickly across the road, saluting when he arrived.

"Sir, conditions in their hospital are deplorable," Captain Bruce reported. "They have no medicines, and a mortar round struck the building, killing half a dozen men, as if things weren't already bad enough the way they were. Doctors are performing emergency amputations with no morphine or anesthetic. It's butchery, sir, but necessary to halt the spread of gangrene, their doctors say. For the sake of decency I'd like to request a team of our surgeons to assist them and give them whatever medicines they need. Men are screaming until pain renders them unconscious. . . ."

"Permission is granted," Thomas said, swallowing a mouthful of bile when he thought about surgery without anesthesia or painkiller. "Send as many units of our medical corps as you think they require. There are hundreds more wounded out there in the snow. Instruct Colonel Riley to have men with stretchers begin looking for them as quickly as possible. I've no stomach for any more suffering by these Rebels. Frankly, I've seen quite enough. Let's provide what help we can give them."

Captain Bruce saluted again and wheeled away. Thomas bit his lip thoughtfully before addressing Colonel Menem. "Have men from the signal corps repair the telegraph lines we severed. I want General Grant notified as quickly as possible that Nashville has fallen. Inform him that Hood's army has been captured, but their condition is such that it would be virtually impossible to march them to Camp Morton in this weather. Ask for further orders in that regard. If the telegraph isn't servicable, send couriers with our message. And please wish General Grant a merry Christmas for me."

28

Their carriage rolled through quiet hamlets seemingly untouched by the war, past peaceful farms in clearings among pine and oak forests covered with snow, small cabins on the sides of steep hills surrounded by pole fences where a milk cow, occasionally a mule and a few pigs, were kept. Although the snowstorm had ended, skies were still gray, threatening, and a chill wind from the north blew beneath the canopy wherever a winding lane they followed lay unprotected by trees. During most of the afternoon they'd driven past hundreds of Confederate deserters carrying what little they had in snow-encrusted backpacks or in burlap bags slung over a shoulder. Few had weapons, not wanting the added weight while plodding through half a foot of fresh snow. Many had no coats, wrapping themselves in blankets and whatever else they had found to keep out the cold. Lorena saw this gloomy procession from her buggy seat, with Clara still cradled in her lap, as their driver pushed his team away from Nashville. A lone cavalryman followed the carriage, a rear guard, she supposed, to keep them from attempting an escape. Even if they had been foolhardy enough to consider any such thing, Clara was in no condition for it—unconscious most of the time, occasionally waking up for brief periods only to lapse back into a deep sleep. Her thin face was florid, made worse by the cold, and her pox appeared to be a darker red. Lorena tried not to think about the possibility her friend was dying, nor did she allow herself to think of Jonathan when she could control her thoughts. For the first hour's drive away from Nashville she had wept silently over their shared fate, a black ending to a blossoming love affair. Even if the fates were kind to him, sparing his life, he would be sent to a Union prison. How ironic, she thought, that her actions had dealt them both the loss of their freedom—*if* Jonathan lived through a Union assault on Nashville. Cruel irony, ending mutual love so sweet and fulfilling that it had a dreamlike quality until its abrupt and bitter final moments last night when Major Canfield had paid his unexpected call on Clara.

The soldier driving their buggy glanced over his shoulder again as they topped a bald knob surrounded by trees. He gazed at Lorena for a few moments, neglecting his team until a carriage wheel hit a stone hidden beneath snow. He clucked to the tiring horses and slapped their rumps with the reins before turning around again to stare at her.

"You're a right pretty gal, missy. I bet you're a hell of a lot prettier without that coat an' dress."

She stiffened, holding Clara to her breast more tightly than ever. "You mustn't talk to me like that!" she demanded.

He chuckled. "Way I see it, I can talk to you any damn way I please, missy. You're a prisoner, a goddamn Yankee spy, an' that means I can say whatever I want. If I wanted to, I could tie your hands an' feet, even shoot you dead if I took the notion. All I have to say is that you was tryin' to escape. Roy Lee back yonder will vouch fer me, 'cause me an' him are real good friends. So, if'n I was you, I wouldn't start out tellin' me how I'm supposed to talk. I'll say whatever I feel like sayin'."

The beginnings of terror turned cold in the pit of Lorena's stomach. This Confederate had none of the politeness nor good manners she had found among most soldiers she'd treated. When he leered at her, she was reminded of men who had stared at her or made lewd remarks along narrow back streets in one of the worst sections of Baltimore where her father owned a cobbler's shop, those dirty unshaven types who whiled away time standing on street corners or in doorways of cheap rooming houses, drinking liquor. Her father had continually warned her not to look at them, and to hurry past whenever she encountered men of their ilk. But she was a prisoner of this bearded soldier, thus there was no escaping his unwanted attention or his crude remarks.

"Please stop staring at me," she said, making her request as firmly as she was able, filling her voice with as much indignation as she could muster, "and please refrain from saying that sort of thing to me again."

His face hardened. "I done told you I can say anything I want. You're my prisoner. Don't tell me what I can do or I'm liable to show you a thing or two 'bout how we treat folks who spy on us. I'll stop this buggy right here an' tear that dress off so me an' Roy Lee can see what's underneath." Now he gave her a cruel grin. "If we wanted, we can cut your teats off an' let you bleed to death. Won't nobody in these parts complain, after we tell 'em you're a damn Yankee spy."

Lorena gasped, "That would be murder!"

The driver wagged his head. "Not fer killin' a spy, missy. This is a war. You're the enemy. We can kill you legal. Won't nobody say a word." He turned back to watch the road, guiding his team down snow-filled ruts as though he intended to give her time to think about his threat.

She looked down at her hands, finding her knuckles white as she gripped the comforter around Clara. Was he planning to kill her? Her heart thumped wildly and her mouth was dry. In a panic she began to search the woods ahead of them for a farmhouse or a cabin where she might cry for help. But would anyone help her if told she was a spy for the Union Army?

The sky slowly darkened with nightfall as the carriage moved deeper into thickly wooded hills. They passed no more farms, nor were there any signs of habitation. Riding close behind was the lone cavalryman named Roy Lee, a rifle resting across the pommel of his saddle.

It was a vacant barn made of logs, its walls leaning, a roof with missing timbers, where the driver stopped sometime during the night. Lorena had been dozing, exhausted by an ordeal that had begun more than twenty-four hours earlier, during which she'd been too frightened to sleep. When the carriage halted, she bolted upright on the seat to watch the driver climb down.

"Keep an eye on 'em, Roy Lee," he said, lighting a small oil lantern. "I'll see if this barn is fit to sleep in fer a few hours. There's a bunch of holes in the roof." He walked to one side of the building holding his lantern aloft where an opening gave a view of what was inside. "It'll do," he muttered, peering in for a moment. "There's straw on the floor. Not too much snow. Git down an' carry that sick woman. I'll fetch the other one while you unharness them horses. Toss 'em some of this old straw. It ain't much fer 'em to eat, but it's all there is."

Roy Lee swung down, tying his horse to a rear buggy wheel. He came for Clara and took her from Lorena's arms, lifting her so easily that he hardly seemed to notice the weight. "Where you want me to put her, Rufe?"

"Over yonder in that back corner. Cover her up real good so she don't freeze."

"I'll see to that," Lorena said, starting down from her seat as Rufe came toward her.

"No, you won't," Rufe warned, pulling a long knife from some hiding place inside his coat, its blade glittering in the lantern glow. "You'll do jus' exactly what I say or I'll cut your throat so quick you won't have time to sneeze." He made a threatening pass with the tip of his knife just below her chin, causing her to draw back against a carriage wheel. "Walk in front of me an' go inside. Don't do nothin' stupid, missy. I'd hate like hell to have to carve you up 'fore we get to Memphis, but I damn sure will if'n you don't do what I say."

Cringing, keeping away from his knife tip, she crept past Rufe and started for the barn. He was right behind her. Lantern light spilled through an opening into a barn littered with straw and scattered piles of snow fallen from holes in the roof. She walked inside, watching Roy Lee place Clara on a pile of straw near one wall.

"See to them horses while I git a fire goin'," Rufe said as Roy Lee came toward him. He spoke to Lorena. "Sit down against that pole. You try an' make a run fer it an' I'll shoot you," he added, opening his coat to show a pistol strapped to his waist.

She walked over to a pole supporting the roof and sat down as he instructed, shivering from the cold—and fear. Rufe hung his lantern on a nail above her head, still holding his knife in a threatening way.

"I'm gonna build a fire," he said. "Remember what I told you. You run, an' I'll shoot." Sheathing his blade, he went to the rear of the barn gathering bits of rotted roof beams and any pieces of lumber he could find. Clearing a place in the old straw covering the floor, he made a pile of wood and struck a match to it.

A minute later, flames licked up the sides of dry logs at the center of the barn. Outside, Lorena could hear Roy Lee working with harness chains, yet she never took her eyes off Rufe, sensing she was in real danger now. Clasping her hands in front of her she trembled, waiting. Clara moaned softly, uttering a few words Lorena couldn't hear, although Clara's eyes remained closed in a fitful sleep. "May I attend to my sick friend?" she asked when Rufe heard Clara's voice.

"I reckon so, but don't be too long about it."

"I have some powders in my trunk."

Rufe pondered it. "I'll have Roy Lee fetch your trunk in as soon as he's done with them horses. Meanwhile, you can see what's makin' her so damn noisy—only I done warned you not to run off." He drew his revolver while squatting beside the flames, holding the weapon loosely in one hand.

She got up and hurried over to Clara, touching her face when she knelt beside her. Clara's eyes were slitted, and her cheek was somewhat cooler than before.

"Are the soldiers coming to take us home?" she asked faintly.

"No, Clara, dear. They aren't coming to help us. . . ."

It was useless to resist and yet she did, struggling to free her wrists while he bound them together with a piece of cord. He was so powerful, it only required a moment to tie her hands before he pushed her down on her back, sitting astraddle her stomach on a pile of straw. She could smell his stale breath and an odor far worse—an unwashed body in filthy clothes. But when he took his knife from a sheath tied to his belt she forgot all else and opened her mouth to scream.

He struck her with such force her mind was reeling. Stars flashed before her eyes. She tasted blood. Her head lolled to one side from the blow.

"Don't make a sound, missy, or I swear I'll cut your gizzard out. Lie real still. This ain't gonna hurt none if you'll stay quiet an' be still. You start to kick an' scream an' it'll be a hell of a lot worse on you. Me an' Roy Lee ain't had us a woman in quite a spell, so we're gonna use you. If'n you behave real nice, we won't kill you, but if you raise a bunch of hell or make too much fuss, I'll slice you open." He showed her his knife and then held it against her throat.

The weight of Rufe's body on her stomach made it difficult to breathe. "Please don't do this to me!" she gasped, swallowing blood oozing inside her left cheek. She saw Roy Lee standing a few yards away watching what was going on with a crooked smile on his face.

Rufe ignored her, bringing the knife tip to a top button of her dress. He cut it off quickly, then another button, until his hand seized a fistful of fabric, tearing the rest of her buttons open.

Now his blade cut through gathering strings holding the front of her bodice, making a popping sound.

"No! Please!" she cried.

He hit her again, slamming the back of his hand into her jaw too suddenly for her to turn away. A ringing in her ears started an instant after her head was jarred to one side.

"Shut up, bitch," Rufe growled. "I done told you what I'd do if you made a fuss."

He tore the front of her bodice open. She felt cold air on her naked breasts and stomach. The second blow to her head left her stunned, dizzy, too weakened to do more than kick feebly when he ripped off her dress and pulled her undergarments down to her ankles as rapidly as he could. With her hands bound behind her she was completely helpless, rolling back and forth on the straw before a tremendous weight fell on top of her. She saw Rufe's beard-stubbled face only a few inches from hers as a moving blur.

He forced her knees apart, spreading her thighs even as she summoned all her strength to prevent it. "Please, please!" she cried. "Don't do this to me!"

A sharp pain began in her groin—she knew what was happening and couldn't stop it. He entered her, increasing the pain. His weight threatened to crush her ribs. A rough hand clamped around her right breast, kneading it, squeezing, until it hurt so badly she screamed. Seconds later she felt his hardened member driving back and forth inside her. Salty tears streamed down her face to the straw beside her head.

She lay on her back staring at the lantern, senses dulled by events she would never be able to forget. Her genitals were raw and bleeding beneath a blanket Roy Lee had tossed over her after he had taken his turn on top of her. Rufe had cut the cord binding her arms when they were finished, allowing her the use of her hands. Yet as she lay there now, she was barely able to move at all. During the terror of their savage lust she had tried to remove

herself from it as much as she could, thinking of happy times in
Baltimore when her mind was able to shrink away from what they
were doing. Pain so intense it almost rendered her unconscious
made it difficult to think of anything else. There had been times
when she had wondered, as all young women surely do, what intercourse would feel like. Nothing in her wildest imagination
might have prepared her for the grim reality of it, or the indescribable pain.

And as she recovered from what they'd done, a blacker
thought nudged the edges of her consciousness. Would she have
a baby as a result? Her mother had never told her about these
things, only that some vague act she called intercourse between
husbands and wives produced a baby. It was a most private matter, she had said, a thing discussed between a wife and a husband.
Lorena's friends at school knew as little as she; however, there
were a few whispered guesses as to what transpired. No one
seemed to know for sure precisely how the coupling was accomplished.

She knew now. Gazing at the lantern, she wished she didn't
know—it had been the most painful and humiliating moment of
her life.

29

At dawn, Rufe made watery mush from melted snow and a handful of parched corn cooked in a small tin pan. In a smoke-blackened coffeepot he boiled tea leaves taken from a store in Nashville, providing them with a weak drink smelling more of tea than tasting of it. Lorena dressed with her back to both men, putting on a spare nursing gown before she took some of Rufe's corn soup to Clara. She found Clara awake, staring blankly at the roof over her head, but when Lorena sat beside her she turned her face.

"I saw what they did to you," Clara whispered. Tears began to brim in her eyes. "It was the awfulest thing I ever saw. I just knew they meant to kill you." She swallowed. "They intend to do the same thing to me, don't they?"

Lorena offered her a spoonful of mush, doing her best not to think about what happened or the dull pain inside her. "They may leave you alone because of your illness, Clara. Don't worry. If you pretend to be asleep most of the time maybe they won't bother you. Anyone can see you're quite ill."

"I'm feeling better. I woke up in a sweat this morning. I cried while they . . . did that to you. I couldn't watch after I knew what they were doing." She took a spoonful of food, lifting her head with Lorena's help. "Where are they taking us?"

Lorena took a deep breath. Clara would be terrified as soon as she learned the truth. "To a prison camp in Memphis. We were discovered by Major Canfield. General Hood ordered that we were to be sent to a Confederate prison named Camp Ford."

"Major Canfield overheard us talking that night, I just knew he did," Clara whimpered softly. "He suspected us all along."

There was no point in telling Clara she had given them away in her delirium. She continued to shed tears while doing as much as she could to cry quietly.

"It really doesn't matter now," Lorena told her, giving her another spoonful of mush.

Clara swallowed and asked in a tear-choked voice, "What will prison be like? Will it be dreadful? Will we be locked in cages like animals?"

"I don't know," Lorena whispered, when she heard a stirring near the fire. Glancing over her shoulder, she saw Rufe ambling across the barn in their direction.

"What kinda sickness has she got?" he asked, frowning when he examined the red spots on Clara's face.

"Typhus. Her case is very serious. Unless she is given the proper care she'll only get worse."

"I heard the two of you talkin'. She's feelin' better'n she did yesterday, ain't she?"

"Her fever has broken, however it may return. She needs to be in a hospital."

"That ain't what my orders say, missy. General Hood himself ordered the both of you to Camp Ford, an' that's damn sure where I aim to take you."

"She could die without medical attention," Lorena warned.

Rufe merely shrugged. "It don't make no difference to me if she does. The two of you are lower'n snakes, spyin' on us like you done. A lot of good men are gonna lose their lives because of you. Seems fair that you oughta die too, seein' as you were the cause of it." He examined Clara's face again. "Damned if she don't look like a spotted frog. She ain't near as pretty as you. Me an' Roy Lee was talkin' last night 'bout how pretty you was, an' how good it was to have a woman like you to buck jump on the way to Memphis." He grinned, revealing yellowed teeth in a shaft of pale morning light beaming through a hole in the roof, a hint of sun even though skies were still gray.

Lorena let anger get the best of her. "It was disgusting, what you did to me! I find both of you revolting, smelling like filthy pigs! You hurt me!"

Rufe took a quick step closer and backhanded her with enough force to knock her to the ground, spilling corn mush all over her clean gown and on Clara's quilt. Her cheek was stinging when she pushed herself up again, but this time she did not cry or cringe away from him.

"Hitting me won't change the way I feel!" she spat. "Does it satisfy you, hitting a defenseless woman?"

His grin faded. "It satisfies me when I poke you, lady. I hit you on account of what you said. You keep talkin' to me like that an' I'll hit you again until you shut your goddamn mouth."

"Don't hurt her anymore!" Clara cried, struggling to sit up on her bed of straw until she collapsed on her back, too weak to rise on her own.

Roy Lee came over. He had a narrow face with close-set eyes that appeared slightly crossed. "You two women better learn to keep your mouths shut or me an' Rufus will have to teach you how to act," he said, his voice high pitched, breaking. A shock of red hair fell below the brim of his hat. His right hand rested on the butt of a revolver holstered at his waist. He looked down at Lorena. "We're liable to poke you again right now unless you pay attention to what Sergeant Cain tells you." He gave Rufe a sideways look.

"Better listen to Roy Lee," Rufe said hoarsely, anger still burning in his eyes. Then he turned. "Harness them horses so's we can get movin' 'fore it starts snowin' again. Sooner we get to Memphis, the sooner we'll be rid of these bitches."

Roy Lee blinked. "We're gonna poke her again, ain't we?"

Rufe nodded slowly. "Can't see no reason not to, only I'll tie a rag over her mouth tonight if'n she don't learn to shut up callin' us pigs. Bustin' her skull don't seem to do no good."

"Maybe you ain't hittin' her hard enough," Roy Lee wondered as he smiled in lopsided fashion. "I'll go hitch up the team an' saddle my horse."

Lorena watched the soldier depart, remembering his cruelty last night, the way he smelled lying on top of her. She looked at Rufe, feeling degraded, humiliated, and deeply angry. There'd been times growing up when she wished she'd been a boy, especially when she was very young. Given the strength of a man for only a few moments now, she would seek revenge against these cowardly Confederates—or if she had a gun, she would make them pay dearly for what they'd done to her. A pistol required nothing more than resolve to equalize the difference in strength between a man and a woman—although she admitted to herself she'd never fired a gun or considered such an act, until now.

"Could be Roy Lee's right," Rufe said. "Maybe I ain't been hittin' you hard enough." He laughed and walked toward the fire.

Clara reached for Lorena's hand. "He has to be the meanest man in the whole world," she whispered. "I'm so frightened, and I'm so afraid of what prison will be like. They'll leave us to die there . . . we'll never see our families or home again. I won't ever see Willard, or my mother. Why, oh, why did we agree to come here, Lorena?"

Lorena touched her cheek where Rufe had struck her. "We came to serve our country because we were asked to volunteer by General Grant. I suppose it's my fault for agreeing to go. But we can't change what's happened, so we'll just have to make the best of it until things get better. Jonathan believes the war will be over soon, and then we'll be let out of prison, I'm sure. Until then we have to be strong and pray for an end to this fighting. God will surely answer our prayers if we pray earnestly."

Clara squeezed her palm. "I will pray fervently for this to stop." A noise near the fire silenced her when Rufe smothered the flames and began packing his gear.

Again, Lorena thought about how things might have changed if she'd had a pistol. Could she have found the courage to pull a trigger? Was she capable of killing someone even for the best of reasons? The question remained unanswered for now, but in the back of her mind she had begun to believe she might be able to do it—she was certainly angry enough. She wondered what it would feel like to have a gun go off in her hands, to know a bullet she fired had taken someone's life, even if it were a man like Rufus Cain who took advantage of his size and strength against women. Most of the night, while she tried to recover from what they had done to her, she dealt with her feelings, a mixture of hatred and revulsion, the wish for revenge matched against fear that Rufe and Roy Lee would force themselves on her again. Looming behind every emotion she had was the knowledge she would never be the same.

"Let's get movin'," Rufe said, inclining his head toward the opening. "Put them clothes back in that trunk an' help the sick woman outside. If she's too sick to walk, I'll have Roy Lee carry her."

"I think I can manage," Clara said to Lorena in a very soft voice, "if you'll let me hold on to your arm. I don't want that evil man touching me."

"I'll help you up. Put your arm around my waist."

30

Chief of Staff John Rawlins sat up in bed when he heard the persistent rapping on his front door. He swung his legs off a four-poster bed quietly so as not to awaken his slumbering wife and put on a robe and slippers. Treading down a narrow stairway in total darkness, he lit a candle on a table near the doorway to see who was outside. As a precaution he took a Navy Colt pistol from a drawer and tucked it into a pocket of his robe before he unlocked the door—Washington had its share of criminals who had no qualms about robbing houses in the middle of the night in the very shadow of the Capitol itself.

"Who's there?" he asked, reaching for the lock, fully awake now and wary after seeing the time on his mantlepiece clock in the candlelight. Who would come calling at a quarter past four o'clock in the morning?

"Lieutenant Bigsby, sir. I have a telegram marked urgent."

Rawlins open his door. "Urgent? Is it from General Grant?"

A uniformed soldier handed him a folded paper. "No, sir, I

was told it came from General Thomas in Kentucky."

Rawlins frowned. "Thomas should be in Tennessee." He broke a wax seal with his thumb and held the candle closer. For a few moments his eyes scanned the page. "Praise the Lord and Pap!" he exclaimed. "Pap has taken Nashville, capturing Hood's army in a single day. May the saints be praised, as well." He looked up at Bigsby. "Summon a carriage for me. I must get a wire off to our commander in Petersburg and inform the President immediately. A decisive blow has been struck for the Union. Hood's troublesome Texans have been smashed. This is a mortal wound to Jeff Davis and the Confederacy."

"Sir, we've just been informed all telegraph lines are cut between Washington and Petersburg. A courier will be necessary in order to reach General Grant."

Rawlins showed his impatience. "Damn the delay! I want him to know about this at once." He abruptly softened his tone with Bigsby, mindful that his aide was a very thorough soldier who paid close attention to small details. "Get me a carriage while I dress to go to the office. I'll prepare a dispatch. Find the quickest way to send it by any means available, Lieutenant. Find out when the President can see me on a matter of utmost importance. I'm quite sure he will greet this news with enthusiasm. Hood was a difficult adversary. Having him removed from the field of battle is a giant step toward ending this war. I'll ask that Pap Thomas be commended."

Bigsby saluted and turned on his heel, hurrying down snow-covered stone steps to mount his horse. Rawlins closed his front door and put the telegram aside before starting back up the stairs to shave and dress. He smiled to himself. John Bell Hood had apparently been handed a sound thrashing by the Army of the Cumberland, a military coup that would make headlines all across the country, both North and South. With an iron grip on Petersburg and Sherman's march to the sea, the end was in sight. Lee couldn't withstand an endless bombardment while cut off from supply lines. The Confederacy would surely fall in a matter of weeks.

Remembering a final line from General Thomas, Rawlins gave a soft chuckle and said, "It will be a merry Christmas indeed when Ulysses hears about this." He climbed the stairs and went to his clothes cabinet for a uniform.

President Lincoln was having breakfast. White House staffers knew he rose early, before dawn, thus the kitchen prepared food at five o'clock and kept it warm until he asked for a tray in his office. When Rawlins was shown in, the President looked up from the previous day's *New York Tribune* while chewing a bite of toasted bread with butter and jam.

"Good morning, John. I hope you bring good tidings. Only yesterday Horace Greeley, a man who calls himself a Republican, continued to feed the wolves bits of my carcass. At the beginning of this war he wrote the nation's war cry should be: Forward to Richmond. Now he writes, 'Our bleeding, bankrupt, almost dying country longs for peace, shudders at the prospect of any further wholesale devastation, or new rivers of human blood.' The press as well as the Congress will not be satisfied until they have my head."

Rawlins paused in front of Lincoln's desk, waiting for the offer of a chair. The President seemed distracted, his pallor that of a tired, sick man. "I do indeed have good news, Mr. President. Nashville has fallen. Hood's army has been captured in a single day. General Thomas reports an unconditional surrender. Hood fled the city before Pap could encircle it, but he is said to be on his way to Texas with plans to resign. The Texas brigades are now prisoners of war bound for Indiana. Even though it was a short battle, Confederate casualties are said to be very high."

Lincoln let out an audible sigh, putting down his coffee cup and newspaper. "On the one hand I feel relief, however my legions of critics will doubtlessly claim we have beaten an army unfit to fight, merely to add to growing piles of corpses littering fields where corn and cotton used to grow. Our victories are certain to be tailored by an unfriendly press to make me the warmonger they say I am. I remain convinced our only reasonable course is to press for outright victory so this country can be reunited. We shall never be able to silence those who keep a tally of bodies. Send my heartiest congratulations to General Thomas. Ask that he show the greatest concern for his prisoners' welfare. If I can win the forbearance of my countrymen through this winter, perhaps General Grant can end it in the spring."

"We have Lee surrounded at Petersburg," Rawlins reminded him, a bit surprised at Lincoln's mild reaction that one of the South's most successful military leaders had been neutralized. "With a concentrated effort against Lee, and Sherman's unmolested march through Georgia, the rebellion must collapse quickly. They have no food in Virginia, no armories. Even the barest essentials are cut off. Our blockade holds, preventing European profitmakers or Confederate sympathizers from sending them any relief by sea. We are strangling them. When Lee can be shelled into submission by ceaseless mortar fire, Jefferson Davis will have no choice but to concede total defeat."

Lincoln's face showed he had doubts. "So many times in the past I've had the same assurances. Let us hope and pray we have finally come to a turning point." He drummed his fingers absently on his desktop.

"We admit we underestimated them in the beginning, but our superior numbers and firepower have taken a steady toll. They are down to their last bread crumbs and grains of gunpowder. It quite simply cannot last any longer."

The President appeared to ignore his remarks. "Do we have a report of civilian casualties at Nashville? My numerous critics will seize upon this as evidence of my inhumanity if casualties among the citizenry are high."

"No report as yet," Rawlins replied, wondering himself about it. A high civilian death loss would only add grist to Democratic mills in Congress.

"Let us pray they are low," Lincoln said quietly. "At the outbreak of this civil revolt I was criticized for appointing inept military leaders who were indecisive, avoiding engagements, men who hesitated when a strike was called for. George McClellan was too cautious, everyone agreed. Now Ulysses Grant is dubbed a butcher for winning battles. The press is preoccupied with grisly statistics, counting bodies, as though wars should be won without mortality. The very same hounds that bayed when we were hesitant are howling over Grant's military successes if we lose a single soldier. There is no middle ground."

"If Lee can't be shelled out of Petersburg, he will soon find himself starved out. We have a net over him from which he cannot escape. When Lee learns of Hood's defeat, he may be motivated to surrender. Only one Confederate army of any size remains in the field to rescue him with his back against the wall. As soon as we locate Jubal Early, Lee's hopes will be lost."

Lincoln rubbed his chin thoughtfully. "My first term taught me never to indulge in optimism. We shall see if Robert Lee is as convinced as we are of the hopelessness of his situation when he is informed of our victory in Tennessee. I rather doubt it. Lee may be cornered, but he's not yet entirely caught. I wouldn't be at all surprised to learn he sprouted wings to escape our clutches yet another time."

Rawlins glanced at a clock ticking on a bookshelf behind the President's desk. The ticking grew louder, or so it seemed then, when Lincoln turned to an office window in silence.

31

Clara had begun to cough violently, the first warning signs of developing pneumonia. As the carriage bumped and swayed over rough, backcountry roads, her condition appeared to worsen when a flush returned to her skin. Within a few hours she was coughing and shivering. Lorena tried to make her comfortable and keep her as warm as possible. She would never forget how David Cobb had died from pneumonia when it struck him in concert with typhus. She wouldn't consider the possibility Clara might die in her arms—somehow her friend would survive, she told herself again and again.

And there were other things she wanted to banish from her mind today if she could—a second night on the road to Memphis, this time on an empty stretch of winding lane beside a shallow stream hidden in a snowy pine forest where Rufus and Roy Lee tore off her undergarments and took her savagely on the buggy seat. Trembling with cold and fear, last night she had not resisted even though the pain was almost unbearable, suffering their cruel lust without so much as a whimper until they left her to boil tea and fry fatback over a small fire. Not long afterward Clara started to cough, requiring Lorena's full attention to keep her tightly wrapped in her quilt. Although Lorena had wept silently later that night while Rufe was asleep as Roy Lee stood guard near their horses, she did so only a short time and then dried her eyes. But as their third day of travel wore on, she thought less of what they'd done to her, finding it too painful to contemplate for more than a moment or two, instead worrying more and more about Clara's steadily worsening condition.

She also wondered about Jonathan, praying he'd survived the Union attack on Nashville. Had the battle already been fought? She longed for him, for the feel of his arms around her, and the tenderness of his kiss. But in her heart she was sure she would never know those sweet pleasures again, even if he came through the attack unscathed. She had deceived him, betrayed him, and when he stalked out of Clara's room that night, she had known he would never feel the same way toward her again.

At midafternoon, under skies still gray with a possibility of snow, Rufe drove the buggy along the crest of a narrow ridge overlooking a broad river valley. In the distance Lorena saw a few buildings on the riverbank where a ferry loaded with men and horses crossed a sluggish expanse of silvery water. When Rufe saw the flat-bottomed barge, he hauled back on his reins to examine men aboard.

"Goddamn bluebelly soldiers!" he exclaimed, wheeling around to warn Roy Lee. "Let's git off this high ground quick!" With a vicious slap of the reins, he drove his team out of the ruts into tangles of brush covered with snow. Roy Lee hurried his horse out of sight and swung down, scrambling back across the road to a lone pine tree, carrying a pair of field glasses.

For a time, Roy Lee studied the scene below. Rufe waited in silence on the carriage seat, fidgeting back and forth, gnarled hands fisted around his reins. Moments later Roy Lee backed away from the tree cautiously before trotting back to his horse.

"Big bunch of Yanks crossin' the Tennessee River," he said,

sounding worried. "That's liable to mean we can't git through to Memphis. What the hell are we gonna do with these women? This damn contraption you're drivin' is slowin' us down so we're sure to be caught if they make a sweep this side of the river."

Rufe chewed his lip. He glanced over his shoulder at Lorena and Clara. "Damned if I know. Our orders say we's supposed to take the bitches to Camp Ford, unless . . ."

Clara coughed in her sleep. Lorena patted her shoulder.

Roy Lee frowned. "The spotted gal is mighty sick. We can say she up an' died, I reckon. If we toss her behind these-here bushes an' unharness the team, you can ride one horse, and we'll tie the pretty one on the other nag."

"You can't do that!" Lorena shouted. "She has pneumonia! She'll die left out in this miserable cold! That would be the same as killing her!"

Rufe gave her a nod. "I bet you got real good marks in a schoolhouse, missy, figurin' that out all by yourself. There wasn't supposed to be no Yanks between here'n Memphis, only now that there is, we got to make a change in plans. This buggy is too damn slow for outrunnin' bluebellies. We got but three horses. Means somebody gits left behind, an' it sure as hell ain't gonna be me or Roy Lee."

"Then you might as well kill us both," Lorena said, her voice calm, pulling Clara close. She said it before she truly thought about what dying would be like, yet she knew she could never leave Clara to die alone in a snowbank. Let them kill me, she thought, suddenly resigned to it. "I would prefer death to leaving Clara by herself."

Roy Lee questioned Rufe with a look.

"That can be arranged, missy," Rufe growled, dropping his reins on the splashboard to reach for his knife. He showed her the wicked blade, turning it to and fro, twisting it the way he might if it were buried in her heart.

"I'm not afraid of you," she said, gripping Clara's quilt with all her might. "Kill me if you wish, but I won't leave her side."

A smoky haze darkened Rufe's eyes. "I can make you wish

you was dead, lady. I know how to hurt you real bad so's you'll be beggin' me to stop."

Somewhere inside her, Lorena felt her fear slip away until it was as if a door had closed, blocking it from her mind. "It's too late for that," she told him. "I already wish I was dead. After what you did to me I no longer care about living. So go ahead, if you must—kill us both. I'd rather die than suffer another night of your disgusting animal behavior. Neither of you can be called men. Pigs have a better smell and better manners—"

He reached across the seat and struck her. She reeled backward, falling sideways when the buggy seat kept her from toppling to the ground between rear carriage wheels. Almost unconscious, she heard a soft moan, her own voice.

A hand seized the front of her coat. A blur moved near her face.

"We ain't got time for that now, Rufe," Roy Lee said. "Them Yanks is likely plumb across the river by now."

Lorena heard noises, the rattling of harness chain. She did all she could to sit up, failing at it, collapsing on her side as soon as she made the initial effort. But even in a badly weakened, half-conscious state, she reached instinctively for Clara to pull her friend close. She cried out feebly when she found no one was there beside her. Forcing her eyelids open, she caught a hazy glimpse of someone carrying a blanketed form into the brush.

Days and nights jumbled together, becoming indistinguishable while slumped on the bare back of a moving horse, rocking with a gait that chafed her inner legs raw until they bled—she felt wetness there, dull pain where her thighs rubbed the horse's sides. Her feet were tied together underneath the rawboned bay's belly. Only at night was she released from her bonds, and that was when they used her, crushing her with their weight, pinching or biting her breasts, moving inside her until their seed was spent. If she cried, Rufe slapped her; at other times when she pleaded with him to go back for Clara, he hit her with a closed fist. Her face was badly swollen where his blows had landed—both of her eyes were puffy and partially closed. She existed in a world of pain, never quite sure where she was or where she was going. Every now and then she was fully conscious long enough to see her surroundings as Rufe led her horse through dark forests or across open expanses. On two occasions she remembered an oily rag being tied over her mouth when they neared small towns, but even then Rufe was careful to lead them wide of these settlements as though he meant to avoid contact with anyone wherever he could. Few travelers were on the road, sometimes a handful of Confederate deserters trudging westward carrying their meager belongings. Rufe always asked about Yankees . . . had they seen any patrols or heard about a Union invasion from the west crossing the Tennessee River? Once she heard him ask about conditions in Arkansas. No one seemed to know. One weary foot soldier told Rufe he'd heard Yankees controlled every mile of the Mississippi River now; then he asked about the woman with them, why she was bound and gagged. Rufe merely said, "She's a prisoner, a Yank spy," before he urged his horse forward again.

And with every mile they traveled she despaired over what they'd done to Clara, abandoning her in the snow like she was nothing more than unwanted baggage. She imagined Clara's terror of awakening from her fevered sleep to find herself alone in the middle of a snowdrift. Fever and pneumonia had probably claimed her life quickly in this terrible cold; or worse, she might have been there for days, suffering immeasurably before she died. How could anyone be so cruel, she wondered, leaving a sick girl to die of exposure like that? Rufe and Roy Lee were the kind of men this war was truly about, men the Union Army wanted to defeat to put an end to their ruthless disregard for human suffering—it had nothing to do with the color of skin or slavery.

If I could, I'd kill them myself, she thought. After what they did to Clara, pulling a trigger would be easy. Or so she told herself just then.

She looked down at her frozen hands. Was she really capable

of using a gun? Clinging to the bay's mane, she considered it as they rode deeper into a pine forest. But no matter how often she tried to envision what it would be like to shoot someone, even a man as loathsome as Rufe, she couldn't quite imagine it. Seeing what bullets had done to so many soldiers only made the idea more repugnant, seem more impossible done by her own hand. She simply was not able to do it, she believed.

Shuddering from the cold, she watched the bulge of a pistol underneath Rufe's coat, trying to convince herself that if she got her hands on his gun, she would find the courage to use it.

Threatening skies grew dark above them. Rufe glanced over his shoulder, speaking to Roy Lee. "We'd better find ourselves a place to spend the night. Looks like it's gonna snow to beat all hell afore long."

"We can poke the woman again 'til the storm's over. Sure do wish we had us some whiskey to go along with it."

Lorena closed her eyes, steeling herself for another violation of her body. While it would not matter to them, she wouldn't allow either man to enter her mind, her thoughts. She willed herself to dream of Jonathan until they finished with her, and until then she would remember what it was like to be caressed by someone who once loved her, to be kissed so gently and passionately the way he had before learning of her treachery.

32

Her hands and feet were tied. She listened to the wind as it howled around eaves and between cracks in log walls of a farmhouse, abandoned by a Confederate widow and her two children when her husband didn't come home from Gettysburg. Flames crackled in a crumbling fireplace while Rufe and Roy Lee slept. They'd been given directions to a settlement called Boles Hollow by a storekeeper who sold Roy Lee a pint of home-brewed whiskey after telling him about Widow Jones's empty cabin. They'd been told Boles Hollow was east of Memphis near the Mississippi state line, and that an outnumbered Confederate force at Memphis had pulled out just ahead of Union troops, retreating westward into Arkansas. But when the storekeeper had related that a detachment of Confederate cavalrymen had passed through describing the recent fall of Nashville, Rufe suddenly became agitated over this bit of bad news.

"What'll we do?" Roy Lee had asked. "Where'll we go?"

"I ain't got the foggiest notion," Rufe had replied, swinging up on his sore-footed harness horse. "Head home for Texas, I reckon, if we can git there without runnin' into more Yanks." He had given their surroundings a nervous glance, like he expected to see the arrival of Union soldiers at any moment.

They'd ridden south from Boles Hollow to this farm only a few minutes ahead of the storm. Wind-driven sleet pattered on wood shingles and log walls while Rufe and Roy Lee had built a fire and drank whiskey. Soon their drinking had made them surly. Lorena had sat near the hearth bound hand and foot, listening to them talk in angry voices, dreading what might come later if more whiskey made Rufe turn mean.

"I reckon that means our whole outfit got took prisoner," Roy Lee had said, tipping the pint back for a swallow. "Damn it all! A bunch of mighty brave ol' boys from Texas are headed fer a goddamn Yankee prison."

"Or killed deader'n pig shit," Rufe had suggested, scowling at a crack in one wall where cold wind whistled through. "They could most all be dead by now. Gen'l Hood wasn't never inclined toward givin' up on a fight. Looks like we ain't got no brigades to go back to. Appears this-here war is over for us."

"I was gettin' sick of soldierin', anyways, Rufe. They hardly gave us nothin' much to eat besides peas. . . ."

Rufe had taken the bottle, drinking deeply, smacking his lips as he slowly turned his attention to Lorena. "If this bitch hadn't told them bluebellies right where we was, we wouldn't be in this fix. Maybe we oughta cut her throat tonight so we'll be finished with her. We could say she tried to escape."

Roy Lee had watched Lorena a moment with his perpetually canted eyes. "I say we poke her some more afore we do that. You an' me ain't never poked no woman pretty as her in all our lives. Ain't no good reason to kill her jus' yet, is there?"

"She's a bother. Besides, she can tell somebody what we did to that other one, the one with them fever spots. She could say we dumped her friend in them bushes."

"Nobody'd believe her over us," Roy Lee had said, after taking another drink. "We'll swear she's lyin'."

"It'd be smarter to kill her. Dead men don't tell no tales. Same goes for women."

"We're gonna poke her first, ain't we?"

Rufe had sighed, gazing at Lorena. "I reckon. She ain't near as pretty as she was, not with her face all swelled up like that. Changes her looks some."

"You hit her a right-smart number of times, Rufe. But afore you made her face puff up she was real pretty to look at. Prettiest damn female I ever set eyes on, might' near."

Rufe had come slowly to his feet, taking the bottle, letting a generous swallow of whiskey slide down his throat. "I hit her on account of her bein' a goddamn spy who sold us out to them Yanks an' because she won't shut up when I tell her to. May as well poke her again. I can't figure out much else she's good for, an' we can't take her to Memphis like our orders said. You can go first this time if'n you want."

They had come for her then, and she hadn't resisted. She had found herself strangely detached from the pain of it this time, suffering their foul odors and rough hands, the press of their bodies, the stabbing entry into her groin, the sticky wetness they left inside her. Now, as she watched them slumbering in front of the fireplace, remembering what Rufe said about dead women telling no tales, she began to work her fingers into the knots binding her wrists. Perhaps because of the whiskey Roy Lee had been careless with her ropes tonight, tying them more loosely. If she could free her hands, she might escape on one of the horses before they woke up.

Unable to see the knots behind her back, she worked blind, slowly, twisting her wrists, using a fingernail to pick strands from the rope until it was frayed. A moment later she pulled a strand through a loop and when she felt the knot relax, a wave of excitement raced through her. Half a minute more and her wrists were free. Quietly, she untied the rope around the tops of her high-button shoes and let it fall to the packed sod floor.

She eyed Rufe's pistol lying beside him, only a few inches from his hand. If she had his gun she stood a far better chance of getting away should either man be awakened by a noise when she crept outside and rode off on one of the horses. Her heart was like a drum beating inside her—did she have the courage to get close enough to Rufe to take his pistol? Would sounds from the storm keep them from hearing her until she had the gun and made it outside to a horse?

Rocking forward to her hands and knees, she crawled toward Rufe with her heart in her throat, moving so slowly it seemed she made no progress at all. But as she neared him she heard snoring above howling winds around the house, and his stale smell filled her nostrils. She saw his face, his mouth slackened by slumber, allowing spittle to run from his lips to the blanket underneath him. Fear gripped her. She held her breath and inched onward until she could reach his revolver. Glancing over to Roy Lee for only an instant, making sure he was asleep, her hand went to the wooden pistol grip and at that moment her heart stood still.

The gun was much heavier than she had imagined it would be when she picked it up, examining it in soft light from the fireplace. Her forefinger curled around its trigger. She found the iron icy cold. Brass firing caps gleamed at one end of the cylinder—she smelled oil and a vaguely acrid scent she couldn't identify, making her nostrils burn. All she knew about pistols came from observation during the Baltimore draft riots, when she had seen a man pull back the hammer on a revolver to fire over his head. He'd pulled the trigger afterward and his gun went off, startling her with its loud report.

Backing cautiously away from Rufe, she sat back on her haunches, placing both thumbs on the hammer. Her hands shook. With her full attention on Rufe's gun she almost failed to see a movement, a stirring beneath blankets where Roy Lee slept.

A pair of dark eyes fluttered open, reflecting light from the fireplace. Roy Lee stared at her blankly for a few seconds as though he couldn't quite comprehend what he saw. Lorena drew in a sharp breath, swinging the gun barrel toward Roy Lee as she pulled the hammer back until it clicked into place. Her hands trembled so violently it was impossible to aim the revolver even at a distance of only a few feet. He started to sit up and she knew the time had come to act—but could she pull the trigger? Thoughts came in a rush, so confusing that they were only meaningless images, like shadows in a terrible nightmare where some fiendish creature was chasing her through dark caverns. She'd never felt so completely alone or so frightened.

Roy Lee tossed his blankets aside. "Put that gun down, you crazy bitch!" he snarled, reaching for the revolver too quickly for her to back away.

She wasn't thinking when her finger pulled the trigger. It was simply a reaction as Roy Lee sprang toward her. She heard a click—the hammer fell—accompanied by a booming explosion. In the same instant she saw a flash of bright light. There was a cracking sound, like splitting timber. Off balance on the balls of her feet, the gun slammed into her palm, driving her backward. She toppled over onto her side, jarred when her shoulder landed on frozen earth. But even as she fell she kept her eyes on Roy Lee and the strange transformation taking place in the middle of his forehead. The skin above his eyes appeared to pucker. Something flew from the back of his skull, a twist of matted hair spiraling away from his head. He was midway through a lunge for the pistol when all at once he stopped, briefly suspended above the ground until he slumped to the floor, groaning, with a fist-sized hole in the top of his scalp, blood streaming down his neck and cheeks.

Rufe bolted up from his bedroll, turning, his eyes bulging. He saw Lorena, and Roy Lee lying facedown on the sod as a cloud of gun smoke wafted in lazy curls toward the ceiling. Whirling over in a crouch, Rufe's muscles bunched as he got set to leap for her.

Lorena, momentarily paralyzed by fear, realized what Rufe was about to do. Lying on her back, shaking, hot tears from the sting of burned gunpowder blurring her vision, she pulled the hammer back with her thumbs again and did her best to steady her aim. She caught a momentary glimpse of the steely gleam of a knife blade, and when she did she let out an involuntary scream as it flashed toward her. A moving shadow came between her and the flames, blocking out light. With her scream dying in her throat, she jerked the trigger.

A blast came, louder than before, and a finger of white light shot out for fractions of a second before Rufe landed on her, forcing air from her lungs. The pistol was trapped between them when he fell atop her ribs and stomach. A searing pain jolted her left shoulder, a hurting so intense, her body went rigid. She screamed again, this time in agony, not fright, before her limbs and spine went slack.

"You rotten whore!" Rufe cried, his features pinched into a pained grimace.

She tried to twist her body so she could breathe, finding him much too heavy to move. He stared down at her, air whispering from his nose and mouth in rapid bursts.

"I knew I shoulda . . . killed you," he gasped.

Something warm spread over Lorena's stomach where the pistol was caught between them. The look in Rufe's eyes was one of pure hatred—shuttered eyelids partially covering a fiery glow. Then a gurgling sound came from his throat. Tiny bubbles of pink and white foam formed on his lips, dribbling down his chin into his beard. His chest expanded and he coughed wetly, sending a shower of spittle over her face.

Again she tried desperately to throw him off of her, though her hands were pinned beneath him still clutching the gun and she found she could not budge him at all. The effort brought renewed waves of pain shooting through her left arm. When she turned her head, she saw his knife buried in the flesh of her shoulder with his fist tightly wrapped around the handle.

Suddenly Rufe's head fell onto her chest. His hand relaxed on the knife. Only then was she able to roll him to one side so her arms and legs were free. He groaned when she pushed him away just enough to wriggle backward. A dark stain covered his shirtfront, and in the firelight she could make out a bullet hole below his breastbone.

Her shoulder ached so fiercely that she feared she was about to lose consciousness. "I have to pull it out!" she sobbed, reaching for the knife handle, gritting her teeth, dizzied by white-hot pains racing down her arm. Closing her eyes, bracing herself for what she had to do, she jerked the blade free and fell back on the floor, shrieking, sucking cold air through her open mouth as rapidly as she could when she could stop screaming.

For a moment she stared at the ceiling, fighting off a swell of nausea, waiting for the pain to subside. She felt the weight of Rufe's gun on her belly. Panting, doing everything she could to remain conscious, she raised her head to see Rufe sprawled on his back near her feet. He was still breathing—his chest rose and fell irregularly, lungs making a rattling sound. A pool of blood around him grew larger as she watched it trickle down his side. "Thank God," she whispered softly, closing her eyes for a second or two, thinking how close she'd come to dying.

Outside, a gust of wind whined around a corner of the house. Bits of ice pattered noisily against mud-chinked logs and shingles above her head. She reached for her left shoulder, touching a tear in her coat sleeve and dress very gently, then a gash in her skin oozing blood down her arm. "I've got to bandage it," she said, when her mind began to clear. She could bleed to death unless she was able to stop the blood. But as she tried to use her injured arm to help her sit up she found it was too painful, forcing her to manage with one elbow and hand.

Gazing across the room, she saw Roy Lee motionless near the fireplace. I killed him, she thought dully. Looking at Rufe, she saw he was gutshot. He would probably suffer a slow and painful death from internal bleeding. "I had to do it," she told herself quietly, shivering now, suddenly very cold. Listening to ice and wind batter the cabin she added, "I didn't have a choice."

She looked down at the pistol. It had most likely saved her life. Her ears were still ringing from its mighty roar, and there was an odor of gunpowder hanging heavily in the air. Last of all, she glanced down at the knife, its long blade coated with blood, her blood. In a matter of seconds she'd killed two men and suffered a serious wound herself, all before she'd had time to think.

For reasons she couldn't fathom then, she thought of Clara, of her friend dying alone in the snow. Perhaps it was justification for what she'd done herself, remembering how heartlessly a sick girl had been abandoned by these two Confederates, left to die a miserable death. "An eye for an eye," she said, recalling scripture her father frequently quoted.

The only material she had for a bandage was her skirt. She picked up Rufe's knife, wincing when movement increased pain in her damaged shoulder, to cut a strip of cloth from her hem. When the blade ripped through her dress the sound made her shudder.

Struggling to her feet, swaying with dizziness, she went to the fire, clutching her bad arm to her side. She knelt near the flames and carefully shed her coat to wrap the strip of cloth around her wound. The sleeve of her dress was soaked with blood, and Lorena suddenly felt faint, light-headed. She sat down and collected herself, breathing slowly, deeply, tying a knot in her bandage as best she could using her teeth and one hand.

When the knot was tied, she rested a moment before draping her coat over her shoulders. Shivering, she watched the fire's red embers as her pain subsided, knowing she faced a difficult ordeal—mounting a horse, then riding through this storm to look for someone who might help her. After losing so much blood she was weak. It would take all the strength she had to sit a horse in such awful weather. And she had to be alert enough to avoid Confederate soldiers while looking for a Union Army camp before she froze to death. The storekeeper at Boles Hollow said Memphis was in Union hands now, but how far away was Memphis? She'd eaten so little since they'd left Nashville, her physical condition was poor to begin with and suffering a wound only made her weaker.

"There's no other choice but to ride for Memphis," she said

to herself, hearing wind and sleet strike the cabin with renewed fury.

Because of the storm she failed to hear the scrape of a foot behind her, or notice a shadow moving closer to her back.

33

A sixth sense warned her of danger and she glanced over her shoulder. Rufe lunged, hands reaching for her like huge, hairy claws. His fingers found her throat before the force of his jump knocked her forward into one side of the hearth. Her head struck fireplace stones, slammed against them by the weight of his body. His fingernails dug into the soft flesh of her neck as she began to fall to the floor, momentarily stunned by the blow to her skull. She reached for the iron grip blocking off her windpipe to pry it loose when suddenly a burst of red sparks flew past her face.

A blood-curdling scream ended Rufe's powerful grasp on her throat. She had fallen to one side, landing on her injured shoulder when Rufe's dive propelled him over her back face first into a bed of hot coals and crackling flames inside the hearth. His head was completely engulfed by fire. His feet thrashed wildly while he pawed at his face with his hands, trying to pull back from the inferno surrounding him. He scrambled backward from the hearth with his hair aflame, screaming at the top of his lungs, slapping his face when fire blazed in his beard. His shirtsleeves erupted like fiery torches. Rocking to and fro on his knees, pawing frantically at his burning cheeks with flaming arms, he roared like a mighty lion and then slumped over onto his back making strangling sounds, legs pumping as though he were trying to run.

The scent of scorched hair and flesh assailed Lorena's nostrils. She lay on her side stunned, watching the grisly scene in horror, unable to move or think clearly after striking her head against mortared rock. As she looked at Rufe's flaming beard and shirtsleeves, his legs stilled, then his feet began to twitch with death throes. The choking noises he made ended, trailing off to a whisper, then silence. A moment later his boots quivered one last time; then his chest stopped moving.

Rising painfully off her shoulder to a sitting position, she reached for a knot swelling on her scalp, finding it impossible to stop staring at Rufe's body or control the icy fear making her arms and legs quake. The fire in his hair and beard sizzled and burned out, leaving his face a blackened mask of scarred flesh. Taking a deep breath, she turned away from the smoking corpse in order to calm herself. This time she was certain Rufe was dead.

She covered her face with her hands, for the moment ignoring sharp pains in her shoulder. "Dear God," she sighed, trembling, fighting back a rush of memories. So much had happened to test her willpower, her strength. Somehow she'd managed to stay alive through all of it. All she had wanted in the beginning was a career in nursing, believing that by doing so she might help others less fortunate. "It wasn't worth it," she said above a howling wind swirling around the cabin. She took her hands from her eyes, looking across a darkened room at two corpses. "If we had only known what was in store for us. . . ." She thought again of what Rufe and Roy Lee had done to Clara, the brutality of abandoning her to die the way they did. Her cheeks hardened. "An eye for an eye," she whispered again, this time with a hint of anger.

She still faced a long ride through a terrible storm to find help, but she believed she could manage it somehow. She was free now, free to look for Jonathan—if he was still alive. All she could do was ask that he forgive her for what she'd done, hoping for his understanding for a decision she made, convinced it was her duty to her country. If she could find him. If there was no grave at Nashville with a marker bearing the name Jonathan Cross.

Three days before Christmas, suffering mildly frostbitten hands and toes and a swollen shoulder, Lorena rode a starving bay gelding to the foggy banks of a river where she happened upon a Union patrol. She had found the Mississippi quite by accident, after riding blindly in aimless circles through an ice storm, then thick fog, missing Memphis by more than ten miles. She collapsed in the arms of Lieutenant Donald Marks from the Army of the Ohio the moment he helped her down from her horse.

34

John Rawlins joined General Grant for an inspection tour of Petersburg reluctantly, not wanting to see too closely how sorely men suffered here. Conditions along the front were deplorable yet clearly inescapable. Lee had to be driven from his trenches—and the only way to accomplish this was to dig in and fight. Reports as to Confederate troop strength and positioning were skimpy, although there was agreement from every source that Lee's men were hungry, sick, short on ammunition, deserting at an alarming rate. Some intelligence said Lee had fewer than thirty-five thousand men, spread out in ever expanding trenches until defending soldiers stood fifteen feet apart near their outermost flanks. If this were true, a determined charge might break through Confederate lines, yet no one seemed quite sure where Lee's men were spread thinnest or where Rebel gun batteries were being moved every few days. Grant was content to wait it out until some visible weak spot showed up.

A cold rain fell on Rawlins and Grant as they rode slowly

through a sea of mud with a cavalry escort to reach command post. Rawlins shivered in his greatcoat every time crisp February winds swept across eastern Virginia's coastal plain. Networked as far as the eye could see, a maze of deep trenches crisscrossed uneven battle lines. Petersburg was under full assault, and burrowing continued to the north and south to prevent flanking maneuvers. But in this labyrinth of ditches where soldiers lived, fighting men had been reduced to an existence only certain farm animals could survive. Mud was two-feet deep in all but a few places. Breastworks bristling with fraises sheltered men from enemy rifles and mortar rounds—the sharpened stakes were designed to prevent a direct assault by infantry. After months of steady combat, hundreds of decomposing bodies lay between Union and Confederate lines where the risk of a rifle ball made removing corpses too great. Swarms of rats fed on the dead daily until most were merely grinning skeletons and scattered bones. From the bottom of muddy trenches came the sound of thousands of soldiers coughing while others made softer sounds— cries of misery and loneliness.

Grant pointed to an earthen pit where stacks of tree trunks kept piles of wet dirt from sliding into the trenches. "This is the creation of Colonel Washington Roebling!" he shouted, to be heard above echoing coughs and the drum of steady rain. "He has dubbed it Fort Sedgwick. Those ramparts have walkways to keep the soldiers' boots dry."

Rawlins didn't see how anything could be kept dry in such a downpour. "A splendid idea," he said without feeling, hunching his shoulders against a sharp gust of wind. Grant had insisted he take a tour of Union lines in Virginia, to be able to enlighten the President with a firsthand report of field conditions when he got back to Washington. As soon as a break came in the weather, Grant planned an all-out bombardment day and night with his heaviest artillery. Huge mortars were now in place that could hurl shells into the heart of Lee's positions up and down the front. One Pennsylvania soldier described these thirteen-inch field guns as "volcanos mounted on railroad cars spitting a ball of red lava larger than a small horse."

Near the perimeter of Fort Sedgwick, Grant signaled a halt to study what lay beyond it. Partly obscured by gray rain were more miles of muddy ditches filled with sodden riflemen. Rawlins thought it unlikely that half these men could muster enough dry powder to fire a single shot. Months earlier, fighting here had occurred with fixed bayonets and rifle butts until Grant and Lee had virtually crippled each other into a stalemate. Neither side would give an inch.

"I'm quite sure I've seen enough to give the President all he needs to know," Rawlins said, hopeful his tour was at an end.

Grant pointed north. "He'll want to hear about our batteries closer to Richmond. When Lee's wall breaks, we'll be in the Confederate capital before Jeff Davis can pack his valise."

"I hope this lousy weather ends soon."

The general nodded thoughtfully. "All of Virginia is unfit for habitation in winter, John. Most of it is swampland. Hardly worth fighting for unless some other merits can be discovered. I never liked living near the coast. Sticking mud when it rains and hot as hell in summer. I wish Lee had picked a more suitable place for this encounter. A place where it's dry and warm."

Rawlins thought about how dry and warm his office would be at this moment. One of the benefits of rank was less field duty. Grant was different . . . he liked it outdoors, and when he couldn't be in the field, as a substitute he continually opened his office windows no matter how inclement the weather. "I'm soaked to the skin," Rawlins protested.

Grant ignored him, spurring his horse forward into a marshy spot where accumulated rainfall stood inches deep between clumps of winter-gray bunchgrass. Rain pattered down on Rawlins's hat brim as they circled Fort Sedgwick from the west to be out of rifle range to Confederate sharpshooters. Grant's enjoying this, he thought. How could any man enjoy being wet and cold in this soup littered with rotting corpses?

*   *   *

A lantern shed soft light on a map of Petersburg's fortifications, which was spread across a cot in Grant's command tent. The rain had ended after dark. General Ambrose Burnside peered at the map following Grant's finger."

"Here," Grant said. "This appears to be a place where they don't set up heavy artillery. For three days nothing much has come from that spot. Direct your guns there and give them bloody hell. Maybe something will give."

Before Burnside could offer an opinion, a cannon roared in the distance. He turned toward the sound, listening. "It would seem Bobby Lee is ready to fight again." A canister whistled across black skies, exploding somewhere to the north. As if the shot were a signal, Union guns set up a deafening roar all along front lines, pounding regularly like the thump of a giant steam engine. In the midst of this roaring a heavier concussion made the earth's crust shudder. "Ah," he sighed, "there's no mistaking Dictator's throaty voice. Its crew has nicknamed their gun as though it were an animate object. It makes one damn big hole in the ground."

Rawlins winced when the huge cannon fired. "They should be able to feel that all the way to Richmond."

"Precisely," Grant remarked, strolling to his tent flap to peer outside. Streaks of orange and yellow light painted the sky overhead as shelling continued. "At the very least it should interfere with Jeff Davis's digestion. I intend to give them something to think about in the weeks ahead."

Rawlins joined Grant at the opening. "Lee's their last ray of hope. If we can batter the Army of Northern Virginia into submission, it will be over. Sherman routed the last Confederate forces in Georgia. His dispatch said Joe Johnston left twenty-six hundred Confederate dead when he withdrew."

"The end is in sight," Grant agreed. "I believe it will only be a matter of days or weeks. If I'm any judge of the man, Lee will make one final dash for freedom. He'll have something up his sleeve—he won't sit there until we devour him. I'm counting on the fact that Davis can't resupply him. We've tightened our net around Richmond. By the time this weather breaks, I expect to see our Stars and Stripes flying over the Confederate capitol."

Rawlins turned his gaze northeast where Richmond lay. "It will be a grand day, indeed," he agreed. "No one will celebrate it more enthusiastically than poor Mr. Lincoln."

35

From her second-story hospital room overlooking the Mississippi River, Lorena rested against downy pillows while a nurse washed her shoulder wound with ammonia solution. For days she had drifted in and out of sleep, a light slumber from which she seldom fully awakened. Fever often gave her chills. Her shoulder was seriously swollen. Angry red streaks ran away from the tear in her skin, announcing the presence of blood poisoning. Her feet and hands were bandaged where frostbite had left its mark, ruddy flesh and an absence of feeling in her extremities. Whenever the bandage was removed from her shoulder, the smell of putrefaction was so strong, she became nauseous. A constant dull pain never entirely left her, despite doses of laudanum three times daily. She remembered being told she was in a civilian hospital in Memphis, operated by a division of the occupying Union Army, although memories of how she got there were vague and incomplete.

"It doesn't look any worse," the nurse said, peering down at her shoulder, gently dabbing ammonia water into the opening. "I think you're on the road to recovery, dear. My, but you've had a terrible time of it. Dr. Arnott believes you'll recover fully in due time, however."

Lorena was barely able to recall the woman's name. "You've been most kind, Mrs. Crosby. I do appreciate your time when you sit at the foot of my bed. It's such a comfort to find you there when I wake up." Mrs. Crosby was in her thirties, heavy waisted, with a friendly manner and a kind voice.

She smiled and put down the pan of ammonia. "You've been in the grip of terrible nightmares lately. You talk in your sleep. I can't help but listen."

What had she dreamed about? "I don't remember my dreams. I hope I haven't said anything too dreadful."

"Some of your dreams are pleasant. You call out a name. He must be someone very special, this Jonathan."

She was mildly embarrassed. "He is. He was. I fear he may have been injured, or even killed, at Nashville."

Mrs. Crosby's expression darkened. "We heard it was real bad there. I overheard some of the soldiers talking about it."

"As soon as I'm well enough to travel I have to go back. I have to know what happened to him . . . if he's . . . still alive."

"You were at Nashville?"

"Before, before the fighting began."

"Is he a Confederate?"

"Yes. A surgeon with Hood's Brigades. I was his nurse."

"Nursing in these times ain't easy. We've had no medicines or linens until the Yankees took this town. Most folks say the war is lost. Yankees control all of Tennessee, or so they tell me."

Lorena made no mention of her loyalty to the North. "We had no medicines, nor was there any food to speak of. Doctors were performing surgeries without anesthesia or painkiller. It was a horrible thing to watch. It might be called a blessing when the Union Army arrived. So many Confederate wounded were suffering because of shortages."

Mrs. Crosby began winding cloth around Lorena's shoulder.

"You must be quite taken with Jonathan. You actually smile when you call out his name, even though you're sound asleep."

Lorena's gaze wandered to the ceiling. "I never knew what love was until I met him. He's the sweetest man, so gentle and loving." She thought about their few tender moments together. "We had so little time to get to know each other and yet somehow we experienced a closeness so complete that it was as if we'd known each other forever. He could almost read my thoughts, and I felt I could read his."

"Is he your first love?"

"Yes, and he is my only true love. I believed I was in love before, but when I fell in love with Jonathan, I learned there was so much more."

Mrs. Crosby said knowingly, "I do understand. When I first met Herbert, we waltzed half the night. I felt like I was floating on air. He whirled me around and around that floor until I grew dizzy. When he looked into my eyes, I saw something I'd never seen before—a man who had feelings, a man who could say more to me with a look than other men could with words. I felt so close to him . . ." A crystal tear sparkled at the corner of her eyelid and her voice fell. "I lost him to the Yankees at Gettysburg," she continued, wrapping more bandage around Lorena's wound. "We never got to say good-bye to each other, but I knew he'd gone to heaven to be with the angels that day. I was out in the garden tending to my tomato plants. It was the second day of July. Herbert was with James Longstreet. A soldier wrote me that he died on Cemetery Ridge. I still have the letter . . . I remember how it read: 'The dead lay upon open fields, in crevices of rocks, behind fences, trees, and buildings, in thickets where they'd crept for safety only to die in agony wherever their weakening legs could carry them. Sergeant Herb Crosby died by a stream from a ball through his heart. He did not suffer much.' I knew it the day it happened. I could feel it while I was standing in our garden on the second of July that he was gone."

Lorena reached for the woman's hand. "How terrible it must have been for you—to know," she whispered.

"I looked up at the heavens and said a prayer for him. I didn't tell the children until that letter came, but they knew something bad had happened."

Lorena's eyes misted a little. "I'm so sorry. I fear the same fate may have befallen Jonathan. It's only a feeling, yet I know something is wrong."

"Feelings can be a warning. For your sake I hope you are mistaken."

Lorena turned to the window. Gray winter skies above Memphis seemed to fit the mood she was in. "I've prayed every day that he's alive and well. I couldn't go on living if I've lost him."

"Folks go on living regardless, my dear. The Lord has His way of testing us," She tied off the ends of the bandage and put Lorena's nightgown over it. "I'm raising three kids on my own and that's a hardship sometimes, but I knew Herbert would want me to see after them the best I can."

Lorena felt a stab of inner pain. Could she face Jonathan's loss as bravely? She felt the need to escape his memory, and yet she wanted him desperately. Something inside her was growing, a feeling that she would never see him again. She wanted to be rid of it, and at the same time she was helpless to stop it, a dark fear that he was dead. God help her, but she had fallen in love with him, and until she knew what had happened to him she would get no rest, no peace. For the past few days she'd been little more than an observer, lying in her bed thinking about him when she was fully conscious. And according to Mrs. Crosby, her mind was on him while she slept, even calling his name in her sleep. "I must get well," she said.

"You'll be well soon enough."

Lorena's uneasiness wouldn't go away. She felt Jonathan's fierce inner power beckoning to her, calling her to Nashville in a voice as distinct as her own. She sensed his presence and his gentleness somewhere just beyond her reach. "I love him so much and I don't know what I'll do if he's . . . gone," she said. She craved his intimacy, his touch, the feel of his lips on hers. She began to shiver convulsively, as though a winter wind had entered her hospital room, when she imagined his voice—that same gravelly voice haunting her at night in the sweetest of dreams. Why had she let herself love a man whose life consisted of danger near a battlefield? She had walked off an emotional cliff, falling helplessly into the arms of a man who now could be dead. A reasonable person would not have allowed such a thing to happen.

"You're cold," Mrs. Crosby observed, covering her with a quilt. "It's your fever."

"His memory is making me shake, wondering if I'll ever see him again, wanting him with all my heart and knowing there is nothing I can do to change what has happened. Until I know for sure what has come of him, I have only his memory."

"Sometimes sweet memories are all we have," Mrs. Crosby said sadly. "But it's better to have those memories than to have had nothing at all. I'll get you some more laudanum. Now, lie still until I return."

"How long will it be before I'm strong enough to leave?" she asked.

"Blood poisoning is slow to heal. Your wound has festered. It may be several weeks before you have any strength."

"I simply can't wait that long, Mrs. Crosby."

The woman took a breath. "I doubt you'll have much say in the matter. You can ask Dr. Arnott when he makes his evening hospital rounds."

She thought about what weeks of waiting would be like. How could she do it? Each day, each hour without knowing Jonathan's fate made her more restless. But was she prepared to face the hard truth? What would it do to her if she found a gravestone bearing his name?

Mrs. Crosby was watching her from the doorway, and the look in her eyes said she understood Lorena's agony. "You can't change what has already happened," she told her softly. "I'll be back with your medicine in a moment."

When the nurse was gone, Lorena let her mind wander back to the first time she had seen Jonathan during the battle at Franklin. Even then, something special had taken place between them. When he had looked up from his operating table, there was some silent communication she felt . . . it had made her uncomfortable, she remembered. He had looked into her eyes in a different way, a way no other man ever had. Until then her experience with men had been limited. Paul was the only man she'd ever known intimately, her first serious suitor. Paul was nice, polite, correct with his manners, a good banker from a good family. Not until she met Jonathan had she even suspected something might be missing from their relationship or that she was capable of feeling with so much intensity. She knew now she didn't love Paul, not enough to become his wife or bear his children.

Lorena suddenly went rigid, clinging to the hem of her quilt when she thought of having children. Could she be pregnant by Rufe or Roy Lee? It was the darkest thought imaginable, to have a child by either of them. They had violated her so many times. Was it possible? Instruction at the academy relating to childbirth had been limited to the birth itself and any potential complications. How women got pregnant had been scarcely mentioned as if it were already understood by everyone.

She couldn't think about it—wouldn't think about it until the time came for her monthly bleeding. Then she would know for certain what lay ahead. "I made them pay," she whispered to her empty room, replacing dread with controlled anger and just a hint of satisfaction when she remembered her escape from the abandoned farmhouse. She had never considered herself a vengeful person, but when she had to make a choice between using a gun or remaining their prisoner to be used to satisfy their animal lust, it was a simple decision, made out of fear. When she pulled the trigger and shot first Roy Lee and then Rufus Cain, she'd done it to save her own life. It was her or them. They'd given her no other way out.

Without wanting to, she recalled what a gun sounded like, how it felt in her hands when it exploded. And she remembered all too vividly the way Roy Lee's forehead puckered as a ball struck him, blood and brain flying from the back of his skull. But by far the most terrible memory of all was of Rufe, his face and hair aflame before he fell to the floor. Riding through the storm trying to reach Memphis, Lorena hadn't been able to forget that sight. It haunted her day and night until soldiers found her wandering beside the river.

"I'll only allow myself happy thoughts," she said to herself a moment later, returning her gaze to the window. "I won't think about the possibility Jonathan might be dead—I simply won't let myself consider it."

She remembered how she had shrank away from him at first, until her heart spoke more loudly than her conscience. In the beginning she believed loving Paul demanded that she turn Jonathan's shows of affection aside. Only after she had looked closely at her relationship with Paul was she able to see things more objectively. Paul's love had been conditioned upon the success of his banking position—hard times at the bank prompted him to put off any commitment he made to her. This wasn't the kind of love she wanted from a man, but not until she had experienced love of another type from a man who gave all of himself to her was she able to see the difference.

She made up her mind to lose herself in fond memories of Jonathan until she was able to travel. It was better to cling to the love she'd known than to worry. Later, when she felt better, she would write to Paul and tell him of her decision to end their love affair. A war, and a Confederate surgeon, had taught her enough about real love to show her how shallow the relationship with Paul truly was. Better to end it than continue trying to make herself believe it was what she wanted from life.

Mrs. Crosby returned with a small bottle and a teaspoon. "This will make you feel better," she promised.

"I feel better already," Lorena said. "I'm taking your good advice."

"And what advice was that, my dear?"

"To cling to my sweet memories of Jonathan, for it may be all I have left. Until I know, I'll remember him the way he was, and how he made me feel when we were together."

*   *   *

April 9, 1865
UNION VICTORY! PEACE!

"The Work of Palm Sunday! Lee has surrendered at Appomattox to Lieutenant General Grant in a final triumph of the Army of the Potomac. If one army drank the joy of victory, and the other the bitter draught of defeat, it was a joy moderated by the recollection of the cost at which it had been purchased, and a defeat mollified by the consciousness of many triumphs. If the victors could recall a Malvern Hill, an Antietam, a Gettysburg, a Five Forks, the vanquished could recall a Manassas, a Fredericksburg, a Chancellorsville, a Cold Harbor."

William Swinton
The New York Times

SPECIAL EDITION
April 15, 1865
PRESIDENT LINCOLN IS ASSASSINATED!

"Our beloved President, Abraham Lincoln, has been murdered! His assassin is still at large. The assassin's stroke at Ford's Theater last night but makes the fraternal bond the stronger. A nation's heart was struck. In sorrowing tears the nation's grief is spent. Mankind has lost a friend and we a President."

The New York Times

*   *   *

36

Grassy hills around Nashville's city cemetery were covered by an array of colorful wildflowers, yellows and pinks, reds, a violet hue here and there. Beyond a rusting cast-iron fence sat row upon row of fresh graves. Many bore no markings, while some did acknowledge who lay below mounds of recently dug earth. She had been told almost a thousand soldiers were buried here after the battle. A caretaker checked a list of known dead upon her request, a short list since so many had had no identification papers when they fell defending the town. He found only one name Lorena recognized when he read, "Goodie Carrothers" in a soft monotone while standing under a giant oak tree outside the fence. But no mention of Jonathan Cross. Gazing silently across so many rows of wooden markers and granite tombstones, Lorena wondered if one of the nameless graves might be Jonathan's, or if she would ever learn his fate. After three months of uncertainty since she had last seen him, with only his memory to comfort her while she recovered in a Memphis hospital, there was something final about visiting this cemetery where casualties of the Battle of Nashville were buried. But was he among them? It had taken all the courage she had to come here seeking answers.

"Sorry, ma'am," the old man said, folding his tattered list. "You could ask that Yankee commander if the feller you're lookin' for was one of them prisoners. They's supposedly got a list of their names." He watched her a moment. "If he got took prisoner, he'll be comin' home shortly, we was told. Somebody said they was shipped off to someplace up in Indiana. . . ."

"I'll inquire with the Union commander," she said quietly, despair thickening her voice as she turned away from the fence. "Thank you very kindly, sir, for your help."

He tucked the paper into an inside coat pocket. "That was a mighty fearsome battle. I was here at the time, hidin' down in my root cellar. It was over in half a day. Hood's boys didn't stand no kinda chance at all. Got shot to pieces, they did. Wasn't long afore they put down their guns an' surrendered. Them Yankees like to have blowed this town off the face of the earth."

She hadn't been paying attention. "I'm sorry. What did you say?"

He nodded like he understood. "I was jus' sayin' how it was a terrible battle. I hope the feller you're lookin' for ain't buried here without his name on a marker. Ask that Yank commander if his name's on the list of prisoners. There's been plenty of womenfolk askin' me an' Colonel Martin as to the whereabouts of husbands an' other kinfolk lately."

"He wasn't my husband," she said, looking toward the skyline of Nashville, remembering a bitterly cold day when she and Clara had been escorted away from the city. A week ago, on her way back to Nashville, she had driven to the ferry crossing on the Tennessee River to look for Clara, driving a buggy provided by the Union commander at Memphis. She'd stopped at the crossing to inquire about her friend, where she was shown a grave bearing a legend UNKNOWN YOUNG WOMAN FOUND IN HILLS. With the aid of an understanding ferryman, Clara's name was carved into a wood plank while Lorena had looked on, unable to cry after so many tears had already been shed over her lost friend. Penning a letter to Clara's parents advising them of her death had been one of the most sorrowful moments in her life. There were times in the hospital when she had wondered if she would ever be able to cry again. She'd written her father and mother, advising them of her safety and a Union commander's assurances she would be escorted home after her wound and frostbite healed. And always, in the back of her mind, was a desperate longing to see Jonathan, coupled with fear . . . fear that she would discover he was among the dead here.

"Pardon me, ma'am, but are you all right? You seem kinda distracted, if you don't mind my sayin' so."

"I'm okay. Thank you again for all your help. I'll make my inquiry with the Union commander, as you suggested."

She walked down to her carriage parked along the edge of a tree-shaded lane leading to the cemetery, wishing she hadn't been so quick to recall finding Clara's grave—or the pain when she had stood there gazing down at her friend's final resting place. She knew she would never quite be able to lose the feeling of responsibility for her death.

Climbing woodenly up to the buggy seat, she drove back toward town. Seeing those streets again where she and Jonathan had walked arm in arm, and the livery stable where he had given her tender kisses while telling her how much he loved her, would be another painful memory she now had to face. The one thing she dared hope for was finding his name on the list of prisoners sent to Indiana, yet it was only a slim hope at best, and she understood this.

When she drove into town, she swung her carriage down a muddy road leading to the river where Union forces were camped, driving past crews of workmen repairing shell-damaged buildings and homes. Men in threadbare gray uniforms lounged beneath shaded porches and on street corners, some of the first Confederate soldiers to return home after General Lee's surrender.

She was directed to the tent of Colonel Theodore Martin by a soldier resting in the shade of an oak tree. An aide helped her down from the carriage and announced her arrival. A moment later, an officer with graying sideburns emerged buttoning his dark blue tunic.

"Pardon me, Colonel," she began, "but I wish to find out if a Confederate physician by the name of Jonathan Cross was taken to Indiana along with the other prisoners. I was told you had a list of names."

Martin bowed stiffly. "We kept a ledger." His face showed a hint of irritation. "I'll look." He disappeared into his tent and came back with a merchant's tally book. "Is this doctor some relative of yours?"

"No. Only an acquaintance," she replied, watching him thumb through the first few pages. When he reached a section of notations, it seemed an eternity as he scanned each line. Lorena felt a quickening of her heart.

"No one by that name is mentioned here," he said, following another cursory examination of his book. "If he was captured by us, his name should be on this list showing he boarded a train up in Kentucky bound for Indianapolis before Christmas as a prisoner of the Army of the Cumberland. General Thomas marched them over the Tennessee border on the fourteenth of December."

Her meager hopes fell. "Could there have been a mistake of some kind?"

Martin frowned. "That's hard to say, ma'am. It isn't very likely. I could send a wire to Indianapolis asking about him, I suppose. . . ."

"I'd be so very grateful, Colonel. I've driven such a long way to find him."

"It will take time. Repairs are being made to miles of telegraph lines all across Tennessee."

"I'll come back tomorrow. Thank you so much for your kind assistance."

He watched her thoughtfully a moment, tapping his canvas-bound ledger with a fingertip. "I'll see what I can do," he said when she smiled. "Come in the afternoon. It's possible his name was overlooked. They'll be headed home shortly, I figure. They may have already been released. Of course, you know there is one other possibility. He may have deserted before the battle."

Her smile faded quickly. "He would never desert!" she said angrily. "Jonathan Cross is a dedicated doctor. He would never leave his patients, not for any reason. I was his nurse, and I am certain he wouldn't abandon suffering men."

Recognition crossed Martin's face. "Are you the nurse who wrote General Grant regarding Hood's whereabouts? I was told by one of the general's officers it was a couple of nurses who led General Thomas here, that they were the spies responsible for bringing about Hood's final defeat."

It was a stinging reminder of her role in so many dark events—Clara's death, perhaps Jonathan's. She looked away, to Barnum's cotton warehouse with her heart breaking. "I wrote the letter," she whispered, as though she spoke to herself. "I wish I hadn't now. . . ."

The colonel seemed perplexed. "You sound as if you have Rebel sympathies."

"Only regrets," she replied, gazing across a battle-scarred city she'd help destroy. Turning for her buggy, she said, "I'd appreciate anything you can do to help me find out if Jonathan Cross is still alive. There is no record of his burial at the Nashville cemetery."

Martin showed more sympathy now. "So many died without any form of identification on them. It may be impossible to know for sure, unless he is found elsewhere."

"I understand, Colonel. All I'm asking is that you try to help me if you can." She strode over to her carriage and climbed up to the seat before gently slapping reins over her harness horse's rump. The buggy lurched away, swaying her back and forth when it crossed deeper mud ruts.

She drove to the old warehouse and stopped, gripped by some powerful need to revisit the hospital where she had seen

Jonathan for the last time. He had been standing outside in the snow, watching her leave Nashville—they had waved to each other, she recalled vividly. Did this mean he'd forgiven her? Or was it simply a way of telling her good-bye without words, without having to say he never wanted to see her again?

Stepping down, she walked to the loading platform before going inside, remembering how he had stood there gazing at her while she was being driven away. That mental image had been locked in her heart ever since, treasured, remembered at times when she felt desperately lonely. Returning to that place now, to the very same spot where he'd been standing, tortured her soul even more with his sweet memory. "I love you, Jonathan," she said in a tiny voice, clutching the front of her skirt to keep her hands from trembling. But she did not cry, nor did she believe she could. She felt too empty for tears, or so it seemed, although in the back of her mind she knew she would certainly cry one more time if she learned Jonathan was dead.

"Tomorrow," she whispered, bracing herself for a walk into Barnum's where more memories awaited her, even though the warehouse was empty now. "Perhaps I'll know tomorrow where he is."

When she entered the building, she saw a corner where shafts of golden sunlight spilled through a huge hole in the roof. Another smaller hole above a doorway facing east allowed more sunlight into the room. Splintered rafters charred by fire and heaps of ashes still lay scattered across the floor. She stared at the spot for a time, until she could bear it no longer. Something told her Jonathan had been here when a Union shell exploded in this place—she could almost feel his presence now as if somehow a part of him was still there.

37

An hour slipped away before she realized how much time had gone by, standing in Barnum's lost in memories. A voice brought her back to the present, a voice she remembered. Across the road a woman swept her front porch while talking to someone paused near the steps. Lorena easily recalled the old woman's name and the kindness she had shown them when Clara was ill—Beatrice Peabody had been a good friend during a very trying time.

She walked through a warehouse door and stood in evening's warm sunlight, shading her eyes with a hand. "Good afternoon, Mrs. Peabody," she called out as a buggy rattled down the street passing between them. She noticed the boardinghouse had a new split-shingled roof and new floorboards across the porch. A fresh coat of whitewash covered the sides of the building. Mrs. Peabody's home must have been damaged by cannon fire, she thought.

The woman stopped sweeping abruptly when she heard

Lorena's greeting. She waited until the buggy went by. For a moment she merely stared across the road without giving any sign she recognized her; then she leaned her broom against a porch post and came down the steps. "Is that you, Miss Blaire?" she asked as she walked across the street.

Lorena wondered if Beatrice might know anything about what had happened to Jonathan. "Yes ma'am. I was on my way back home, now that the war is finally over. I thought I'd inquire as to the whereabouts of Jonathan Cross on my way through Nashville. I drove out to the cemetery first, hoping the worst hadn't befallen him. I was told many of the graves aren't marked."

"Why would you care about him?" Beatrice asked, stopping before she reached the warehouse steps. "You're the one who gave him away to them Yankees."

She knew she should have expected the accusation. She bowed her head and looked away. "Yes ma'am, I am. At the time I believed what I did was right. I was told all Southerners were my enemies, enemies of the United States. I wanted to help my country by being an army nurse. Instead, I was sent to Tennessee to become a spy. I should have known better, that I wasn't suited for that sort of thing. Neither was my friend, who died because of it. We were both terribly sorry we came."

"Nurse Brooks passed away?"

"Yes."

"From her illness?"

"Not directly. Two soldiers who were taking us to Memphis abandoned her during a snowstorm because they felt she was slowing them down. Clara probably froze to death. She was much too weak to find help on her own."

Beatrice rested her hands on her hips a moment. "That would be a mighty terrible way to die, freezin' to death. There may be some who'd say she had it comin', I suppose, bein' she was a Yank spy an' all. I'm not sayin' I feel that way, but a lot of good men died here in December."

"I know, Mrs. Peabody," Lorena said softly. "Neither Clara

nor I wanted things to happen this way. We didn't really understand what was being asked of us at the time."

"They blasted hell outta my house," Beatrice snapped angrily, tossing a look over her shoulder. "Preacher Johnson got a lump on his head, but the rest made it out okay. The room where Miss Brooks was stayin' got hit worst of all. She'd have likely died in there if she'd been in that same room."

"I'm sorry," Lorena said, "about your house."

"We got it fixed back reasonable well, considerin'. Most of the lumber was given to me by them Yankee soldiers. Now that the war's over, maybe things'll be back to normal pretty soon."

She remembered the damage to the warehouse roof. "I see the cannons also struck this hospital. I hope Dr. Cross wasn't seriusly injured."

"Roof beam fell on him," Beatrice said. "Crushed his chest like he was made outta matchsticks. Six men died in yonder that day."

"Oh no!" Lorena cried, whirling around, staring up at the hole in Barnum's roof. Her hands flew to her face. She grew dizzy. In her mind she could almost see falling timbers and hear screams coming from dying men underneath a pile of rubble. She gasped for air, feeling her knees grow weaker. "I loved him," she said as her voice began to break. Now she knew her worst fears had been realized. Jonathan was dead. Indulging in sweet dreams of him during her hospital stay had given her hope, and now she knew all hope was lost.

"There was a fire got some of 'em," Beatrice added. "They was burned alive. Folks all over this part of town heard them screamin'. . . ."

"Please don't tell me any more!" Lorena begged. "I don't care to hear how it happened. I loved Jonathan Cross with all my heart, and I'll have to live with the knowledge that a letter I wrote was responsible for his death." Letting herself go, a rush of pent-up emotion leaked hot tears down her cheeks. "I killed him!" she sobbed. "The only man I ever truly loved is dead and I'm to blame!"

A moment passed before Mrs. Peabody whispered, "I never said nothin' 'bout him bein' dead, Miss Blaire, only that his ribs got crushed when the roof fell in."

She couldn't quite trust her ears just then—she turned so she could see the woman's face. "You told me six men died here, and you said something about a fire. . . ."

"Never said Dr. Cross was one of 'em, did I?"

"But his ribs? You said his ribs were crushed."

Beatrice nodded. "He was hurt real bad when we found him. We helped put out the fire an' took them timbers off his chest. Yanks was all over the place by then, holdin' guns on everybody, so we carried him over to my root cellar an' hid him out so they couldn't find him. They was takin' all the Confederate soldiers to prison camp somewhere, an' we didn't want that nice doctor in no prison if we could help it, so we tended to him ourselves, me an' Preacher Johnson. Hid him out real good, we did, so's no one knew he was down there. He's been a mighty sick man over the past few months, but he'll make it. Soon as he was able, he told us what to do for his broken bones."

Lorena's heart leaped with joy. "May I see him?" she asked, glancing across the street to the root cellar door where she and Jonathan had shared a few wonderful private moments. "I'd like to have a chance to explain myself, if he'll listen."

For the first time Beatrice smiled. "I reckon he'll listen, all right. He's talked about you prett' near ever since he woke up the day after we found him. He's plumb crazy in love with you, so I don't figure you'll have to explain yourself all that much."

She started down the warehouse steps, wiping tears from her eyes.

"He ain't down in the cellar no more," Beatrice said. "Soon as word came the war was over, we moved him upstairs to that room you an' Miss Brooks occupied, only we ain't told them Yankees we been hidin' him out. He'll be sorry to hear your friend passed on. He was wonderin' about her from time to time when his head was clear. He's been through a lot of pain, but the worst is over. Takes a spell for ribs to heal, he told us. He was in bed quite a while, till just lately. He gets around some now with a walkin' stick reasonable well."

Lorena hurried past Mrs. Peabody across the road, flying up her front steps two at a time. She rushed through the door, down a familiar hallway to Clara's room. There she stopped long enough to brush strands of hair off her forehead and smooth a few wrinkles from the front of her dress. Then she tapped lightly on the door feeling her pulse race.

"Come in," a soft voice said.

She took the doorknob in trembling fingers and turned it. A floorboard creaked with her weight when she pushed open a newly painted door and let herself in.

On a brass-framed bed she saw a bearded face. Blond hair, much longer than she remembered, tumbled in neglected curls over Jonathan's broad shoulders. He is so much thinner, she thought, and his beard has small streaks of gray. But he is alive!

His face changed the moment he recognized her. "Lorena!" he exclaimed, grinning. "You came back! I wondered if I'd ever see you again."

The sweet melody of his voice thrilled her . . . a voice she'd longed to hear all those months while recuperating in a dreary Memphis hospital. "I had to know what happened to you," she said, doing her best to resist an urge to run across the room to his bedside. "I've been living with the most awful guilt for what I did ever since they took us away from here. I wanted to tell you how sorry I was for what happened. We didn't know . . . I didn't understand what our letters would do. I wouldn't have done anything to cause you harm, Jonathan. I loved you so very much . . . I still love you with all my heart."

"Please come here," he told her gently, patting the edge of his mattress. A linen sheet covered him from the waist down. "I think we should talk about it, about feelings and loyalty to a cause, about a great many more things. People can be blinded to the truth of matters, by fevered rhetoric and a sense of belonging to something. We both knew too little about what this war would do to us."

She came to the bed, seeing a layer of bandages around his ribcage where his shirt hung open in front. Looking deeply into his eyes, she thought she saw behind those bright blue irises remnants of the pain he'd suffered. She sat on the edge of his bed feeling giddy, foolish for staring at him the way she was then, yet she found she was unable to take her gaze from his face until modesty forced her to look away for a moment, to the window. "I was so afraid you'd been killed," she said quietly, fidgeting as she spoke, toying with her dress.

He reached for her hand, and when he held it, a tingle went up her spine. His callused fingers encircled her palm, gripping it in a firm but gentle way.

"I also feared for *your* life," he said. "I learned a great deal more about Major Von Bulen, the prison camp director. You are most fortunate to be alive."

She squeezed his hand. "We never got to prison," she told him. "The men guarding us left Clara to die in the woods when we encountered a Union patrol. They took me to an abandoned house. My hands and feet were kept tied and they . . ." She couldn't finish what she had started to say, too ashamed to tell him what they'd done to her. "I escaped one night after they'd been drinking. I loosened my ropes while they were asleep. They woke up as I was leaving. I was forced to use a gun, although I wasn't sure how to do it. I took one of their pistols and fired when they came after me." Her voice had begun to quiver. "It was awful. I did something I didn't believe I was capable of, shooting those men. But I was utterly terrified."

He smiled with understanding. "You don't need to tell me about it now. We've other things to discuss. I'm sorry to hear about Miss Brooks." Footsteps in the hall made him pause.

Beatrice looked in on them. "No need tellin' you you've got a visitor, Doctor. I'll close the door so you can talk private."

"Thank you, Mrs. Peabody," he said. "I've been waiting for this moment a long time, as you must already know."

The old woman grinned. She closed the door quietly and walked away.

Using his free hand, Jonathan pushed himself up carefully on the mattress, wincing a little. His face was only a few inches from hers now, and his nearness became somewhat unnerving—but in a distinctly pleasant way.

"We've so much to talk about," he said, holding her hand as he spoke. "We've both been through a terrible experience. If I only could, I'd erase all your bad memories." His eyes searched hers a moment. "We can't let pain from our recent past destroy our chances for a future. If you'll allow me, I'll try to show you how much I love you, how much I've missed you. It doesn't matter about the letters you wrote, not to me. It's best forgotten. There is no war now, no cause to defend. Our country is reunited, although at an unthinkable cost in bloodshed. We must find a way to put it behind us."

"I've missed you terribly," Lorena whispered, leaning closer until her mouth almost brushed against his. She wanted to kiss him but dared not be so forward, so bold. He seemed able to read her mind when his lips slowly parted. He kissed her tenderly, so gently, and the thrill of it raced through her from head to toe.

"And I have missed you, my darling Lorena, more than you'll ever know. Not a day or a night passed since you left Nashville when I could put you from my mind. All my thoughts have been of you, and there were nights when I couldn't sleep. You came to me in my dreams so often that I preferred sleep to loneliness without you. If I sound foolish, then so be it. My heart speaks for me now . . . laugh at my childishness if you will, but know my words are sincere."

"Oh, Jonathan," she whispered, reaching for his cheek with her fingertips. "I do love you so." She kissed him lightly, letting her mouth linger a moment before she drew away. "I can't change what happened, nor will I ever stop feeling remorse for the pain I caused you. But if you'll give me the chance, I'll prove my love for you is genuine. I've done a lot of growing up since I came to Tennessee. I suppose I lost some of my innocence. The one thing I'm sure of is the way I feel about you . . . if you can ever forgive me for betraying your trust, I'll prove it to you."

"There is nothing to forgive, my darling," he said, placing his arms around her without allowing pain from his movements to show. "We needn't discuss forgiveness again. None is needed."

She rested her head against his shoulder, being careful not to touch his damaged ribs. It felt so good to have Jonathan's arms around her. She let her mind drift, back to the abandoned farmhouse, to a moment in time when everything depended on an act of courage, the courage to pull a trigger on a gun. Until then she couldn't have imagined taking someone's life, not even the lives of men like Rufe and Roy Lee. Had the war changed her?

"I feel safe with you," she said.

He kissed the back of her neck and spoke with his mouth against her skin. "Someday I hope you'll agree to share the rest of your life with me . . . as my wife. I promise to keep you safe for as long as I live."

Those were words she'd wanted to hear for such a long time, or so it seemed. Lying in a Memphis hospital, she'd had plenty of opportunity to think about her life, and the way she felt about Jonathan. Falling in love with him had been like a dream, almost too perfect, too complete, and all of it occurring in a breathtakingly short number of weeks. She knew she had been right to question it then until enough time had passed, allowing her to think clearly. In the end she had had no doubt, only fear—fear that he might not be alive. "I've thought about it," she admitted as she drew back to look at him closely. "I think any woman would feel proud to become the wife of Jonathan Cross."

"Then will you marry me?" he asked.

Her quick smile and scarlet blush answered for her. "I will if that's what you truly want. If you're absolutely sure."

His kiss removed any doubts she might have had.

38

John Rawlins watched puffy clouds drift across a pale-blue sky beyond Ulysses Grant's office window while the general went to his sideboard for another whiskey. Their discussion centered around Grant's concerns over the new President's reconstruction policies. So soon after Lincoln's death, Andrew Johnson might be excused for his many uncertainties when it came to rebuilding Southern states while the rest of the nation was begging for any form of relief from a war-ravaged economy. Johnson vacillated on too many issues, Grant believed. Those who had the President's ear usually got what they wanted, but only until another voice spoke against it. From time to time, Grant wondered aloud about making a bid for the Presidency himself, although he kept this ambition from the public. But as his frustrations grew over a lack of consistency in Johnson's policies, Rawlins believed Grant was edging closer to an announcement that he would run for office, despite his well-known aversion to politics, on a platform pledged to peace, honesty, and civil rights.

Grant tossed back a gulp of bourbon and took a puff from his cigar. "I'll ask for an appointment with the President," he said wearily. "After our rebellion, when so many young men were at liberty to return to their homes, they find they are not satisfied with the farm, the store, or the workshops of the villages, but want larger fields. Our economy cannot be rebuilt without a measure of assistance from the government that helped destroy it. Every state in the Union has been devastated. So little is left on both sides. We must offer a sound plan, a workable plan we can implement immediately." He scowled. "Johnson won't hear a word I have to say, but I must make the effort. Let's move on to other matters, John, before my stomach further upsets itself."

Rawlins studied a stack of papers on his lap. "I have the commendations for our nurse spies ready for your signature. As you may recall, two are given posthumously. Misses Ruth Ann Waldrop and Clara Faye Brooks are deceased. Miss Waldrop died from a reported case of acute dysentery in Georgia while she was with Bedford Forrest. The team of spies with Forrest were never able to give us information we could use. Miss Brooks died of exposure and typhus in Tennessee. Miss Bessie Mae Higgins and Miss Lorena Blaire are alive and well. Miss Higgins has returned to Maryland, I believe; however, you may find it an oddity when I relate what happened to Miss Blaire. She's the one who gave Pinkerton's people the location of John Bell Hood. It seems Miss Blaire fell in love with a Confederate surgeon while she was with Hood. Dorothea Dix informs me they intend to marry this summer in Texas. Curious, that enemies will become marriage partners."

Grant sauntered to a window, blowing smoke into a gentle spring breeze, gazing thoughtfully across Washington. "It may serve as a reminder to all of us that we were never truly enemies in the first place. More and more it occurs to me that this war was fought over nothing more than the right of a state to secede. As to Miss Blaire, I wish her all happiness. She and her brave counterparts performed with remarkable courage despite my premonitions to the contrary. Their performance, and my wife's quite considerable badgering on the subject, have forced me to take a somewhat different stance on a woman's role in the military."

Rawlins envisioned trouble. "That posture could be damaging to your political ambitions," he warned. "Most men would develop a case of the rigors over the notion that women might serve in a uniform. Surely you have in mind a lesser role. . . ."

Grant offered no immediate reply, sipping whiskey, smoking his cigar. "It wouldn't be popular," he finally agreed, following the flight of a robin from its nest in a nearby tree. "All the same, we should give those nurses due credit. Without them, we might still be chasing Hood from hither to yon. Send the commendations along with my warmest regards, and in the case of Miss Blaire, perhaps I should also send a wedding present."

Rawlins placed the commendations on Grant's desk. "Whoever her future husband is, we can deduce he has a forgiving nature."

The general rocked back on his boot heels without taking his attention from the scene below. "Our reunited country must learn forgiveness. I forsee a very difficult time ahead. It will not be repairs to our economy that shall trouble us most, I fear. Putting aside our hatreds, our grief, so that inner wounds can heal promises to be a long and painful process."

Rawlins held out a pen and blotter. "Your signature, sir, on these commendations. I'll send them off right away."

Grant came to his desk, frowning at a name inscribed on the piece of parchment as he took the pen. "Send Miss Blaire a gift of some sort, something appropriate, along with my congratulations. She has done this country a valuable service that may open new doors of opportunity for women."

Again, Rawlins was troubled. "You need to master the art of keeping more radical views to yourself if you decide to take aim at higher office. Women are not voters. Most men prefer to have their women at home preparing meals and taking care of children, not marching off to war. Men want women in their proper place at home, minding their own affairs."

Grant scrawled his name at the bottom of Lorena Blaire's commendation. "Try telling that to my wife," he said, pressing the blotter lightly over his signature.

39

Aided by a walking stick, Jon took small, careful steps along the edge of a shady lane running beside the Cumberland River. Lorena was by his side carrying their picnic basket. It was late April and spring flowers bloomed everywhere, scenting warm breezes with so many sweet smells, no single odor had its own identity. It felt good to be strolling outdoors after all those weeks bedridden. As they passed rows of tents where Union occupation forces camped, he remembered the battle and the sight of blue uniformed soldiers and the din of gunfire in a blinding snowstorm the day Nashville fell. At a bend in the Cumberland west of town, he found a grassy spot for their picnic beneath a magnificent oak towering above surrounding forests.

"This is a perfect place," he said, walking stiffly to the edge of the riverbank.

Lorena set her wicker basket next to the oak trunk and took a thin blanket from it, spreading it over a bed of soft grass. A blue jay shrieked from a nearby branch before it took off with a rustle of wings for higher limbs.

Jon settled slowly to the blanket and smiled, although pain radiating across his ribs throbbed fiercely from exertion, bringing beads of perspiration to his brow. "It's so quiet here," he added, glancing around them, listening to a silence interrupted only by the soft gurgle of water brushing against the river's shores.

She knelt in front of him to wipe sweat from his forehead with her handkerchief. "Your ribs hurt, don't they?" she asked.

"Some. It isn't all that bad. Besides, I'm blessed with a lovely distraction—a very beautiful woman somehow makes my pain seem less."

Her smile made him forget his ribs for the moment. She came closer and kissed him lightly.

"Men are so shallow," she teased him, feigning annoyance. "A woman's physical appearance is no measure of her worth any more than a man's good looks should be. Real beauty comes from deeper within, from the soul." She handed him a slice of warm bread and a piece of cured ham; then she took a jar of pickled peaches from her basket and opened the lid. The smell of spices mingled with the aroma of wildflowers. "In many ways, being considered pretty can be a curse. I suppose that's a part of what I wanted to tell you this afternoon. I haven't told you everything about . . . about what those men did to me." She lowered her voice and cast a look toward the river. "They brutalized me, Jonathan. If I tried to resist, they beat me. They made me their . . . concubine. They did this to me frequently, almost every night when they found a place to make camp. I couldn't bring myself to keep track of the number of times they . . . had their way with me. I honestly think this was what made me believe I was justified when I got my hands on a gun. I killed them, and felt no remorse. Ever since, I've had the feeling that I did something so terrible that I cannot be forgiven for it."

"You needn't tell me about it," he said, putting his sandwich aside to reach for her hand. "It must be dreadful having to remember what they did to you. No one could blame you for using a gun to defend yourself."

"I wanted you to know what happened . . . I wanted you to know the truth."

"It doesn't matter. It doesn't change the way I feel about you. I love you and nothing can change that."

"But there is more," she continued hoarsely, unable to look him in the eye. "Soon after I reached Memphis, I discovered I was with child. I lost the baby, Jonathan. An army doctor there said I might not be able . . . to have another. There was damage. He told me he can't be certain of it, but there's a possibility I won't be able to bear children."

He stared across the river himself for a time, wondering if a childless marriage would make a difference. Finally he said, "I can honestly say it is of little consequence to me, but I fear it may be a far greater concern of yours. And the doctor may be wrong. In any case, it won't change the way I feel about you. If we can't have children, we have each other."

She looked at him then. Most of the color had drained from her face. "I keep telling myself it wasn't my fault. But there are times when I wonder if God is punishing me for taking those soldiers' lives."

"You punish yourself, thinking that way. You did the only thing you could under the circumstances, and I don't believe you deserve punishment for it. I don't claim to be a cleric, but I'm quite sure God understands."

She lowered her eyes. "I wonder if you will still love me if I can't give you a child. You tell me it doesn't matter, yet I question it, that it might make a difference later on."

He put one arm around her shoulder, gently stroking the back of her neck. "Marry me. If we are to have children, it will only add to our happiness. I love you. Almost from the moment we met I have known our lives would be entwined. Destiny has brought us together . . . a Confederate and a Yankee who made peace before Grant and Lee declared it. We can be happy. We can begin new lives and forget about the horrors we've been through."

Lorena appeared to be lost in thought. "Don't most men wish for a son to carry on their name? Or a doting daughter to sit on their knee?"

He chuckled. "Most men would rather be happy."

She finally looked at him. "I do love you so, Jonathan. I thought of you so often while I was on the way to Memphis, and while I was there in the hospital. You were always in my heart and in my prayers. A thousand times I wished I could have made you understand why I came to Tennessee under false pretenses. I knew it could be dangerous, yet I believed it was worth the risk. All I wanted was to help end the war. I didn't stop to consider that my actions would cause men to die. When I fell in love with you, I finally understood. Those letters I wrote could have killed someone I loved." Anguish clouded her eyes. "I thought you were dead when your name wasn't on the list of prisoners. I prayed it was some kind of mistake. When I came back to the hospital and saw that hole in the roof and those ashes, I just knew. . . ."

"I owe my life to Beatrice Peabody," he said. "In all the confusion I might have been buried there, or been consumed by the fire like the others. But you mustn't blame yourself for that cannon shot or anything else. You did your duty as you were asked. It was wartime, and in most respects you were no different than me or any other soldier."

She kissed him again, tracing a fingertip down his unshaven cheek. "I'm so glad you're alive. I wasn't sure what I'd do if I found out you were dead. I don't think I could have lived with myself."

"It's a part of the past. Forget about it. We have plans to make." He held her, staring into her eyes.

She'd scrubbed the floors with lye until there was no trace of blood anywhere, although no amount of scrubbing could erase so many memories associated with Confederate ambulances. Jonathan had been given the decrepit wagon by Colonel Martin, who had seen to it that a few badly needed repairs were made. One wheel still wobbled slightly, and the wagon box groaned over rough terrain, yet its canvas roof and sides kept out all but the worst rain and sun, which allowed Jonathan to rest comfortably on a bed of quilts and sack cloth when he became too tired to ride with Lorena on the wagon seat. Loaded with their few belongings and a gift of provisions from the Union mess, they drove westward across Tennessee following roads Lorena had traveled with Rufe and Roy Lee on her way to Memphis. She hadn't wanted to head for Texas by this route, but it was the shortest way and easier on Jonathan's slowly mending broken ribs. An old gray mule with collar-marked withers drew their converted ambulance slowly over miles of hilly roadway Lorena remembered all too well, a road filled with sad memories of Clara and bitter recollections of two Confederate soldiers who introduced her to terror beyond anything she had ever known. As the wagon rattled and bumped over every forested hill, she relived that terrible journey in her mind, until Jonathan noticed her lengthening silences and a change in her expression.

"You're remembering this road, and Clara, aren't you?" he asked, as the wagon rumbled past a group of men walking single file along the edge of the lane, Confederates returning home in mismatched uniforms with a few personal effects slung over their backs.

She tightened her grip on the reins. "Yes. I can't help myself. Those were Clara's last days on earth. I suppose I must have sensed it, that she wouldn't survive, only I believed then it would be her illness that would take her. I wish I could stop thinking about her . . . about how she died. She must have suffered an agonizing death. And she was all alone."

"It won't help to remember it," he assured her. "Nothing will be changed. You did your best for her. What happened was not your fault."

She took her eyes off the road to stare at him. "I cannot simply forget about it, Jonathan. She was my friend. When we come to the ferry, I'll visit her grave for the last time, and if God is willing, perhaps then I can put her memory to rest."

He gave her an understanding smile, touching her arm. His cheeks, shaved clean now, still looked pale and sunken. He wore a boiled white-linen shirt and mended cavalry pants tucked into worn stovepipe officer's boots reaching his knees. He glanced to the sky. "It looks like it'll rain soon. Let's find a place to make camp before the rain starts."

"It isn't far to the ferry," Lorena promised. "If you can stand a few more miles, I'd like to get there today. I'd planned to cut flowers for her grave. It's something I have to do."

"Of course, my dear. You needn't explain. A few more miles won't make any difference to me. I feel fine."

Accompanied by the rattle of harness chain and the bang of iron-rimmed wheels over hard ground, the ambulance started up a wooded hill as the sun lowered in front of them. Lorena remembered this part of her previous journey vividly. In the distance, on a tree-studded ridge overlooking the Tennessee River, they would pass the spot where Clara died. Steeling herself, she drove toward it with her mouth set in a grim line. Off to the southwest a bank of black clouds lay above the horizon.

Gentle rain fell on a newly cut pine plank marker behind a trading post where the wooden ferry was tied. A plume of sweet-smelling hickory smoke curled from the log building's chimney. Puddles of rainwater formed where a mound of earth over the body of Clara Brooks rose above a carpet of spring grass. Raindrops trickled down the plank, momentarily diverted where letters were carved until each niche filled with accumulated water, shedding it like tears down the face of the marker whereupon it pooled and grew to larger puddles as the rain continued. Nestled against the base of the plank, a handful of flowers wilted sud-

denly when raindrops struck colorful petals. Lorena paid no attention to the wilting flowers or the rain falling on a sunbonnet
given to her by Mrs. Peabody, for she was lost in dark memories.

Jonathan put his arm around her shoulders. Rainwater fell in
tiny rivulets from the sodden brim of his cavalryman's hat, pool-
ing around his boots. The patter of raindrops grew louder as the
spring storm worsened. From the south, thunder rumbled in a
muffled voice from the heart of the thunderstorm, still many
miles away.

"Sometimes it helps to cry," he said. "My mother told me it
cleanses the soul to shed tears."

She turned away from the grave. "I find I am unable to cry
now. I feel as though I should, and yet I can't. I feel so sad. I
miss Clara with all my heart. Ever since I came to this region it
seems as though I've been crying, and now I can't. Is something
wrong with me?"

"Maybe you've begun to heal inside. It happens a little at a
time. You never truly forget, but you begin to realize things are
often beyond your control. You couldn't save Clara any more
than you could save yourself from the men who took advantage
of you. Accepting what has happened may be the first step you
take to understanding it later on for what it really was. You've
been blaming yourself when it wasn't your fault." A chain of
lightning brightened the sky, crackling before it faded. "I've had
the same feelings about men who died while they were in my care.
I did the best I could, and still I couldn't save them. I am a doctor, but I can't work miracles. At the beginning of the war I felt
responsible, until battle hardened me to the truth. Armies were
out to destroy each other, and there was nothing I could do
about it. I served my country the best I knew how, and so did
you, and so did Clara. She was a casualty of war. You weren't responsible for her death any more than I was responsible for my
patients' injuries. It always saddened me when I couldn't save a
soldier's life, but toward the last I finally understood that I'd done
all I could to help them."

Lorena watched the grave a while longer, ignoring her damp clothing and water dripping from her bonnet. A clap of thunder above the river startled her, yet even as the rainfall increased, she wouldn't seek shelter in the trading post. Her gaze wandered along the inscription again. "I hope Clara knows I did all I could for her . . . that I would never have left her to die in the cold."

"She knows," Jonathan said. He tightened his embrace around her shoulders. "Let's go inside."

She allowed him to lead her away, walking through wet grass and puddles to the front porch. They climbed the steps side by side, arm in arm. But before she would consent to go any closer to the door, she halted to look across the river. "I'll be leaving everything behind to go with you," she said, "my family back east, my friends in Baltimore. I'm sure I'll miss them from time to time. I'll always miss Clara and carry her in my heart." She turned to him. "What I found here is far more precious than anything—someone I love, someone who loves me. Wherever you're taking me, I'll go willingly. I discovered nothing is more dear than sharing my life with someone who truly cares for me." She listened to the splatter of raindrops on the roof. "I promise to give you all my love in return."

Jonathan's blue eyes sparkled when a bolt of lightning arced from the sky. He waited until the accompanying thunder ended to speak. "I'll always love you, darling Lorena. Never doubt that. I pledge to remain by your side forever . . . as long as I live. We have shared a terrible experience, and from it has come a bond so strong, nothing can tear us apart. You are right to believe there is nothing more precious than another's genuine love. We are the fortunate who know what love really is." He took her in his arms and kissed her passionately. A breath of wet wind swept his hair away from his forehead when he drew his lips from hers. He gazed into her eyes and she saw his love, a soft light burning behind his pupils like the warm glow of a candle's flame.

She nestled her cheek against his shoulder. Jonathan was right, she thought. There were few who knew what love was about. Amid the bloody realities of war a man and a woman had discovered each other and feelings so deep that even betrayal and differing loyalties could not destroy what they shared. "You are so right, Jonathan," she said quietly, knowing theirs was a love that would last.

Author's Note

This is historical fiction. For the most part I have tried to remain faithful to what is known about the battle at Franklin and the battle of Nashville, although I took liberties with some geography for dramatic effect by placing the final engagement at Nashville inside the city, rather than five miles to the south of town.

General John Bell Hood, a Kentuckian by birth, led Hood's Texas Brigades and a combined army of Tennessee units at Franklin, then at Nashville, after which he resigned. The battle at Franklin is an anomaly in Hood's military career. Noted historian Shelby Foote states his belief that "There is a strong suspicion John Bell Hood was trying to discipline his army by staging those disastrous charges at Franklin. He was exasperated by what had happened at Spring Hill shortly before that and the idea was to put the iron to his men." His army was shattered and the defeat at Nashville was a result of heavy losses at Franklin. At Nashville, the flower of the Southern army was no more. The beginning of the end for the Confederacy was not far off. Hood may have been driven mad by years of pain from numerous injuries and habitual use of morphine during the final years of the war. In any event, his behavior at Franklin was uncharacteristic of his military brilliance and scholars still debate what caused him to sacrifice so many of his troops over what was apparently meaningless territory. John Bell Hood died quietly with his wife and a daughter in the New Orleans yellow fever epidemic of 1878.

His nemesis, Ulysses S. Grant, whose actual birth name was Hiram Ulysses, died of throat cancer while penning his memoirs in 1885, bankrupt and unable to speak. Union General George "Pap" Thomas was responsible for Hood's final defeat. The characters of Dorothea Dix, Ulysses Grant, his chief of staff John Rawlins, and others are faithfully depicted; however, Dorothea Dix did not take part in any covert spying operations for the Union. This was creation on my part. Other characters are fictional, and Hood's betrayal at Franklin by nurse spies is also fiction, although women did serve as spies on both sides in later years of the war. Copies of anonymous medical records from both armies allowed me to create a realistic picture of treatment and medicaments from the period. Over six hundred thousand men died during the war, two percent of America's population in 1864.

I'm indebted to a number of excellent sources: *Hood's Texas Brigade* by Harold B. Simpson (Waco, Tex.: Texian Press, 1972); *Military Memoirs of a Confederate* by Edward Alexander (Bloomington, Ind.: 1962 reprint); *Advance and Retreat* by John Bell Hood (New Orleans, La.: PGT Beauregard, 1880); *Hood's Texas Brigade* by Mrs. A. V. Winkler (Austin, Tex.: Von Boeckmann, 1894); "Medicine of the Civil War" by Alfred Bollet, M.D. (*Staff Physician,* July 1994); and to James M. Thompson, M.D., and Judith Piner, D.O., for their invaluable medical expertise. And lastly, to perhaps the best of all histories of the Civil War, *The Civil War: An Illustrated History* by Geoffrey C. Ward, with Ric Burns and Ken Burns (New York: Knopf, 1990).